O9-ABF-250

CHARLOTTE
HUGHES

Night Kills

AVON BOOKS
An Imprint of HarperCollinsPublishers

This is a work of fiction. Names, characters, places, and incidents are products of the author's imagination or are used fictitiously and are not to be construed as real. Any resemblance to actual events, locales, organizations, or persons, living or dead, is entirely coincidental.

AVON BOOKS
An Imprint of HarperCollins*Publishers*
10 East 53rd Street
New York, New York 10022-5299

Copyright © 1998 by Charlotte Hughes
ISBN: 0-380-79220-6
www.avonbooks.com

First Avon Books paperback printing: December 1998

Avon Trademark Reg. U.S. Pat. Off. and in Other Countries, Marca Registrada, Hecho en U.S.A.
HarperCollins® is a trademark of HarperCollins Publishers Inc.

Printed in the U.S.A.

10 9 8 7 6 5 4

*This book is dedicated with much
love and appreciation to Patricia Shipley.
May all your kindness come back to you tenfold.*

ACKNOWLEDGMENTS

Many thanks to Ralph Baldwin, attorney and friend, for his assistance on this work. And to my agent and friend, Richard Curtis, for lending me his shoulder when I needed it. And to Laura Tucker, for her irreverent sense of humor.

Also, to my very dear friends, who've seen me through some trying times: Kazue Hathcox, Rebecca George, Gail McClam, Joy Hager, Terry Green, Carl Yeager, Lillian Collings, Inge Merker, Cheryl Conte, Jim Brannon, Wanda Cook, Bob and Bettie Hudson, Brenda Rollins, Alfie Thompson, Patty Reese, BJ James, and Janet Evanovich. Thank you for your love and support. I am truly blessed.

SHE WAS beautiful, he thought, watching her sleep. Even stunning—thanks to a plastic surgeon in Hilton Head who'd cut away the scars from years spent with a husband who tended to use his fists when he drank. And he'd been drunk often.

Conversation stopped when she entered a room. People stared. At thirty-five, she passed for a woman in her late twenties. Women envied her as much as they despised her. She had taken more than one married man to bed, only to flaunt the affair in his wife's face afterward.

She was ruthless. And he hated her for it.

He approached her bed, a hideous, Chinese-red lacquered thing with cylindrical posts, each topped with a brass lion's head. A leopard-skin bedspread had been thrown back, exposing red satin sheets purchased from a specialty house in Atlanta. Overhead, an ornate mirror had been affixed to the ceiling so she could watch herself mate like an animal.

A whore's bedroom.

A steady beating filled his head, like the sound of war drums. He realized it was his own heartbeat. His anger escalated; he choked it back. It would not do for him to lose control. Not now. Not when he'd planned this so carefully.

The smell of expensive Scotch whiskey and cigarette smoke mingled with the ever-present scent of gardenia, her signature fragrance. In spring and summer, the saccharine-sweet flowers grew in abundance in the flower beds surrounding the house. Inside, they found homes in tall Waterford vases and antique water pitchers. That smell was in her soap and talcum power and perfume; even the white Jaguar she drove carried a hint of it.

There was no escaping that smell, just as there was no escaping what she was. Yes, she was beautiful—but with her facial muscles slack and her mouth hanging open from the pills and booze, she reminded him of a baying mare.

She shifted in her sleep, startling him. He took a step back, watched her for a moment. Her black slip rose high on her thighs, exposing a black garter belt and silk stockings. The black dress she'd worn earlier was a shapeless wad on the floor. She began to snore.

Whore. Whore. Whore.

The pillowcase he held suddenly felt heavy. In it was everything he needed. He cocked his head to the side and studied her face as an art lover would a masterpiece. He almost regretted what he had to do.

She awoke while he was taping her mouth with duct tape, and she managed to get out a couple of good screams before he silenced her with a blow to the temple. He'd been thinking ahead when he'd removed the blunt paperweight from her writing desk.

She was unconscious when he strapped her wrists and ankles to the bedposts, but the first cut to her face yanked her out of her stupor. A brief moment of confusion, then stark terror when he held the box cutter before her eyes. She bucked on the bed, tried to pull free, but the tape held fast, just as he'd known it would.

The blade flashed in the light as he brought it

down and went back to work. Her eyes rolled back in their sockets; the veins on her forehead bulged beneath her porcelain skin.

He laughed softly. "Relax," he said. "I'm going to give you a new look."

Two

LEE CATES woke from a bad dream to a freezing cold bedroom and decided, as days went, this one was starting out rather sucky. The nightmare was the result of a childhood trauma; the cold room due to a prehistoric furnace that had crapped out last winter.

As she lay in her grandmother's antique iron bed, Lee considered, not for the first time, putting the place up for sale. She could list it with Francie Nettles. Everyone knew Francie slept with her clients, which was why she was the top realtor in town. Nobody was surprised the day ol' Francie received her Lifetime Multi-Million-Dollar Producer Award. Folks couldn't help but wonder if she was packing knee pads in the trunk of her Town Car. Lee figured Francie could convince some Yankee businessman with a thick wallet to buy her house and turn it into a bed and breakfast.

Not that she relished the thought of strangers traipsing through her grandparents' massive turn-of-the-century Victorian, mind you, but the damn house was falling apart before her very eyes. If it'd been a car, someone would have removed the tires and set it up on cinder blocks. If it had been a horse, they would have just shot the damn thing.

Lee tried to wiggle her toes to keep the circulation

going, not an easy task considering she wore three pairs of tube socks. They were the perfect accessory for her orange sweats and brown knit cap. Her older sister, Lucy, would have taken one look at her, shaken her head, and said something like, "Lee, you look like you've been beaten with an ugly stick," or, "Lee, you're so ugly you'd have to sneak up on a glass to get a drink of water." All corny sayings left over from their childhood, and Lucy would just be kidding her, of course, but Lee would believe it because her sister was gorgeous and she wasn't.

And then there was her mother. "You're never going to catch a man looking like that, Lee, honey. You need to get out of those blue jeans, put on a dress and pantyhose, and do something with your hair." As if Comfrey, South Carolina, was crawling with eligible bachelors. Unless you counted seventy-year-old Melvin Bennefield, who'd just got him one of those penile implants. He was half blind and couldn't hear worth a cuss, but he walked 'round town with a semi hard-on, scaring some of the blue-rinse ladies so badly they'd skitter six blocks out of the way to keep from passing him on the sidewalk.

Lee tried to disentangle the thermal blankets that had wound themselves around her long legs during the night like a wild potato vine growing up a fence post. She jerked the old wedding ring quilt to her chin and cursed the bone-chilling temperature in her bedroom once again, a result of an early cold snap in the Carolina lowcountry, and, of course, the good-for-nothing furnace.

No telling what it would cost to replace the blasted thing.

She shoved her thoughts aside and burrowed deep in the feather mattress, which was about the only thing she could rely on these days. The fact that she had to pee was not enough reason to venture out from beneath the covers. She'd just begun to doze again when the phone rang. She muttered something foul under her breath and ignored it. Anybody who called at 6 a.m. was either drunk or crazy.

Then she thought of her father. Having suffered a stroke almost a year ago, he kept his wife and younger daughter on edge for what would happen next.

Just one more thing, as she saw it.

Lee struggled to get free of the covers, grabbed the phone on the fourth ring, and mumbled the closest thing she had to a hello before her first cup of coffee.

"Aunt Lee?"

Aunt Lee? At first she was just thankful it wasn't her mother calling with bad news. She blinked several times, pulled off her cap so she could better hear the person on the other line, who had to be her nephew—a frail, dark-haired boy with brown eyes that had always seemed too large for his face. "Stevie, is that you?" Ridiculous question; who else called her Aunt Lee? Not that she was much of an aunt, mind you. She seldom saw the kid, would've had a hard time pinning down the last time they'd shared more than a handful of words.

"Stevie?" she repeated, when she was met with silence.

"Y-you have . . . to come. I don't know what . . . to do."

His voice shook uncontrollably, his breathing was erratic. Lee's muscles tensed. "Calm down, Stevie," she said, coming to a sitting position so quickly it made her dizzy. Her brown, shoulder-length hair tumbled into her face. She shoved it back impatiently. "What's wrong?"

He choked on a sob. "She's all . . . bloody. Her face."

Lee gripped the phone tighter. "*Who's* bloody?"

"It's Mom. I think she's . . . dead."

An immediate adrenaline rush followed. The phone slipped from Lee's grasp and hit the floor. She lunged for it. "Stevie, what the hell are you talking about?" she demanded. He had to be on drugs, having delusions or something. It was bound to happen now that he was a teenager.

He gulped. "She's got a hole in her chest. Someone must've . . . stabbed her."

Lee's limbs suddenly turned liquid, her mind instantly rejecting the idea. No way was Lucy dead. Her sister was just hurt, and Stevie was overreacting. "Have you called for an ambulance?" She climbed from the bed, stumbled. It was all she could do to stand. The old heart pine floors were icy, the cold seeped right through her socks, made her toes ache something fierce. Her need to relieve herself suddenly became paramount.

"I didn't know what to do," Stevie said. "There was a man here. I don't know who he was."

Something in his voice had changed. Lee feared he was going into shock. *A man.* "Where is he now, Stevie? Is still in the house?"

"I dunno."

She could imagine a stranger lurking in the shadows. Fear jolted her into action. "Get out of the house," she ordered.

"What about . . . the . . . ambulance?"

His words were slow and disjointed. Lee would have shaken him if she'd been there. "I'll call. Just get the hell out!"

She jumped when he slammed the phone down in her ear. Her fingers trembled and her bladder felt as though it would burst as she dialed 9-1-1.

Sheriff Holden Cates was snuggled next to his pregnant wife when the phone rang. At first he thought it was the alarm. He reached over, slapped the button. The ringing continued. He grunted, slapped it again.

"Phone, Holden," Debbie mumbled.

Like a blind man, he searched with his hand and lifted it from its cradle. He brought it to his ear. "Cates here." His mouth was dry and tasted like a barn stall. One of his deputies spoke from the other end. He listened as a cold knot formed in his windpipe and cut off his breathing for a minute. He lay very still, his dazed brain trying to process the information. God, the things people did to one another, he thought.

Holden wiped his hand across his face and raised up on one elbow. "You say the boy's missing?" He knew his wife was listening so he chose his words carefully. Two miscarriages had made him protective of her. Once again he listened, but as he pictured the scene that'd just been described to him, he wanted to lash out, put his fist through a wall. He wouldn't, of course. Folks just naturally expected him to be cool-headed at all times.

"You got backup?" he asked his deputy, using his sheriff's voice. No one would suspect how shaken he was inside. Except Debbie, of course, unless he was careful. "Okay, secure the house. I'm on my way." He hung up and climbed from the bed.

"Who died?" she asked.

Holden hesitated. He should have taken the call in the kitchen. "Lucy."

Debbie raised her head slightly and gave him a startled look. "Your cousin Lucy?"

"Yeah."

She rolled onto her back. "Oh, Holden, I'm so sorry. That poor family. Seems only yesterday that fire claimed Bill's life."

Holden gave a grunt. "You ask me, that's the best thing that ever happened to Lucy and the boy. Only thing Bill Hodges was good for was getting lickered up and beating the hell out of them." Holden wished he'd kept quiet the minute he said it. Debbie was probably the only person in Comfrey who pitied the mean drunk that'd died in a house fire started by his own negligence. It would have taken his family with him if one of the firemen hadn't risked his own life going in after them.

"What happened?" Debbie asked softly. "How'd Lucy die?"

He rounded the bed and dropped a kiss on his wife's forehead. He'd sometimes shared his work with her in the past, but those days were over. At least for now. "Try not to think about it, honey," he said, using the same tone he used when he was forced to tell someone they'd just lost a loved one in a car wreck or a bar shooting. He adjusted the covers, patted her huge stomach, and thought about the baby that was snuggled deep in her womb, presently insulated from the harsh realities of life. Debbie's due date was two weeks away, and he'd looked forward to spoiling her these last days. A helluva time for something like this to happen.

"Now, be a good girl and go back to sleep," he said. "You don't have to get up for another hour." He started for the bathroom, then paused at the door. "I wish you'd quit your job, honey. I'm afraid it's too much for you. You need your rest."

"It'll make the time go faster," Debbie said sleepily.

He knew there was no sense arguing; they'd had this conversation before. Besides, her doctor said she was healthy as a horse. Holden could only hope. He headed for his shower, dreading the day ahead.

Eighty-year-old Hyram Atwell was already awake when the sirens shattered the early morning silence in a neighborhood where nothing much ever happened. After working in New York City for forty years and rising long before dawn to catch a train into the city, he'd never gotten out of the habit of getting up with the chickens, as they called it here in the South. He knew some of his neighbors thought him strange skulking about his property at that hour, but he didn't care. It was his favorite time of day; unhurried and peaceful, he could just sip his morning coffee and reflect.

Only today had been different. A nightmare. Something out of a horror show. Even now, he wished he could turn back the clock. He would have done things differently.

He pitied the poor soul that would have to gaze upon what was left of Lucy Hodges.

For once, he was glad his Margie wasn't alive. He would never be able to live with himself if she knew what he'd done.

The sirens were louder now, startling the hundred or so snowy egrets that nested on the other side of the drab brown salt marsh, sharing space in knobby cypress or tupelo trees, feeding off fiddler crabs, shrimp, snails, and a multitude of insects. From the back window in his bedroom, Hyram watched the birds leap from the trees and soar upward, stark white against a pewter sky.

The Carolina lowcountry had seemed the perfect place for a burned-out CEO to retire. He and Margie had fallen in love with the quaint town and surrounding wetlands, with its whimsical tidal pools and oyster beds, and woodlands where deer roamed in herds and often ventured into backyards to graze. He remember fondly the day Margie had awakened to find the blooms stripped from her Confederate jasmine and wisteria vines. And finally, the beaches where one could walk for miles without seeing another person.

After today, no one would ever feel secure in the little town of Comfrey.

Hyram imagined his neighbors—doctors, lawyers, engineers, all professionals—tumbling from their beds, throwing on silk bathrobes, and rushing outside to see what the commotion was about.

He stood and gazed at his reflection in the mirror over the dresser, smoothing the wrinkles from his clothes. He'd already showered and dressed for the day. His pajamas and the bathrobe his housekeeper had given him last Christmas were soaking in hot sudsy water. He would have to wash them several times to get the stains out. He combed the few strands of white hair remaining on his shiny, liver-spotted head, and he wished old age wasn't such a hardship.

Lucy Hodges would never know what it was like growing old, of having her mind slip away from her, taking with it her best memories. She wouldn't fear slipping and falling and having her brittle bones snap like twigs, of losing control of her bladder in a public place.

Perhaps Lucy was the lucky one.

Then he remembered how Lucy Hodges had looked as she lay dying, and he knew that nothing, not even the fires of hell, could have been worse.

Three

THE STREET leading to her sister's house was blocked by a young black deputy holding a long-handled silver flashlight. Lee cursed and glanced away as he shone it in her face. He apologized and listened as she gave her name, then immediately got on his radio. Lee thrummed her fingers impatiently on the steering wheel. Finally, he touched the bill of his cap respectfully and waved her through.

Lee gunned her engine and sped past him, whipped around a bend and saw patrol cars and a single ambulance parked in the driveway of her sister's lowcountry-style home. She sucked her breath in sharply at the sight. Suddenly everything seemed so real. She parked, climbed from her truck, and ran blindly toward the front porch, only to have someone step in her path and grasp her shoulders. She found herself looking into Holden Cates's somber face.

Her cousin seemed taller and more authoritative in his sheriff's uniform, not at all like the young boy who'd challenged her in watermelon seed–spitting contests when they were kids. And it was Holden who'd given her her first cigarette at fourteen and a taste of moonshine at fifteen. How he'd made sheriff was beyond her; back then he'd seemed destined to grow up a gangster.

"Not so fast, Lee," he said, his usual southern drawl sounding clipped.

Her panic rose. Why was he stopping her? She struggled to break free. "Dammit, Holden, let me go. I have to see—"

"I can't let you go barging in on a crime scene, hon. That just ain't the way it's done."

"Since when do you tell me what to do, Holden Cates?" She realized struggling was useless and gave up. "Is Lucy dead?" she demanded, hands on hips. "And don't go giving me some song and dance routine, just give it to me straight."

"Yes. Lucy's dead."

Lee felt as though she'd just received a blow to the chest, like a hot air balloon suddenly deflating in midair and hurtling to the ground. The shock of it made her stagger like a Saturday night drunk. Holden reached out, steadied her. "Are you sure about that?" she asked. " 'Cause if you're not—"

"I'm sorry, sweetheart."

A chill black silence enveloped her as she tried to come to grips with what she'd just learned. "What happened?" she managed in a voice that sounded nothing like her own. It was the voice of a woman whose soul had been yanked from her, leaving her as hollow as a pair of long johns flapping in a breeze on the clothesline. "Was there some kind of acci-dent?"

Holden sighed. "She was murdered, Lee. Stabbed in the heart. One of the paramedics pronounced her dead ten minutes ago."

She clenched her hands tight, her nails biting into her flesh. Her chest felt as though it would explode. "No," she said, unable to speak above a broken whisper. "No way are you going to convince me Lucy is dead. Somebody screwed up." There was a ring of finality to her words, as though saying them made it real.

His look was grim. "I personally ID'd her."

"Oh, yeah? When's the last time you saw my sister?" she demanded, trying to find a loophole in his story. "Were you aware she had plastic surgery? She didn't even look like her old self."

"You're only making this harder on yourself, sweetheart."

Tears stung her eyes as the truth began to register, despite her mind and heart screaming otherwise. She dug the heels of her palms against her eyes, felt Holden's arms encircle her. Lucy murdered?

A thought hit her. She glanced up quickly, and her fear shone in her eyes, as stark and vivid as the scene around her. "Oh, my God, where's Stevie?" She looked around frantically. "Has anybody seen Stevie?" She made for the house once more.

Again, Holden stopped her. "You're going to have to settle down, Lee. Stevie's missing. I have to tell you, it doesn't look good that he took off like that."

His words didn't register at first. Lee stared back at him, blank-faced. "What do you mean, it doesn't look good?" Realization jolted her. "Jesus Christ, Holden, you don't think Stevie is responsible for killing his own mother! Are you out of your blasted mind?"

"Not so loud," he said. "No sense getting the neighbors all worked up." He lowered his voice. "Frankly, I don't know what to think."

Lee clutched his jacket. "But you don't understand. I told Stevie to get out of the house when he called. I *ordered* him out."

Holden pried her fingers loose. "That's another thing I can't figure. Why didn't he just call nine-one-one himself?"

"He was in shock, that's why. I could tell by the sound of his voice. Good God, he's just a kid."

"He's seventeen years old. An adult."

Lee was shocked. She would have guessed her nephew to be no more than fifteen. Of course, he'd always been small for his age. And scrawny as a scarecrow. "He said a man had been in the house. I was afraid for him." She went on. "Dammit, Holden, somebody needs to find out who else was in that house last night, instead of doing all this finger pointing at my nephew. And somebody needs to get off their ass and find him!"

She glanced around quickly. "We can put together a search party—give these nosy neighbors something to do. I've got a pair of rubber boots in the back of my truck. I'll comb as much of the marsh as I can." As she turned for her pickup, Holden grabbed a fistful of her sweatshirt and pulled her to a halt.

"Just cool your heels, Lee," he said. "I'm not letting you go off half cocked. Besides, I've got the K-nine unit coming in—"

"You're sending *dogs* after him? What, are you trying to scare him to death? You know Stevie's terrified of dogs. Have you forgotten he was bitten several years ago?"

"I was there when it happened, and the boy brought it on himself by mistreating the animal." Holden released her. "These dogs won't hurt him. But if there's a possibility someone *was* in the house and that person abducted Stevie, we'll want to find him as soon as we can."

"Did you question the neighbors? Did you bother to talk to any of these assholes standing around with their thumbs up their butts?" She glared at the neighbors standing in their bathrobes, gawking at her as though she'd just landed her spaceship in the middle of the street.

"I don't need you telling me how to do my job, Lee," Holden said sternly. "And you need to watch your language in front of my deputies."

She would have laughed if she hadn't been so pissed off. "Very funny, Holden. I've heard your men once they get started."

"Well, that's no way for a lady to talk. Come with me." He all but dragged her to his patrol car and put her in the passenger's side. "Have you had coffee yet?" he asked, joining her in the front seat.

Her look was incredulous. "You think I took time to brew coffee?"

"A simple no would have been sufficient." He reached for his thermos and poured coffee into a plastic cup. "I wish I had a shot of whiskey to go in it or one of those elephant guns with a tranquilizer dart, but this is the best I can do at the moment."

Lee knew he was trying to put her at ease, but he was wasting his time. Yet as she held the cup with both hands, she drew small pleasure in its warmth. She tried to raise it to her lips, but her hands shook so badly some of the hot liquid sloshed onto her jeans. She'd raced out of the house without a jacket, and her thin sweatshirt offered little protection against the cold.

"You're shivering," Holden said, climbing out to retrieve a blanket from the trunk.

Lee thanked him as he laid it across her shoulders. "This can't be happening," she said. "I know I'm going to wake up any minute and find out it's all a bad dream." She started to cry.

Holden reached for a pocket-sized package of tissues. He pulled out a couple and handed them to her. "You feel like answering a few questions?" he asked, when the worst of the tears had passed.

"I don't know what I can tell you."

"Can you recall the conversation you had with Stevie? Word for word?"

Lee did her best, wondering as she did so if he was still alive. She would not allow herself to think otherwise. More tears. "The poor kid is going to end up in a mental institution after what he's been through," she said. "Shuffled from one foster home to the next, only to end up living in a house with an abusive drunk. And that awful fire." She shook her head. "And now this."

Holden looked thoughtful. "Lucy once told me she felt guilty for adopting Stevie in the first place."

Lee nodded and wiped away a stray tear. "But she wanted children so bad. She treated Stevie like her own from the beginning. She gave him everything his heart desired. To sort of make up for the way Bill treated him—or should I say mistreated him."

"I know she took some punches for the boy," Holden said.

"That's right." Lee sniffed hard and looked at him. "And you think for one minute Stevie would ever harm a hair on her head? No way, Holden. He worshipped her." She was quiet for a moment, then moaned. "Oh, God. How am I going to break the news to my parents? My dad won't live through it."

He reached for her hand and squeezed it. "I know this is hard, honey. I'm so sorry. I loved Lucy, too."

Lee nodded. Slumped in the seat with her head bowed over her cup of coffee, she asked the question she'd wanted to know from the start but was afraid to hear answered. "Did Lucy suffer?"

He hedged. "I'm not an expert at this sort of thing, Lee."

She saw the sadness in his eyes and felt bad for giving him such a hard time. "But if she was stabbed in the heart, death would have been immediate. Even I know that much."

Holden glanced out his window. "Yes, a stab in the heart would have been quick and painless."

Lee felt momentary relief. "At least we can be thankful for that much." Her voice quavered when she spoke again. "But why would anybody want to kill Lucy in the first place?"

"I intend to find out," he said.

"But first you'll find Stevie."

He nodded. "Here comes help," he said, seeing the headlights aimed their way. He opened the door. "Stay put while I take care of this. I'm going to send a deputy over to take your statement."

Lee reached for his hand, and he glanced at her. "Could Lucy have been asleep when it happened? Is there a chance that maybe she didn't even know what was coming?" she asked desperately.

Holden squeezed her hand. "That's my guess, hon." But he refused to meet her gaze.

Lee watched him walk away, his ambiguous answer no comfort at all.

Across the yard, Holden greeted the county coroner, Albert McPhee. Besides serving as coroner, McPhee also owned Perpetual Care Funeral Home and Gardens. At forty-eight, he was overweight with a sagging middle, a chronic case of gout, and a tendency to sweat despite the coldest temperatures. He had a ruddy complexion and was bald, save for a small island of red tufts on either side of his crown.

Holden, who was thirteen years younger, was glad he'd remained active, and he was careful to watch the needle on the bathroom scale. He still had a full head of hair, thick and brown as the pecans that fell in his parents' yard, but his temples were almost completely gray. Debbie claimed she liked it, so that was all that mattered to him.

"Nice address," McPhee said.

"Yeah." Holden knew what the houses went for; they were way out of his league. "This one's bad, Albert. I haven't seen such a mess since Johnny Sample's grandson fell off the tractor and got caught in the blades."

"Just what I need this morning," the man said.

They entered the house and paused in the living room, where deputies were dusting for fingerprints and vacuuming for trace evidence. Holden couldn't help but admire the furnishings. He and Debbie had never owned anything so nice; in fact, they'd be lucky to get the crib and changing table off layaway before the big event. He'd never get rich in law enforcement and Debbie would never make a bundle working in a day care center, but they enjoyed what they did, so he figured that had to count for something.

McPhee walked over to a glass cabinet that held an assortment of clocks. "Don't believe I've ever seen so many clocks in one place," he said. "She put some money into them, too."

Holden joined him. Lucy had obviously become a collector. There were close to a dozen in the cabinet, all in different shapes and sizes. Another half dozen sat on a small, round table which had been draped in a linen cloth.

"What do you suppose it means?" he asked.

McPhee looked at him. "It means she liked clocks. Know what your problem is, Sheriff? You're always trying to read something into every little thing."

"A woman's got a couple of dozen clocks in her living room and you don't think that's strange?"

McPhee sniffed. "Smell that? Gardenia."

"Yeah, the house reeks of it."

"That her?"

Holden followed his gaze to the large oil painting over the fireplace. Lucy Hodges was regal in a deep red satin gown, holding a bouquet of gardenias in her hands. "Yeah. She was my cousin, you know."

"Sorry to hear that, Holden," McPhee said, his tone genuine. "I reckon in a town this size you're going to come across a relative sooner or later. She was beautiful, I'll give her that. Is there a husband?"

Holden shook his head. "You remember that house fire a couple of years back on Frazier Street? The husband was drunk. Passed out in bed with a cigarette in his hand. One of the worst fires we've ever had."

"I remember. Wasn't much left of him."

Holden pointed to the portrait. "She and their son almost died in that fire. She got burned on the face."

"So the portrait was painted before the fire?"

"After. She had plastic surgery. Lots of it."

"You ask me, the surgeon knew what he was doing."

"Yeah, well, she has a completely different look now," Holden said, his tone grim. "Once you see it, you're not likely to forget." He led the way to the master suite.

As McPhee walked to the bed, he just stared. "Holy Mother of God."

"Told you."

McPhee set his bag down and pulled out a pair of thin rubber gloves, but his gaze remained fixed on the victim. "Jesus," he muttered. "I've seen some bad ones, but this makes them look like a picnic in the park."

Holden paused in the doorway and reached into his pocket for the gloves he'd worn earlier. "Best I can tell, the wounds are confined to her face, the exception being that stab wound in her chest, of course." He approached the bed slowly. He'd already seen the carnage and was in no hurry to look at it again. "What do you make of it, Albert?"

"Damned if I know. He examined the chest wound briefly. "If the guy was looking to make a quick kill, he'd have gone straight for the neck, to a major artery. If I was a bettin' man, I'd put fifty bucks on the fatal stab wound bein' an afterthought. Looks like he wanted her alive while he rearranged her face."

Holden nodded in agreement. "Which explains why she was bound and gagged." He paused. "Check out the ceiling."

Albert glanced up. "God Almighty. I've heard tell of folks bolting mirrors to their ceiling, but this is the first time I've actually seen one."

"Know what it means, don't you?"

"Hell yeah, I know what it means. He made her watch."

The two men simply stared at one another for a moment. Holden was the first to speak. "So why'd he kill her? She would have bled to death eventually."

"Hard to figure. Was there anyone else in the house at the time?"

"Her seventeen-year-old son. He's the one who found her. He's also missing at the moment." Holden paused. "Do you think a kid could do something like this to his mother? His adoptive mother?" he corrected himself.

Albert pulled a needle-nose thermometer from his bag and inserted it between the dead woman's ribcage. "Depends on the kid. Does he have any priors?"

"Been in and out of trouble the past year or so. Mostly for fighting and disobedience in class."

"Ever use a knife on anybody?"

"Not that I know of."

"Drugs?"

"No indication. A couple of deputies tossed his room, didn't find anything."

Albert pulled out the thermometer and checked it. "She's fairly fresh, Holden," he said, his tone all business now. "I can tell just by looking at her." He examined the body briefly before pulling a small Dictaphone from his pocket and recording his findings.

"The victim is a white female, approximate age—" He paused and looked at Holden.

"She's thirty-four or thirty-five."

"Mid thirties," McPhee continued, then went on to give the date, estimated time of death, and list her injuries. "The deceased is waxy and there's lividity, but it's not fixed. There's no rigidity, but I wouldn't expect much at this point except for maybe in her eyelids and facial muscles. And under the circumstances, it's hard to tell. Have to run further tests once we take her in." He snapped off the recorder.

"What's all that gobblygook mean?" Holden asked.

"Means somebody was madder'n a brown bear with a mouth full of bumble bees when he got his hands on her. You got a weapon?"

"A box cutter. The killer went through two blades. It's over here on the night table. I wouldn't let anyone in the room until you got here, since you have a tendency to whine like a woman if anybody messes with anything."

Albert had rounded the bed and was studying the weapon. "Well, that might have been what cut her face, but it didn't put this here hole in her chest," he said. "Looks like it was meant to go straight through her heart, but I won't know for sure till I see an x-ray. Weapon was probably a common butcher knife. I'll have to get back to you on blade size."

"There's a wooden block with knives in the kitchen. Brand name, Chicago Cutlery. One's missing. I figure it should be easy enough to check."

There was a tap at the door. Holden looked up to find one of his deputies standing there, a young guy who hadn't been with him long. "What's up?"

"The dogs are here."

"Good. Grab something from the kid's room." The deputy hurried away, and Holden exchanged looks with Albert. "That guy's as dull-witted as ol' Floyd

Becket who sweeps up at Kramer's Grocery. Cain't turn my back on him for a minute." He sighed. "Hell, I better go back and see what he's doing. Knowing him, he'll grab one of the kid's suits from a dry cleaners bag. I'll be right back." Albert chuckled as he hurried off.

When Holden returned a few minutes later, after finding one of Stevie's outfits in a dirty clothes hamper in the bathroom, he found Albert studying the victim closely and recording more of his finding.

The older man looked up. "Tell me what you know about her cosmetic surgery."

"Not much. Only that it was performed by some doctor in Hilton Head, and it made a heck of a difference in the way she looked and acted."

"How she acted?"

"I'd only seen her a few times since she'd had it done, but she was a lot more confident." He paused and gave a half smile. "You might even say she liked to flaunt it. Not that I blamed her after what she spent on it."

"That husband of hers. Seems I remember he was abusive?"

Holden nodded. "I locked him up a couple of times for knocking her around. Usually after a bout of drinking. Broke her nose bad. It was as crooked as that slick-talking salesman over at Fankie's Used Cars. I reckon that's why she had plastic surgery on it." He shook his head. "Damned if this world ain't full of crazy bastards. You don't think her murder had anything to do with her plastic surgery?"

"Well, look at her," Albert said. "You ask me, the killer was trying to perform his own type of surgery." He glanced around the room. "I see she was having a nightcap," he added, nodding toward a bottle of Scotch and a glass.

"Yeah. We'll check it for prints, naturally," Holden said. He glanced away. He couldn't stand looking at Lucy another minute. "I'll dismantle the whole damn room if I have to. If there's anything to find, I'll find it." He lifted tormented eyes to McPhee. "I don't want anyone to see her like this, Albert. Can we go ahead and cut her loose? Get her out of here?"

McPhee reached into his bag for something sharp while Holden brought out his pocket knife. Once they cut Lucy free, they bagged her hands and wrapped her in the sheet so no trace evidence would get lost. "I'll need the rest of her bed linens," McPhee said.

Holden nodded. "Let's just get her in a body bag." His voice cracked.

McPhee studied him. "You might want to think of letting someone else work this case, my friend."

Holden knew the man meant well, so he didn't take offense. "It's too late for that, Albert. I've got to see this one through. After all, she's family."

Four

HYRAM ATWELL knew who was standing on the other side of the front door before he answered it. Deputy Willis Green, as his name tag read, was a young black man who looked too serious for his age. He wore his hair cropped close to his skull, and his khaki uniform was starched and ironed to such perfection that Hyram wondered if the man ever sat down and put creases in it. Grace, his housekeeper, would have approved. Grace believed in starch.

"Mr. Atwell?" the young man asked.

"Yes." Hyram was glad he'd taken a mild tranquilizer. He felt calmer, more in control. "I was wondering how long it would be before you visited me. I heard the sirens and saw all the commotion next door when I stepped out to get my newspaper. I would have come over, but I was afraid I'd be in the way." He smiled kindly. "Would you like to come in?"

"Thanks." The deputy stepped inside. "I wouldn't have bothered you at this hour if it weren't so important. But I noticed your lights were on." He looked around. "Lovely house you have, Mr. Atwell. Have you lived here long?"

"Some twenty-odd years. Have a seat, Deputy Green. Would you like coffee?"

Green sat on the edge of the sofa. "No, thanks. I just need to ask you a couple of questions, and I'll be out of your way."

"Was there some kind of accident next door?" Hyram asked, reclaiming his chair.

"How well do you know the Hodgeses, Mr. Atwell?" Green asked, avoiding the question.

"Hardly know them at all. See the boy walking home from the bus stop once in a while, that's about it. I never see the mother around much. Is somebody hurt over there?"

"There's been a fatality, sir. Mrs. Hodges was killed sometime during the night." The deputy paused and looked at him.

Hyram wondered if the man was waiting for a reaction. "Oh, how awful! And she appeared to be so young. Is the boy okay?"

"We're not sure." He glanced around. "Is there a Mrs. Atwell?"

"My wife has been dead some years now."

Deputy Green nodded and studied his surroundings. "I see you have a lot of windows in this room. You must have a beautiful view of the marsh."

Hyram knew where the questions were leading. "Yes, it is beautiful. Unfortunately, I have to keep them closed because of my glaucoma. The light hurts my eyes, you see."

"That's too bad."

Hyram shifted in his chair. He wasn't a good liar, but he knew the deputy would have no reason not to believe otherwise. "Losing my hearing too," he added, motioning to the hearing aids in his ears. "But I figure at my age I have to be thankful for what I've got."

"That's a good attitude to have, sir." Deputy Green made a notation on his note pad. "Do you wear your hearing aid when you sleep, Mr. Atwell?"

"Oh, no. I remove everything before I go to bed.

My teeth, my glasses, my hearing aid." He chuckled, then wondered if it was proper under the circumstances. "I reckon I'm a good ten pounds lighter when I climb between the sheets each night."

The deputy smiled, then became all business. "What I'm interested in knowing, sir, is whether you heard or saw anything last night."

Hyram shook his head. "Not a thing, Deputy. It wouldn't be that easy for me to hear even if I didn't have problems. See, my bedroom is on the opposite side of the house. Like I said, first I knew there was a problem was when I heard the sirens. I didn't have no problem hearing those, of course. Sounded like they were coming through my front door."

"Do you have any pets?"

"No. My wife was allergic to animal fur. I wouldn't mind having a dog, but at my age I'd probably forget to feed it."

"So you didn't hear any dogs barking during the night or early morning?"

Hyram was getting tired of the questions, and the tranquilizer was making him sleepy. "No sir. Nothing."

"And you didn't notice any strange cars in the neighborhood or parked in Mrs. Hodges's driveway?"

"I'm sorry I haven't been much help."

"Thank you for your time, Mr. Atwell," Deputy Green said, standing and pulling a card from his pocket. "Please call me if you think of something."

Hyram took the card. He could feel beads of sweat popping out on his forehead. "Yes, I will certainly call you," he said, "if I happen to think of something. Next time you visit, plan to stay for coffee."

Willis Green made for the door, then paused with his hand on the knob. "Would you mind if I looked about the property?" he asked. "It's just routine."

Hyram shrugged, as if it made no difference. "Help yourself."

"Thank you, sir." Green touched the bill of his cap and let himself out.

Hyram stood there, staring at the closed door, as the first waves of panic gripped him.

It was only a matter of time.

Lee had just finished giving her statement to a young deputy when Holden came out of the house. She could see the tension in his shoulders, the stiff way he walked. Another person might not have noticed, but she did.

The door on the driver's side opened and he slid in. A muscle worked in his jaw. Something was wrong. But what could be worse than what she already knew? She stirred uneasily in her seat, her fingers clenched tightly in her lap. She was suddenly consumed with a sense of dread and foreboding. "I want to see my sister, Holden." She waited, watched him warily. In the distance, she could hear the bloodhounds.

He gave an anguished sigh. "They're loading her up to take her to the morgue. It's not a good time."

The hurt and longing was heavy in her chest. "Then I'll see her there," she said with determination. "I have a right to see my own sister, Holden. You can't stop me." She hadn't realized how loud she was speaking until she stopped.

"Lee, please don't put yourself through this."

"I'm going to see her anyway at the funeral home."

He closed his eyes momentarily. "I wouldn't plan on that. Most likely, Albert McPhee will insist on a closed casket."

An alarm went off in her head, some oddly primitive warning that told Lee her cousin was guarding a secret. "What the hell are you talking about, Holden? You said Lucy was stabbed in the chest. That's easy enough to hide. Why wouldn't her family be permitted to see her?"

He looked at her for the first time since he'd joined her in his patrol car. "It's not that simple."

Something flickered far in the back of his eyes, some emotion Lee was not sure of. "You're hiding something, Holden Cates. What the hell is it?" Even as she demanded an answer, she wasn't sure she wanted to know. But the doubts and uncertainties in the back of her mind refused to let go. "You're beginning to piss me off, Holden, and you really don't want to piss me off right now. Not on top of everything else!" She was shouting.

He glared at her. "What are you going to do, take a crowbar to my windows? That's the problem with you, Lee. You've always been so goddamn bossy and high strung. For once in your life can't you try to be rational?"

"Rational? My sister is inside with a butcher knife in her heart, and you expect me to act *rational*? You know what *your* problems is, Holden? You've become hardened. You see a dead body, and it's just another case to you. Well, this is my sister we're talking about, and yes, I might just take a crowbar to your windows if you don't tell me the truth!"

"You think this is just another case for me?" he demanded. "Lucy was family. I watched her grow up. I shared in her life just as much as you did. So, don't sit there and pretend you are the only one suffering, because I feel like shit too."

Lee saw the anguish on his face and realized he was hurting as much as she was. She longed to touch him, but she feared simple human contact at the moment, feared it would shatter the small hold she had left on her sanity. "Tell me, Holden."

He wiped his face with his hand. He looked defeated, wearied by all he'd seen that morning and the task that lay before him. "Aw, Lee, I wanted to save you from this, but I reckon you'll find out anyway. Lucy had other wounds."

She swallowed with difficulty. "What kind of wounds?"

"To her face. This person . . . this animal . . . took a box cutter to her face. Cut her pretty bad."

She felt the blood drain from her face, felt her composure slip away like tiny grains of sand through an hourglass. She was so horrified she could only stare back at him like a mute. Finally, when she was able to speak, her words were choked. "You said she was killed with a butcher knife, Holden," she said, measuring her words carefully, as though by doing so she would be able to control her emotions as well. "You said death was immediate." Tears spurted from her eyes. "You never *ever* said anything about someone carving up her face like a goddamn Christmas ham."

"Lee—"

She swiped at her tears. "You'd better not be bullshitting me."

"I would never—"

Anger sharpened her voice. "I hope Lucy fought the bastard. I hope she clawed his eyes out." She paused. "You're going to check beneath her fingernails, right? She could have scratched him. We should be looking for a man with scratches on his face."

Holden didn't look at her, and when he spoke his voice was flat, emotionless, but his eyes were tormented. "Lucy was bound and gagged. There was no fight. He—" Holden swallowed. "He didn't kill her until afterward."

A glazed look of misery and despair spread across Lee's face as his meaning set in. She shrank against the door, trying to make herself small. She wouldn't, she *couldn't* accept what Holden was saying to her now, because it would mean living with the knowledge and trying to cope with it for the rest of her life. That was no way to live. Already she could feel a hot fist, twisting and turning inside of her, destroying flesh and organs and everything vital.

"No, Holden," she said, trying to talk over the suffocating knot in her throat. Her voice was reproachful. "You're not telling me some sonofabitch butchered my sister while she was still alive? Is *that* what you're trying to tell me? Is it?" she demanded, nostrils flared.

Holden didn't meet her gaze. "Yes."

Her cry sounded as though it had been ripped from her throat. Pictures, too horrible to imagine, came at her like a slide show, clicking on and off, on and off. Lee couldn't catch her breath. Just like in her dream earlier, she was being swallowed up. The car was shrinking. She grabbed the door handle, wrenched it open.

"Lee, wait!" Holden reached out for her, but she snatched her arm away, not wanting him to so much as touch her. He opened his own door and jumped out. "Lee!" She tried to climb out of the car, but her legs collapsed beneath her and she fell to the ground. The grass was wet and cold against her face, she could smell its sweetness, and the rich dirt below. Lucy would never smell those things again. "Oh, God!" she cried, unable to bear the image of her sister's torn face a moment longer. She felt sick.

She heaved into the grass, but there was nothing in her stomach except the coffee she'd just drank. Big hands gripped her shoulders, but she pushed them away. They reappeared, struggled to pull her up, put her back into the patrol car. Sobs racked her body. She heard sounds, muted and sharp, was vaguely aware of Holden's voice as he started the car and pulled out of the driveway.

''It's going to be okay, Lee,'' he told her over and over again.

In her heart, she knew it would never be okay. Never.

Five

JACK MCCALL raised his dark head from the pillow, and mouthed an obscenity as an arrow of pain shot through his skull and threatened to take the back off on its way out. His stomach gave a lurch, as though he'd been eating green apples and they'd turned on him. He rode the waves of nausea and tried to remember when he'd last been so hungover. Who was he kidding? It had become a way of life for him. If he had a buck for every Cuervo Gold shooter he'd tossed down his gullet the last couple of years, he'd be a rich man.

Funny thing was, he didn't recall drinking all that much the night before. And this wasn't a typical hangover. He felt confused and disoriented, his entire system out of whack. Like maybe he was coming down with a bad strain of flu.

Trying to hold his head as still as possible, he looked about the room. His square jaw tensed. He didn't recognize it. Only thing he knew for sure was that it was a motel room. He'd seen a hundred others just like it—cheap, but serviceable, not to mention on the tacky side. Probably had a couple of pink flamingos out front. The fact that he knew precisely the kind of place it was didn't speak well for him, he decided.

He had vague memories of checking in, of walking into the office as dawn split the night sky, of a man in a dingy tee-shirt and angry-looking red hair scowling at him as he tried to make sense of the registration form.

He tried to remember how he'd spent the evening. Drinking in a bar in Hilton Head, meeting a gorgeous woman and driving her home. After that, *nada*.

Jack looked around for his watch, then discovered he was wearing it. Nine o'clock. His appointment was in two hours, and he felt as though he'd had no sleep. He reached for the phone, dialed the front desk. A man answered on the third ring. Probably the same guy as before.

"This is Jack McCall," he said. "What town am I in?" If the man on the other end of the line thought it an odd question, he didn't say so. He paused and listened. "Comfrey, huh? Could you tell me how far I am from Hilton Head? Less than an hour? Thanks."

He hung up. Cautiously, he raised up from the bed and stumbled to the bathroom. Once he emptied his bladder, he turned on the shower, stripped, and stepped in. A hot shower and a cup of coffee, and he'd be good as new. God knows he had it down to an art by now. As he stood beneath the hot spray, eyes closed, he had a sudden mental image of a red four-poster bed with brass lions heads on top.

Now, where the hell had that come from?

Six

LEE WAS surprised to find herself at Holden's house when the car came to a stop. "What are we doing here? I've got to go tell my parents."

"Not till you calm down," he said.

"I don't want Debbie to see me like this."

"Debbie's at work."

He climbed out of the patrol car and came around to her side. "Careful," he warned, as he helped her up the walk to the front door.

Lee noted a camellia bush in the flower bed that still had a few blooms on it, and she wondered how they'd survived the cold. How would she survive this? She sniffed. She had cried so hard that her head hurt. "Where's my truck?"

"I told you—a deputy will bring it around shortly. You don't think I'm going to let anything happen to that old rattletrap, do you?"

There was a time Lee would have come right back at him over a remark about her truck. But that part of her was gone now, perhaps forever. Once inside the house, she headed for the bathroom where she washed her face and finger-combed her hair. Still, she was a mess. Her mother would've said she looked like something even the cat wouldn't drag in. Holden opened the door a crack and shoved a clean sweatshirt inside. "It's Debbie's," he said. "Hope it fits."

Lee thanked him and closed the door once more. She glanced down at her own shirt and saw that it was covered with dirt and grass stains. Her jeans weren't much better. She didn't want to think about how she'd lost it back at her sister's place, how she'd fallen apart right in front of the other deputies and neighbors. She knew it would be all too easy to let it happen again, but she had to pull herself together—in a few minutes she would be facing her parents with the terrible news.

Holden was waiting for her when she came out, a bottle of whiskey in one hand, a glass in the other. He poured some of the liquid into the glass and offered it to her. "It'll calm you."

Much to his surprise, Lee ignored the glass and took a hefty swig straight from the bottle. She shuddered and coughed once, then took another slug.

"Hey, go easy on that," Holden warned her. "I don't want one of my deputies pulling you over and charging you with DUI."

"Trust me. Jail sounds good right now. I could climb in my cot and pull the covers over my head." Lee could already feel the whiskey taking hold. She sat on an old plaid sofa and buried her face in her hands. Her soul felt bleak and sorrowful. "This is going to kill my father."

"He's stronger than he looks." Holden took a chair opposite her. He waited until she looked up. "Lee, do you know anyone that might be capable of doing those things to your sister?"

She looked at him. "I don't know anyone capable of doing something like that to anybody. Do you?"

"Frankly, no. I've dealt with a few shootings and stabbings, but I've never seen anything like this." He paused and looked thoughtful. "Can you think of someone who might have resented her for having plastic surgery?"

"You think that's what this is about?"

"The thought certainly comes to mind, considering the killer went after her face first."

Lee rubbed her forehead with one hand as though that might coax her mind into action. "There were people who were against the surgery. My mother was afraid something would go wrong. My father kept reminding Lucy how beauty was skin deep and all. There were the town biddies, of course. They thought it was absolutely sinful for Lucy to spend her dead husband's insurance money to make herself beautiful. They'd obviously forgotten it was his fault she needed plastic surgery to begin with. But I can't imagine anyone resenting it so much that they'd . . ." She shuddered. Her throat ached from trying to hold back her tears. and she had never felt so hopeless, so filled with despair.

"Do you know if she was seeing anyone?"

"Your guess is as good as mine, Holden. Lucy cut off all contact with the family last Christmas Eve, if you'll recall."

"I'd heard there was an argument."

"More like a yelling match between Lucy and Dad. She never forgave him for not helping her and Stevie escape that hellhole they lived in when Bill was alive. Lucy had wanted to leave for a number of years, but Bill claimed he would prove her incompetent to raise a child, and he'd get custody of Stevie."

"How did he plan to prove her incompetent?" Holden asked.

"Because she was seeing a psychiatrist and taking medication for depression and anxiety. Who could blame her, knowing what she lived in? But as much as she wanted out, she wasn't about to risk losing her son. She and Stevie had been through too much together.

"My father refused to help her, said it was her own fault for quitting school and running off with Bill in the first place. His feeling was, she'd made her bed, and now it was up to her to lie in it. He also told her Stevie wasn't her problem, and he should be sent right back where he came from. Stevie was eight years old at the time, and he overheard the whole conversation."

"How nice." Holden's lips were pressed into a grim line.

Lee felt like crying all over again at the memory. "Lucy said the kid didn't sleep for weeks. No matter how she tried to convince him otherwise, he kept worrying that if he fell asleep he'd wake up in a foster home where they'd been mean to him." Even as she said it, Lee ached for what her poor nephew had gone through, and felt ashamed of herself for not being a better aunt.

"You remember what the poor kid was like when Lucy and Bill first adopted him," she went on. "Jumpy as a jack rabbit, wouldn't talk to anyone. Skinny as a fence post, but he could never seem to get enough to eat," she added. "And worst of all, he was a bed wetter." Not only did it break her heart to remember these things, it made her furious. "Lucy told me Bill used to make the boy sleep on his soiled sheets, night after night. Wouldn't let Stevie take a bath. Said it served him right to go to school smelling like piss. The kids made fun of him, of course. But if Lucy tried to help him, Bill would backhand her and order her to stay out of it. Said she was turning the boy into a big pussy." She shuddered. "God, I hated that man."

"Bill was a mean sonofabitch, that's for sure," Holden said. "Makes you wonder why he ever agreed to the adoption to begin with."

"So he would have a hold on my sister," Lee told him. "He knew she was unhappy because she'd miscarried. Lucy didn't tell me until later that Bill threw her down a flight of stairs during her fifth month of pregnancy. There were complications, and she was told she'd never conceive again. I think Lucy would have left after that, but Bill buttered her up. Said he would stop drinking, and they would adopt a baby. Lucy agreed to give him another chance, even though I begged her to move out and come live with me.

"Anyway, last Christmas Eve, Lucy arrived at my parents' house slightly drunk. The shit hit the fan, so to speak. She told my father what she thought of him, and one thing led to another until we had a regular shouting match going on at the table. It got so bad I ended up dragging her outside to calm her down. I think she thought I was taking sides, but I wasn't. She ordered Stevie in the car, and they left." Lee was quiet for a moment. A family torn apart by old hurts that would never heal. "A month later, Dad suffered his stroke."

"Lucy felt responsible for it," Holden said. "She told me as much."

"I wouldn't know. She refused to take my calls, and once, when I drove to her house, she wouldn't answer the door. I finally gave up." Lee was thoughtful. "As for whether she was seeing anyone, I once heard she was involved with a married man. I don't know if it was just gossip, but the woman who works for me pretty much has the goods on everybody in town."

"What's her name?"

"Carol Szarmach."

"You know who the man was?"

"No. I made it clear to Carol that I wasn't interested in gossip about my sister. I figured what Lucy did was her business. I only hoped she'd be discreet so it wouldn't get back to my parents."

Holden pondered it. "You'll have to admit the money and surgery changed her," he said. "Luxury home. Custom Jag. Designer clothes."

"What changed her was knowing she finally had control of her life, that she didn't have to take abuse any longer. You ask me, I think she deserved every bit of pleasure she could get."

"I'm not faulting her," Holden said quickly. "If anyone deserved it, Lucy did. I'm just wondering if her lifestyle change had anything to do with her death." He glanced toward the window. "Your truck is here. Do you want me to go with you?"

Lee stood. "I think it'd be better if I told them alone." She put her hand on the door, then turned. "Holden, I want to help in the investigation."

He frowned. "No way."

"I can find out things. Carol Szarmach practically has an FBI file on everyone in town."

"Stay out of it, Lee. That's an order."

"Fine," she snapped. "But if I suspect for one minute that you're dragging your feet on this case, I'll be on you like white on rice." She closed the door behind her.

Lee's parents had lived in the same house for as long as she could remember: a brick ranch with hunter-green shutters, surrounded by azalea bushes that lit up the yard for a few short weeks in spring. They had bought the place for less than ten thousand dollars, when property and interest rates were ridiculously low; it had recently appraised for close to one-hundred grand.

The area was within walking distance to town. As children, Lee and Lucy had walked to the theater for Sunday matinees. She'd felt so grown up, peeking into the windows of Millie's Dresses, where the latest styles—at least by Comfrey's standards—were fitted on mannequins with stiff, unnatural-looking hair. There was Marty's Hardware, a massive, musty-smelling store with wooden floors that creaked like something out of a haunted house; Deal's Department Store, owned and operated by Frank and Alma Deal, who fitted her and Lucy in school shoes each fall; and Jazzie's Beauty Shop. Lee had gone there for her first real hairdo the day of the senior prom. Her mother had made a big to-do over the whole thing, then carried on something fierce when Lee stuck her head beneath the kitchen faucet and washed it out.

"Don't make such a fuss, Mama," Lucy had said. "You know darn good and well Lee don't go for those fancy styles." Lucy was already married by then, but she spent more time at home than she had before she'd moved out.

"But it's the senior prom," Shelby Cates bawled like a lost calf as she watched her youngest comb the tangles from her long hair. "You'd think she could just this once try to look like a lady."

"Jazzie's the worst beautician in town," Lee blurted. "All she works on is old ladies. She wouldn't recognize a modern-day hairstyle if it came up and bit her on that old bubble butt of hers."

"Come on, Lee," Lucy said. "I'll do your hair up nice for you. You don't need much, you're already the prettiest girl in Comfrey."

Lee knew her sister was just being polite, but it was a nice compliment coming from the one who'd always outshone the other girls—until Bill Hodges had come along and snatched her up. Lucy had thought he was the cat's meow, and they'd eloped three months before her graduation. But it wasn't long before her sister changed from a lovely, bubbly young woman to someone who seldom smiled. Lee suspected Bill was sometimes mean to Lucy, but her sister refused to talk about it.

"I don't know why Mama has to make such a big deal out of a dumb ol' prom," Lee hissed on the stairs that day. "I wouldn't even be going if I weren't afraid she'd have a danged heart attack over it. And you should see the dress she picked out without even discussing it with me first. It's got more lace on it than old lady Henderson has on all her windows put together."

"That's a lot of lace," Lucy agreed.

"And guess who I'm going with? That ugly Andy Johnson."

"Do they still call him crater face?"

"Yeah. Ain't that some shit? Ugly dress, ugly date." She could always count on Lucy being sympathetic to her plight, and often wondered what she'd do without a big sister. It was Lucy who'd managed to get her a special charm, or root, a few years back, from a black woman who was said to have been related to the original root doctor of days gone by. The amulet, made of special herbs and fashioned into something that resembled a carrot, was supposed to keep evil spirits away and was guaranteed to put a stop to the nightmares Lee had suffered since childhood. It had worked, until her mother discovered it and had a conniption fit. Shelby Cates was certain her daughter had become a Satanist. She'd burned the root, along with Lee's *True Confessions* and *Modern Romance* magazines. Sure enough, the bad dreams came back. They crept up on her during times of stress or illness and sometimes when she least expected.

Now, as Lee parked in the drive behind her parents' house, she glanced at her wristwatch. Seventhirty. With any luck her father would still be asleep. Once an early riser, he now often slept till nine or ten because of the medication he took. She saw her mother peer out a curtain as she climbed the back steps, obviously curious to see who would be visiting at such an early hour. The look on Lee's face must've startled her because she opened the door immediately.

"You've been crying. What's wrong?"

Lee kissed her cheek. "You got any coffee?"

"Have you been drinking?"

Lee wished she'd thought to take a breath mint on the way over. "We have to talk, Mama."

Shelby Cates wore a worried frown as she backed out of the way. Lee entered the beige and white kitchen and headed straight for the coffee pot. She suddenly regretted not bringing Holden. He had experience in this sort of thing. One of the hardest parts of his job, he'd once told her, was telling someone they'd lost a teenager or spouse in a car accident. "It just doesn't get any worse than that, Lee," he'd told her.

"Something has you very upset," her mother said. "You're white as a bed sheet. Come sit down, honey. Whatever it is, I'm sure we can work it out if we put our heads together."

Lee carried her coffee cup to the table. She noted that the white priscilla curtains at the windows were in desperate need of washing. Her mother had been an immaculate housekeeper before her husband was rendered helpless by his stroke; now all her time was devoted to caring for him. And although Lee helped out as much as she could, there was always more to be done. She suspected it would be up to her to plan her sister's funeral.

"Where's Daddy?"

Her mother joined her at the table. "Still sleeping. He was up and down a lot last night. Okay, let's have it. Does this have anything to do with the fact you're wearing a sweatshirt with a picture of a stork on it?"

Lee glanced down at her shirt and discovered her mother was right. How she'd missed noticing the stork was beyond her. In its beak was a blanket holding a baby; below, the words, "Baby On Board." Now she realized why it was so big. "It's Debbie's," she said. "I borrowed it because I got my own sweat-shirt dirty."

"Oh." Shelby nodded as though it made complete sense.

Lee regarded her mother. She wore a house dress that was faded from too many launderings. Her hair had long ago turned to gray, and she appeared washed out from months of staying indoors with a stroke victim whom she believed would one day be normal again. Lee knew life would never be normal again.

"I'm afraid I have terrible news, Mama." The muscles in her throat constricted as she tried to say the words. "It's worse than terrible, and it breaks my heart to have to tell you." She saw the fear in her mother's eyes and knew there was no kind way to say it. "Lucy's dead."

Her mother looked at her in disbelief. "Lucy dead? Lee, that's utter nonsense. Why, Becky Myers just saw her the other day and—"

"I know it's hard to believe, Mama, but it's true. Holden personally identified her this morning."

Silence. The woman wore a dazed look.

The muscle tightened and knotted in Lee's throat, making breathing difficult. The kitchen had shrunk in size, sucking the floor up with it like something out of a crazy cartoon. Panic rioted inside of her, but she pressed forward. "Someone came into the house during the night and stabbed her," she managed.

A single gasp, pure wretchedness. Any color that was left in Shelby Cates's face faded abruptly. Lee reached for her hand. It was cold and lifeless. "I'm sorry," she said, her voice breaking with emotion. Her mother had withered in those few seconds— like a daylily yanked from the soil and left to die.

Her shoulders sagged; the skin on her face appeared to lose more of its elasticity.

"Do they know who did it?"

"Holden is investigating."

"Was she—" Her mother paused, as if she couldn't bring herself to say the words.

"She wasn't raped," Lee said, suddenly realizing she was perspiring. "This . . . this monster put a knife through her heart while she slept." She almost choked on her own fury as she imagined someone doing such a thing to her sister. "Death was instantaneous," she added. "Lucy never knew." It was a lie, of course, but Lee had already decided her parents would never know the truth.

From somewhere, her mother produced a wad of tissue. "What about Stevie? What's going to happen to him?"

Lee didn't hesitate. "He's fine. Someone's looking after him right now." Another lie, but she felt it was as necessary as the first one. "I'm so sorry, Mama. So sorry."

Her mother didn't answer. She just sat and cried softly in the tissue while Lee tried to comfort her. She no longer felt sad and bereft; all those emotions had been replaced with white-hot anger, an all-consuming rage that made her wonder if she were on the verge of losing control. So what if she did? *So fucking what?* Her sister was lying in a body bag sliced to smithereens, and God only knew what had happened to her nephew. She had a right to be pissed.

"Did Stevie see anything?"

Lee snapped her head up at her mother's question. She tried to calm herself, to concentrate on the matter at hand. She would simply have to deal with her own emotions later. "I'm sure they'll question him."

"This is going to kill your father," Shelby said.

"It's going to finish him off. He'll never get any better."

Lee suspected it was only a matter of time before the man would be completely helpless, and they would be forced to put him in a nursing home. But this was not the time to go into that.

"Do you want me to stay while you break the news to Daddy?" she asked, wondering how much he would comprehend.

Her mother shook her head. "I'll do it." She blew her nose. "We'll have to ... have to plan ... Lucy's funeral."

The funeral. Lee felt something squeeze her heart painfully. "I'll take care of it." She paused. "I think we should have a closed casket," she said, as casually as she could manage. But her voice wavered. Her mother looked up, obviously surprised she would suggest such a thing. "It's what Stevie wants," she added quickly, trying to keep her expression closed as her mother searched her face for answers that Lee had no intention of giving.

"Surely you can't be serious," Shelby Cates replied. "It means I won't get to kiss my daughter good-bye or see her for the last time. Why, Lee, it's simply not done."

Lee felt panicky again. "I think we should respect Stevie's wishes, Mama. After all, he's lost both parents within two years of one another. We have to think of him. Lucy was the only mother he ever knew. He wants to remember her the way she was." She said it as though it made perfect sense, and it had sounded logical in her mind on the drive over, but she was not prepared for the pained expression in her mother's eyes or the fact she might lose this battle and have to come forward with the truth.

"She was my daughter," Shelby replied. "How could you even suggest such a thing?"

Lee took another approach, even though she knew

it might be painful. "Face it, Mama," she said sharply. "Lucy was murdered. *Murdered*. Do you want to put her on display so every busybody in this town can parade by her coffin? Lord, we'll have a three-ring circus on our hands. There'll be reporters and TV cameras and only God knows what." She had to stop to catch her breath. "And how do we know the person who killed her won't be there? Oh, he'd love to see his handiwork, don't you think? And stand among the grieving family. That's what these sick bastards do, Mama. It gives them a thrill."

She saw the anguish in her mother's eyes and hated herself for putting it there. But there was no choice. Her own eyes teared; once more she felt her heart break. "I want my sister buried quietly and with as much dignity as possible. Stevie and I want a closed casket and a private graveside service."

Shelby was clearly shaken by her daughter's outburst. "Okay, dear," she said. "I'll go along with whatever you decide."

As they shared a moment of silence Lee's breathing became normal again, and the kitchen floor no longer felt as though it would suck her in. But she was hurting bad, and she suspected she would hurt for a long time to come.

Finally, the older woman sighed. Her face crumpled. "Oh my God. What are we going to do with Stevie?"

Lee gulped, swallowing fresh tears. "I'll see to him. That's what Lucy wanted. She even put it in her will."

See that he gets a good education, Lucy had said. *I didn't go to college like you, Lee, and that's why I was scared to leave Bill and try to make it on my own.*

The sun had been shining that day and Lucy had been the picture of health. Lee had agreed, then put the matter aside, knowing it would never come to that.

But the time had come, and Lee was faced with taking in her troubled nephew, a boy she barely knew.

After leaving her parents' house, Lee drove to the nearest pay phone and called her assistant. Carol Szarmach had worked in her stained glass studio almost from the beginning, waiting on customers and ringing up sales while Lee designed her creations in the large workshop in back. Carol was a mite of a woman in her late forties, with long red hair, who talked incessantly and at warp speed. But she had a heart of gold, found humor in everything, and the customers loved her. She answered on the first ring.

Lee wasted no time with preliminaries. "Carol, I have a family emergency and—"

"What is it, what is it?"

"Never mind, I'll tell you later. I won't be in today, but I'll call."

"Your dad had another stroke, didn't he? I knew it, I just knew it. Your mother should have tried a more holistic approach. That doctor of his is a quack. I could tell you stories—"

"It's not my father," Lee said, "but I don't want to discuss it over the phone. Grab a pencil and paper and write this down." There was some shuffling from Carol's end of the line. Lee tapped her toe impatiently.

"Okay, shoot."

"Call Leslie Rhett and tell her she can pick up her Tiffany lamp."

"It's finished? You must've worked all weekend, bless your heart. Of course, she was set on giving it to her mother for her birthday. If my mother was as mean as that old crone I wouldn't give her the time of day."

"And find the number for Southern Contractors."

"The people building the Catholic church? Lord knows where they're going to find enough Catholic members in a town filled with Baptists."

"Tell them I've got three window panels ready and one on the work table if they want to take a look. I should complete the other four in about eight weeks."

"That's going to be a real feather in your cap, Lee," Carol said. "Once everybody sees what you can do, you'll have orders coming out the kazoo. You'll never have to worry about sleeping in a cold house again."

"Speaking of which," Lee went on, "please call Allen Brothers Heating and Air and tell them I need an estimate on a new furnace. There's a key to my house under the front door mat in case they need to get in."

"I'm glad to see you're safety conscious, Lee," the other woman muttered wryly. "You want them to just go in whether you're home or not?"

"Yeah. I've known those guys all my life. Tell them I'm going to have to do something quick with the temperatures dropping the way they are."

"Anything else?"

"See if you can find Rob," she said. "Tell him I have some soldering for him on the work table."

"Find Rob-the-Jerk," Carol said. "Honestly, Lee. I don't know why you bother with him."

"I'll call you later," Lee said, knowing she would never get off the phone if Carol got started on Rob Hess, her part-time employee. She hung up the phone, climbed into her truck, and took off.

The Comfrey County Sheriff's Department was located in the basement of the courthouse, only a few blocks from Lee's shop. As she crossed the parking lot, passing men and women in business suits, she felt self-conscious in her old jeans and sneakers. Not

to mention a maternity sweatshirt that would probably set all the tongues to wagging by lunchtime.

The reception area of the sheriff's department was
nothing more than a square room lined with hard
plastic chairs and no smoking signs plastered on bat-
tleship gray walls. Holden was not in but was expected shortly.

Lee grabbed an old *Newsweek* from a magazine
rack and sat down, but after several unsuccessful attempts to concentrate, gave up, her thoughts too
chaotic. How had her father taken the news of
Lucy's death? Had he really been able to comprehend the situation? And the funeral. She slumped in
her chair, the weight of it literally bearing down on
her. She'd have to discuss her plans with Stevie before proceeding. *If* he was still alive. She shuddered.
A second death would be more than she could take.

Holden arrived some twenty minutes later looking
haggard. He motioned for Lee to follow him to his
office. "We found Stevie," he said the minute he
closed the door.

She went weak with relief. "Oh, thank God. Is he
okay?"

"A few scratches is all. The dogs lost his scent a
couple of times sniffing the salt marsh. Took a while
for them to pick it up again." He paused. "I have to
tell you, Lee, it doesn't look good."

She blinked rapidly. "What? What doesn't look
good?"

"We found blood on his pajamas."

"That surprises you? Good God, Holden, he probably tried to resuscitate his mother!"

He shook his head. "Lucy's mouth was taped."

Lee shuddered again and tried not to think about
it. If she allowed herself to wonder and ask questions she would go crazy. "I'm sure there's an explanation. Did you ask him?"

"He claims he laid his hand on her chest to see if her heart was beating."

She bit back a sob that threatened to escape. Her life had suddenly become one bitter struggle after another. Didn't Holden realize she had enough to contend with at the moment? Why would he even suggest her nephew was capable of such a thing?

Holden sighed. "I'm sorry, Lee, but we're going to have to hold Stevie for further questioning. And I'll want to see what the lab reports show."

Disbelief flashed in her eyes as she met his gaze. "Holden, what the hell do you think you're doing?" she sputtered, bristling with indignation. "You're picking on an innocent seventeen-year-old while the real killer is running free." She stood up to pace. None of it made sense. But the last thing she needed to do was to fight with her cousin. Holden had always been a stubborn cuss, and it wasn't likely anything she said would influence his decision.

She stopped pacing and turned, resigned. "May I at least see my nephew?" She saw the tension in his eyes turn to relief and knew he was glad she wasn't going to put up a fuss.

"Not right now, Lee. He's being processed. Listen, are your folks okay? How'd they take the news?"

She tossed him a dark look. "My mother cried. She told me to take care of Stevie. I imagine she'll shed a few more tears when she learns her grandson is in jail for murder."

"Stevie has not been charged with anything," he replied tiredly.

"Then let me take him home with me," she demanded.

"Not yet."

"What possible reason could he have to kill Lucy?" She quickly held up her hand. "Wait, before you answer that. Let's say he got angry, freaked out, and killed his own mother in a fit of rage."

"His adoptive mother," Holden interrupted.

"That doesn't matter. You know as well as I do what kind of bond they shared, Holden Cates," she said, struggling once more with her anger. "Knowing that, do you honestly believe Stevie was capable of mutilating my sister, then plunging a knife through her heart?" She shook her head emphatically. "No way, Holden. No fucking way."

"Lee—"

"This is the work of a madman, someone who has spent a lot of years hating women."

"Did you know Stevie was on medication?"

"He's being treated for ADHD. He's been on Ritalin for years." She gave a snort. "Jesus, Holden, do you know how many kids are on that stuff? I used to teach school, remember? A kid acts up, that's the first thing the doctor puts him on."

"It's a little more serious than that." Holden picked up a sheaf of papers from his desk. "He's been in and out of trouble for a couple of years now. Fighting, punching teachers, skipping school, starting fires. He came close to expulsion when they caught him with a pocket knife."

"And that makes him a cold-blooded killer? A lot of kids carry pocket knives."

"That's not all. Someone killed a bunch of white mice in the science lab at school. Stevie's name came up, but they couldn't prove anything."

Lee didn't like the sound of it, but Holden wasn't going to convince her her nephew was a killer. "Why didn't someone tell me Lucy was having problems with the boy?" she asked, though she didn't know what she could possibly have done to help. She had left teaching because she'd lost patience with kids who misbehaved, parents who didn't care, and a school system that could do nothing about either.

"Lucy didn't want anyone to know. She tried to

protect Stevie as long as she could, but the boy refused to cooperate. Started inflicting wounds on himself. Lucy finally realized she was in way over her head. She was making arrangements to put him in an adolescent treatment facility before she died. He would have been locked up, in other words."

Lee was stunned. "Inflicting wounds on himself?" she asked.

"Self-mutilating." Holden tossed the papers on his desk. "So the kid isn't a stranger to knives or blades, or any other kind of sharp object for that matter. And he knew his mother planned to put him away. You asked for motive, Lee. There it is."

She felt as though she would be sick.

Seven

JACK WAS still feeling the effects of the night before as he pulled into the parking lot of Hill and Crane Associates shortly before ten o'clock. It irritated him that he had little to no memory of the previous night, but he supposed he owed it to all those months sitting on his ass drinking tequila like it was going out of style. All his brain cells were shot to shit.

Maybe it was time to stop feeling sorry for himself. But it had become a way of life for him, and he feared change as much as he did sobriety.

He parked his car and climbed out, noting the Mercedes Benzes, Cadillacs, and BMWs. The two-story building was stuccoed and topped with red roof tiles reminiscent of southern California. It sat on a lawn that looked too perfect to be real.

Inside, the reception area was decorated by someone who had a taste for quality and the money to afford it. He found a pert receptionist sitting behind a half circle cherrywood desk. She wore a headset and spoke into a thin wire. Jack watched in fascination as her fingers danced over the switchboard. Finally, she glanced up and smiled.

"I'm Jack McCall," he said. "I have an appointment—"

"Mr. Hill is expecting you," she said. "I'll let him know you've arrived."

David Hill entered the lobby a few minutes later, a tall, angular man with silver hair and impeccable clothes. From the lines on his face, Jack guessed he was in his sixties. His handshake was firm.

"Ah, Mr. McCall, so good of you to come. I'm sorry we were unable to reach you in time for your father's funeral. I knew you'd left your practice in Atlanta, but I had no idea you were living in the Florida Keys." A shadow of annoyance crossed his deeply tanned face.

"I wasn't aware that I was supposed to keep anyone posted of my whereabouts," Jack responded with cold indifference.

The attorney smiled, but it was forced. "No, of course not. Will you please come into my office?"

Jack followed him into a room that did not resemble any law office he'd ever seen. For one thing, the only books he could see were glossy, oversized books placed on a coffee table in a sitting area that looked out onto the water.

"Please sit down, Mr. McCall." Hill indicated a chair in front of his desk. He waited until Jack was seated before doing the same. "Would you like coffee or tea?"

"What d' you say we just get down to business, Mr. Hill? I've come a long way, and I've got things to do and places to be."

David Hill leaned back in his chair and made a steeple with his fingers as he regarded the man across the desk from him. "Settle down, Mr. McCall, settle down," he said, as though he were talking to a child. "We both know you don't have a place in the world you have to be." He chuckled. "Unless you intend to fly back to the Keys in time to make happy hour at the Sandbar in Islamorada."

Jack tossed him a hostile look. "Do you have a point, old man?"

Hill smiled. "Your father was gravely disappointed when you tucked your tail and ran like you did, instead of giving that bastard in Atlanta a run for his money."

"Well, I've never been out to impress my father."

"He would have helped, you know, had you decided to fight."

"Not that it's any of your business, but some things just aren't worth fighting for."

"Was it worth losing your license to practice law, Mr. McCall? You were reputed to be the best assistant DA the city'd had in a long time. You have friends in high places; you could have called in a few favors."

"I don't beg, Hill. Unlike my mother, who was forced to at times, because of our dire circumstances. And the subject of Atlanta is not open for discussion. So if you have nothing further, I'll be on my way." He got up.

The older attorney stood as well and quickly moved to a cabinet. He opened it to reveal a fully stocked bar. "It's getting on in the day, Mr. McCall. If it's a drink you require—"

Jack's eyes clouded in anger. "Fuck you, you old bastard. I don't have to take this from you or anybody else." He started for the door. The other man chuckled. Jack spun on his heels. "What's so damn funny?"

David Hill straightened his shoulders. "Mr. McCall, I am trying very hard to make you a wealthy man, but you don't seem the least bit interested. Why is that?"

Jack didn't let his surprise show. "I've had money before. It didn't get me jack-shit."

"Not the kind of money I'm talking about, my friend. But then, you've probably grown accustomed to your present lifestyle. What was your last job title, Mr. McCall? Repo man, I believe? And before that, you were a process server. Makes one wonder why you struggled so hard to get through law school to begin with, not to mention graduating at the top of your class."

"How much money?" Jack said.

Hill smiled. "You've got your father's disposition. He would have been proud."

"Fuck my father."

The attorney paused and readjusted his glasses, obviously undeterred by the remark. "Your father, uh, Mr. Wardlaw, has bequeathed to you his entire fortune. Which, including his vast real estate holdings, art, furnishings, and an eighty-foot yacht, should put you in the neighborhood of about eight million dollars."

Jack let out a low whistle. "Jesus. That's a nice neighborhood to be in." He suddenly looked suspicious. "What's the catch?"

"No catch. You're his son, you're entitled to it."

Jack gave a grunt. "I've never been a whiz at math, but by my calculations, he's about thirty-three years late in claiming me."

"There were extenuating circumstances. It was nothing personal."

"My mother took it personal."

The attorney shrugged. "Perhaps your father did as well. But he was a married man at the time and—"

"And his wife held the purse strings. I've heard the story a dozen times before," he said in a bored tone. "Sounds like a soap opera."

"That's why he visited you after her death. He wanted to make it up to you. He would gladly have put you through school, and when he learned of that unfortunate business in Atlanta, he prayed you would turn to him."

"Funny, I have trouble imagining Zachary Wardlaw praying about anything. Was he always a religious man or did he have a sudden change of heart as he lay dying?"

"You're a very bitter man for one so young," Hill said. "But I imagine under the circumstances it's to be expected. I assume you were innocent of the charges they filed against you in Atlanta."

"That's where you're wrong, old man. I was guilty as a whore in church, and they proved it. Now, tell me what I have to do to collect this fortune, and I'll be on my way."

David Hill gave him a knowing look. "You weren't guilty. Your witness simply got away. Your ex–father-in-law was a smart man. A devious man."

"Maybe. But I got back at him in my own way by divorcing his daughter. I would have ripped out my lungs to get rid of her, but she hung on, if for no other reason than to make my life miserable. The scandal was too much for her, and now she's somebody else's problem. So what if I was disbarred in the process."

Hill sat down. "Makes me wonder why you married her to begin with."

"She was a great piece of ass in the beginning. Unfortunately, she was a spoiled daddy's girl, and I wasn't looking to be somebody's daddy." If the insolence in his voice was not convincing that he'd suffered enough indignities in the past, the thunderous look in his eyes was.

Hill cleared his throat, obviously uncomfortable with the angry display and at a loss for words. He picked up a stack of papers and hunched his shoulders forward. "Well, I suppose we should get down to business."

Hill read Zachary Wardlaw's last will and testament, then explained it more fully to Jack. "Everything has already been put in your name," he said.

"It was Mr. Wardlaw's wish to move quickly on the matter." Hill shoved a sheaf of papers in front of the younger man. "These are the properties your father owned. They're yours to do with as you wish."

"Which one was his personal address?"

The attorney put an asterisk beside it. "It's an oceanfront villa with some five thousand square feet. Beautiful house, just beautiful. The servants are already in place. It's up to you if you wish to hire new ones, but these people were devoted to your father." He paused and pulled an envelope from the center desk drawer. "I expect you'll need some cash to hold you over for the next few days. I took the liberty of seeing to it for you." He offered it to Jack. "You'll have to visit the bank and various other lending companies to establish your signature. I can have my associate go with you to introduce you to the right people. Our firm is at your disposal, of course."

Jack noted there was ten thousand dollars inside the envelope. "Looks like you thought of everything. How good are you at speeding tickets?"

The other man looked surprised. "I beg your pardon?"

Jack pulled two slips of paper from his shirt pocket and placed them on the desk. "I got one last night, and another today. Folks in these parts are pretty serious about their speed limits."

The attorney glanced at them and made a tsking sound. "I'll certainly see what I can do, Mr. McCall, but I hope you don't make a habit of this. Your insurance rates will soar. Of course, now that you're rich, that doesn't really matter, does it?" He looked up. "Anything else?"

"Just one question. How long did you work for my old man?"

He shrugged. "Some thirty-five years."

"Did you consider yourself his personal advisor as well?"

"I like to think he listened to my advice, yes."

"And did you advise him as to his dealings with my mother? Were you responsible for the legal threats aimed her way?"

Hill suddenly looked uncomfortable. He reached for his tie and loosened the knot. "I merely tried to prevent a scandal, Mr. McCall."

"You obviously did an excellent job. My mother hanged herself when I was twelve years old."

The man cleared his throat. "Yes, we were informed of that most unfortunate incident. In Mr. Wardlaw's defense, I must say he was devastated."

"Which explains why he forgot to send flowers."

"It was never our intent to cause the lady harm."

Jack stood. "Thank you very much for your time, Mr. Hill. I trust you'll see to these matters immediately. After that, I want you to get my father's files together. I'll collect them in twenty-four hours."

Hill looked confused. "Might I inquire as to why you need these files in such a rush?"

"Because, as of today, you're fired." As Hill gaped in shock, Jack started for the door. "By the way, I see from these real estate holdings that you've been renting this building from my father."

"Y-yes, we've been here five years now."

"You got a lease?"

"It wasn't necessary. We've always rented month to month at a cut rate because we handled all your father's business matters."

"Not anymore you don't. You've got thirty days to get out."

Hill's face suddenly turned a bright red. "That's absurd. You can't just throw us out on the street."

"I can do anything I want, pal, including sue your bony ass if you don't vacate the premises thirty days from receipt of my eviction notice. Which I intend to file this afternoon."

"Your father and I had a gentlemen's agreement. I assumed you'd honor that."

"One problem with that, Hill: I'm no gentleman. You should have gathered that from all the spying you did on me." Jack walked out.

Eight

LEE WAS exhausted by the time she pulled into her driveway that evening. She had spent the day at her parents' house, taking calls, making arrangements, and seeing to her mother's well-being. The news had obviously affected her father; he'd seemed more agitated. He'd remained in his chair in front of the TV set, fidgeting with the buttons on his sweater.

Now, as Lee turned off the engine and gazed at the old Victorian, she longed for the days when her grandparents had been alive, and their presence had made the house a warm and cozy place to be. She could still see her grandfather pruning his garden and laughing as an ornery blue jay chased a playful wren from the elaborate birdbath that had been a fiftieth wedding anniversary gift. And her grandmother in her sewing room, surrounded by bolts of fake fur that had been donated by various churches to make stuffed animals for needy children. And the sun-catchers. She had taught Lee to design and create the miniature scenes that they would later tape to a window, and marvel at the way the sunlight turned the stained glass into jewel-like scenes. Together, they fashioned almost one hundred stained glass ornaments for the children's Christmas tree at the hospital, and somehow still managed to make teddy bears and puppies out of stuffing and fur. Lee was only eleven years old at the time, but the memories were still fresh within her.

But those days were gone. One by one, relatives had died or been placed in nursing homes. Cousins had married and moved away.

Now the place seemed monstrous, what with three floors to take care of. Part of the attic floor had been converted to a small apartment after her grandfather retired and decided to take in a boarder to help make ends meet. Lee seldom went up there because the ceilings were so low that she felt closed in. She'd developed a bad case of claustrophobia as a child when one of her cousins had locked her in a trunk in the attic and gone off and forgotten about her. Her grandmother had found her, terrified and gasping for breath, having wet herself a number of times.

Which explained the dreams.

The cousin had been duly punished, but Lee remembered the experience as though it had occurred yesterday. She only had to step into the small apartment to have a full-blown panic attack, so she hired a high school girl to sweep and dust when she felt it needed attention.

The house was much too large for one person, and it required constant repair. But it was hers and paid for, and she couldn't bring herself to sell it. Sometimes she wished she'd inherited land, like the rest of the grandchildren. As it was, she barely kept up with the cost of owning the place.

She thought of Stevie, who would probably be coming to live with her soon, and her stomach took a nosedive. Perhaps she had been too quick to agree to take him when Lucy had asked. Perhaps it would have been better had Lucy asked Holden to take him; after all, Stevie desperately needed a man in his life.

Lee mumbled an obscenity under her breath. What was she thinking? She couldn't break a promise to her dead sister, and she certainly wouldn't impose on Holden and his wife when they had a new baby on the way.

She truly believed in her nephew, no matter what he'd done in the past. Holden should never have told her those things. What had he hoped to accomplish? Stevie had loved Lucy. If her sister had been considering sending the boy away, Stevie would have known it was for his own good. It was Lucy who'd taken him in when nobody else wanted him, Lucy who'd given him unconditional love from the start.

Lee shrugged out of her coat, then slipped it on again once she discovered how cold the house was. She hoped Carol had been able to get in touch with the Allen Brothers; she didn't want her nephew to catch a chill on top of everything else.

Hearing a car in the driveway, Lee peeked out the window and recognized her old friend, Wade Emmett. He knocked once, then stepped inside, his dark blond hair mussed from the wind. He took one look at her face and pulled her into his arms.

"Oh, Lee, I'm so sorry. Holden called me at home with the news. I can't even imagine what you're going through."

She buried her face against his jacket and took comfort in just being held for a moment. She and Wade and Lucy had grown up together, and it was Wade, in his capacity as rescue worker and volunteer fireman, who'd pulled Lucy and Stevie to safety the night of the fire. It was also Wade who'd risked his own life going back into the flame-engulfed house for Lucy's husband.

"I heard it was on the news," Wade said, "but I've been tied up in budget meetings all afternoon, so the first I knew of it was when Holden called me. Otherwise, I would have come."

"That's not the worst of it, Wade," she said, trying to choke back tears. "They're holding Stevie for questioning. Holden thinks he killed Lucy."

He pulled back, and a scowl marred his handsome face. "Holden didn't mention that part. What kind of proof does he have?"

She swallowed with difficulty. "They found blood on Stevie's pajamas. Stevie claimed he was trying to help his mother."

"Well, of course he was. That's the first thing you learn in emergency preparedness: assist the victim. From what I've learned of the murder, this is the work of some deranged person. Not a kid." He glanced around. "Jesus, Lee, it's like an icebox in here. Why don't you turn on the heat?"

She explained about the furnace. "Carol was supposed to call the Allen Brothers today to see about installing a new one."

"I know how Carol tends to get sidetracked. I'll follow up first thing in the morning. In the meantime, I'll build you a fire. Oh, and here—" He held up a white bag bearing the name of a local chicken restaurant. "I brought you something to eat."

Touched by his thoughtfulness, she blinked back tears. "Oh, Wade, you shouldn't have."

"Hey, it's no big deal," he said, hugging her against him.

Fifteen minutes later, they were sitting before a blazing fire sipping coffee. Lee was nibbling on a piece of chicken as a courtesy to Wade, but she had no appetite. She recounted all that had happened that morning, the awful details of her sister's murder, pausing from time to time to wipe tears from her eyes. "I called the funeral home today. They say they probably won't get Lucy's body back until

Wednesday, Thursday at the latest. I guess that means they'll do an autopsy."

Wade put his arms around her and pulled her close. "So tragic," he said. "She was a beautiful woman. I remember how kind she was to me after the fire."

"You saved her life. Not to mention her son's." Lee was thoughtful for a moment. "Wade, do you know anything about the trouble Stevie got into at school?"

"You must be talking about the science lab incident." He nodded. "My information is secondhand, of course. I know the coach at Stevie's school. Way I heard it, someone broke into the lab, tore the hell out of the place, and killed some mice in the process."

"Stevie was a suspect?"

"Only because he was a student teacher's assistant and had a key to the door."

"I've never heard of giving keys to the students. We didn't do it when I was teaching."

"You have to understand, Stevie's in the gifted programs, the college prep courses. I understand he has an IQ that'll knock your socks off. When a kid shows that much initiative they're usually given more responsibility."

"So you're saying Stevie was a suspect simply because he had a key, and not because anyone saw him do anything wrong," Lee demanded.

"Right. Of course, he'd already been in a couple of fights by this time, and they'd caught a knife on him, so the teachers naturally pegged him as a suspect. My friend thinks Stevie was set up."

"By whom?"

"Well, it's just speculation, but there's another senior who has it in for Stevie, and he's been making the kid's life hell for some time now."

"What's this kid got against Stevie?"

"Stevie's considered a nerd because he's so smart. This senior is a jerk and a no-brainer," Wade replied.

"I thought The Academy only accepted unusually bright or gifted students."

"That's their claim. They used to have a student teacher ratio of ten to one. But the new headmaster, Herb Henderson, is a greedy SOB from what I've heard, and the school is hurting for money. The computer lab looks like something out of the dark ages, and the library is a joke. My friend says Henderson doctors the scores on the entrance exams so that nobody is turned away. Which accounts for the fact that there are a number of undesirables attending the school now."

The sound of a car pulling into her drive made Lee look up. "Wonder who that could be?" she asked.

"Are you expecting someone?"

"No." She got up from the sofa and peered out the window. "Oh, Lord, it's Holden," she said. "I hope it's not more bad news."

"I think you've had your quota for the day," Wade said, having followed her over. "Perhaps he's just stopping by to check on you on his way home."

Lee opened the back door before Holden could knock. He looked tired. "What's wrong? Did something happen to Stevie?"

Holden nodded a hello to Wade and put his arm around Lee. "Aren't you going to offer me a cup of coffee before you interrogate me?" he asked, dropping a kiss on her forehead.

"I'll get the coffee," Wade said.

Holden led Lee to the table and waited for her to sit down before he took the chair next to her. "I've good news, hon," he said, taking her hand in his. "We've got a lead. And it doesn't point to Stevie."

Lee gave a hoot of victory. "I knew it!"

Wade looked impressed. "So soon? Wow, you

guys don't mess around." He set the coffee on the table.

Holden thanked him and took a sip from the steaming mug. "Man, I really needed this. It's been a long day."

"Tell me what you've got," Lee said impatiently.

"Some of it's confidential."

She waved his comment aside. "So tell me anyway and save me the trouble of breaking into your office."

Holden looked at Wade. "I think she would actually stoop to that."

"I *know* she would," the other man said.

"Okay, what we've got is this. We found a couple of strands of black hair on the pillow next to Lucy's, as well as fingerprints on a glass in the bedroom. The hair has already been sent off for a DNA analysis, but that'll take a while. However—" He paused and smiled. "We put the fingerprints through the AFIS and got a hit."

Lee pounced on it. "Who is he?"

"A disbarred lawyer with a drinking problem and a history of spousal abuse."

Lee shook her head sadly. "Could Lucy choose 'em or what?"

"That's not all. Come to find out, one of my deputies gave the guy a speeding ticket shortly after midnight the night your sister was killed. There was a woman in the car with him at the time, and my guy says she fits the profile of the victim."

"I hope you're here to tell me this guy is behind bars."

"We haven't located him yet, but he got another speeding ticket the following morning in Hilton Head." Holden sipped his coffee. "We'll find him, Lee."

"What about Stevie?"

Holden didn't hesitate. "Just because this guy was

at your sister's place doesn't mean he murdered her. He's still innocent until proven guilty."

"You're cutting him more slack than you have my nephew," she said sharply.

Holden sighed. "I'll release Stevie in the morning. There'll be terms and conditions, of course. I don't want the boy leaving town for any reason."

"Like he's going to go someplace on foot."

"One more thing. Toxicology discovered that the Scotch on your sister's bedside table was laced with a drug."

"What kind of drug?"

"Something from the benzodiazepine family."

"Come again?"

"Trade name Xanax. I'm sure you've heard of it. I spoke with Lucy's doctor, and he confirmed that he'd recently given her something for anxiety. We haven't found the bottle, but going by what the doctor said he prescribed, she would have had about thirty pills left."

"Would she have felt the effects in just one drink?" Lee asked.

"I would think so, since the Scotch bottle was less than half full. The pathologist will be able to give us more once he has her autopsy results."

"This could be good news, Holden," she said. "If Lucy ingested a substantial amount of the drug, then she may not have been aware of what was going on." Her eyes suddenly teared. "She may have been unconscious when this monster cut her."

"That's a distinct possibility. The pathologist found a nasty lump on her head. She may have come to at some point, and the killer knocked her out."

"So why was she bound and gagged?" Wade asked.

Holden shrugged. "Maybe that's how this guy gets his kicks." He glanced at his wristwatch and stood. "I've got to go. Debbie's keeping my dinner warm for me." He made for the door, then paused. "Is it me or is it freezing in here?"

"My furnace has kicked the bucket. I'm getting a new one. Soon, I hope." She stood when he opened the door. "Holden, wait." She stepped closer. "When you find this sonofabitch lawyer, I want to get a look at him."

"Forget it, Lee," he said, looking stern. "I've shared a lot more with you than I should have, simply because we're family. Don't make me sorry I did."

At 2 a.m., Lee awoke from a bad dream. She saw the fireplace and the hot coals, still glowing, and remembered she'd made up the sofa so she could sleep in front of the fire to keep warm. She got up, grabbed a couple of logs, and put them on the grate, then stuffed newspapers beneath them until she had a blaze going.

That one task sapped all her strength, leaving her depleted physically and emotionally. Tears stung her eyes as she climbed beneath the mountain of blankets. Her misery was so great that she feared she would never find her way out. Tears were not enough, yet they were all she had to express her grief.

"Lucy," she whispered. She buried her face in her pillow and released an anguished sob.

Nine

THE LAP of luxury, that's what it was.

Jack McCall gazed about the expansive bedroom as he enjoyed a hearty breakfast served on fine bone china and crystal on a silver tray. He'd slept in the master suite, the very bed on which his father had taken his last breath just a few days ago. The housekeeper had wanted to put him in a guest room, explaining the master was not ready because it was being aired after his father's lengthy illness. Jack had insisted and waited for the woman to make it up for him.

A brief tour of the villa, all five thousand square feet, convinced him that his old man had at least possessed good taste if not compassion. The floors and walls were done in white Italian marble, the sofas and bedspreads a deep emerald that matched the bay outside. There was even a rotunda in the entryway, an enclosed, European-style swimming pool, and a regulation tennis court. The man had lived like a king. Still, there was no warmth about the place. To Jack, it felt more like an exclusive hotel than a home.

He realized he was gritting his teeth. All that money. It pissed him off royally that his mother had worked shit jobs to keep them fed and clothed while his father had lived like a king. He choked back his rage, and pressed the channel button on the remote control to find something on the big-screen TV that would hold his interest. Nothing but talk shows. He paused for the local news, hoping to get a look at the weather.

Good thing about living in the Keys, the weather pretty much stayed the same year-round. He'd exchanged most of his suits and preppy-style clothes for jeans and cut-offs when he'd told everybody in Atlanta to kiss his ass and headed south. But up here in South Carolina, a cold front had come through, and he didn't have the clothes for it.

Jack suddenly laughed. What the hell was he thinking? He had enough money to outfit everybody in town if he pleased.

Someone knocked on the door. "It's open," he called out.

The butler stepped inside with two men on his heels. Both wore dark suits. Jack knew without being told they were cops. "What the hell do you want?"

"Jack McCall?" They moved toward him, one on either side of the bed.

"I'm McCall. What's going on?"

"Mr. McCall, I'm Carl Smith, and this is Dave Wright, from the Hilton Head Police Department. We have a warrant for your arrest for the murder of Lucille Hodges."

Jack stared back, wondering if he'd heard right. "Who the fuck is Lucille Hodges?"

One cop looked at the other, a smirk on his lips. "How quickly they forget."

Carl Smith pulled out handcuffs. "You have the right to remain silent. Anything you say can and will be used against you in a court of law . . ."

Jack sat there for a moment in stunned silence. Lucille Hodges? Lucy? A face suddenly appeared to him like out of a fog. The girl with the red Chinese bed? The detective was rambling. "I know my goddamn rights," Jack said. "Save your breath."

"Okay, then," the other man said. "Let's ride."

Holden thrummed his fingers against the desk as he waited for the Hilton Head Police to deliver Jack McCall. Someone tapped on his window, and he glanced up to find his deputy, Willis Green, standing outside his office. He motioned him in.

"You got a minute, Sheriff?"

"That's about all I've got. What's up?"

"I've questioned Lucy Hodges's neighbors, some of them twice, and I have a funny feeling about the old guy. Hyram Atwell's his name."

Holden leaned back in his chair and cupped both palms behind his head. Willis Green was a good deputy, although he tended to go off half-cocked at times. Wouldn't give up on a case till he'd turned it upside down and inside out. "I'm listening."

"When I told the neighbors there'd been a fatality, every one of them wanted to know what happened— whether it was an accident or a break-in. That's the way it usually is; folks like the details, especially if they're gory."

"I know that, Willis. That's why I'm sheriff. Now, what's your point?"

The deputy looked embarrassed. "Sorry. This Atwell fellow didn't ask questions. He expressed his regret, but he didn't seem at all curious when I told him there'd been a death."

"I hope you're not hanging your suspicions on that one little peculiarity," Holden said. "The guy's got to be what, seventy-five or eighty? Looks like he might blow over in a strong wind."

"That's not all," Green said. "He's got windows all over his house, yet the blinds and curtains are closed tight. Says it's 'cause of his glaucoma. But I stopped by the library, read everything I could get my hands on about glaucoma, and I can't find anything that says light is bad for it. Even more curious, his recliner is situated so he can enjoy the views. And one of those views would be the house next door. Lucy Hodges's place." Green paused. "And you know how it is when curtains are pulled open for some time—they form pleats? These curtains had very distinct pleats. Those pleats would have softened or fallen out completely if the curtains had been closed for any length of time. And if those curtains stay closed all the time, tell me how come there are several plants sitting in front."

"Where'd you get your training, Green? Quantico?"

Green smiled. "Don't I wish."

"So you think this guy, Atwell, may have seen or heard something after all, and he's giving you the runaround?"

"He claimed his hearing was bad, that he wears two hearing aids, although he did claim to hear the sirens. Said he knew there was trouble when he went out and got his newspaper. Only problem with that is, we had the roads blocked. The newspapers weren't delivered that morning."

"A lot of inconsistencies there," Holden said.

"And you want to hear something weird? The man has a little cemetery at the back of his property."

"Maybe that's where he buries his pets after they die."

"He doesn't have a pet, and he claimed he has never had one. Said his wife had allergies. Besides, there's twenty-five or thirty markers back there."

"He could be burying dead birds or squirrels. Did you ask him?"

Green shook his head. "No."

Holden looked thoughtful. "Okay, I'll let you snoop around, but don't do anything to upset him. I don't want the press accusing us of picking on old folks." Holden suddenly saw a familiar face on the other side of the window. Lee knocked on the glass. "Oh, shit, here comes trouble."

The deputy stood. "I'll be going, then."

Lee opened the door. "May I come in?"

"Might as well. Everybody else has." He looked at Deputy Green. "Follow up on that and get back to me."

The deputy nodded at Lee and stepped out. She approached Holden's desk. "I've come for Stevie."

"I told you I would deliver him personally. I haven't had a chance to process his exit papers yet."

"I'll wait." She sat down in a chair in front of his desk. She was exhausted from lack of sleep, and her eyes felt gritty and swollen from all the crying she'd done. Where was the relief it was supposed to have brought her? She was as heavy-hearted now as she'd been the day before.

"This really isn't a good time, Lee," Holden said. His secretary tapped on the door and opened it. She smiled at Lee, then turned to Holden. "The two detectives from Hilton Head just came through the back door with the suspect. You want them in room two?"

Lee perked up, her weariness chased away with an adrenaline rush. "Is this the guy you were telling me about last night? You've found him?"

Holden stood. "Teresa, bring Miss Cates a cup of coffee. She looks like she could use one." He looked at Lee. "I'll have another officer process the exit papers so you can take Stevie home. You can wait here."

"It *is* him, isn't it?" Lee's heart beat faster. The tense lines on Holden's face told her she was right. She bolted from her seat and yanked the door open while Holden shouted for her to stop. "No way," she yelled. "I want to see the piece of dog shit that killed my sister."

"Goddammit, Lee, would you stop being a pain in the ass and do as I say!" He hurried out the door and slammed into his secretary. Hot coffee scalded them both, and he paused briefly to apologize and help her up from the floor before he took off again.

Lee raced ahead. Reckless anger pushed her through a set of swinging doors that led to another part of the building. Holden called out to her angrily from a short distance behind, but she ignored him. Her eyes blazed, and her breath was ragged in her own ears as she searched blindly through the corridors like a mouse in a maze.

She pushed through another door, and there he was.

He was easy to distinguish from the policeman in his faded jeans, tee-shirt and windbreaker. His hands were cuffed behind him. He looked like a murderer: hair black as sin, falling well past his collar. His skin was brown and weathered, as though he'd spent too much time in the sun. A construction worker, perhaps, who traveled from town to town and killed. He looked annoyed, and when his gaze found hers, his look was disparaging. *A woman hater.* Lee's face paled with rage and shock, and her eyes froze with icy contempt. Hatred flashed through her as swiftly and fiercely as a thunderbolt.

They stared at one another as a chill black silence surrounded them.

She closed the distance between them. "My name is Lee Cates," she said, her voice trembling with a numbing fury. He stared back at her, his blue eyes hard as stone. The eyes of a cold-blooded murderer.

Finally, he shrugged. "Is that supposed to mean something to me?"

Holden came up behind her, touched her shoulder. "Let's go, Lee."

She ignored him and stepped forward. The detectives on either side of him looked curious, but they didn't try to prevent her from getting closer. "I'm Lucy Hodges's sister." There was a faint thread of hysteria in her voice. "You remember Lucy? The woman you butchered? Does *that name* mean anything to you?" She brought her knee up, fast and hard, into his groin. As his eyes and face registered pain, he uttered a string of obscenities and bent double. The detectives didn't so much as make a move to stop her. One grinned.

"Lee, goddammit!" Holden grabbed her arm. "Come with me!"

Her insides shook. "You'd better hope they keep your sorry ass locked up," she told the man, "because I'll take great pleasure in cutting off your balls and shoving them down your throat if I get half a chance."

Jack raised up and glared at Holden through pain-filled eyes. "Is this how you interrogate people in this town, Sheriff?" he demanded.

Holden dragged Lee down the hall as she struggled to break free. By the time they reached his office, they were both out of breath.

"That was real ladylike," he shouted. "You just violated my prisoner's rights."

"Fuck your prisoner," she yelled. "And fuck his rights. He doesn't even deserve to live." Lee realized she was fast losing control, but she didn't care. The anger was spewing from her, and she wanted revenge.

"Listen to that mouth of yours," Holden said. "You'd better get a grip because I'm two seconds from locking your ass up."

"You wouldn't put me in jail," she sputtered indignantly.

"Try me."

Her brain was in chaos, but she knew Holden would put her behind bars if he felt she was out of control. And then where would Stevie go? She sat back, tears welling up and falling to her cheeks as he waited for her to settle down.

"I mean it, Lee," he said. "If you don't pull yourself together, I'll handcuff you and drive you to the mental hospital in Columbia for observation."

Lee was too hurt and angry to respond.

Holden looked at the female deputy who'd appeared to help. "Keep her here until I come back." He shot Lee a dark look before adding, "And if she tries to escape, shoot her." He slammed out the door.

Some minutes later, after Holden had signed a number of forms accepting Jack McCall into custody and releasing the Hilton Head Police Department from all responsibility, he sat across from the man at a wooden table in the interrogation room. It was a somber room, devoid of pictures, the window barred. No longer handcuffed, Jack's arms were crossed, mouth clenched tight, and a look of pure resentment on his face.

"Would you like a cup of coffee, Mr. McCall?" Holden asked.

"How about we just get the show on the road."

"I understand you've been notified of your rights, and that you waived your right to an attorney."

"For the time being. I have every confidence we can clear up this misunderstanding."

"Okay. Let's get started." Holden pulled a photo of Lucy Hodges from a folder and showed it to him. "You ever seen this lady before?"

Jack nodded. "I met her at one of the clubs in Hilton Head."

"You remember the name of this club?"

Jack thought a moment. "The Anchor Club. Pretty snazzy compared to what I've been in lately."

"Did you talk to anybody else while you were there?"

"I talked to a lot of people. Then this gorgeous brunette walks up to me—" He paused and motioned to the photo. "And asks me to buy her a drink. Naturally, I gave her my full attention."

"What time was this?"

He shrugged. "Ten o'clock."

"The night before the murder took place? November fourth?"

"Yeah." He nodded. "After about an hour, I realized she'd had too much to drink so I offered to take her home. I had no idea she lived an hour away."

"What happened after you got to her place?"

"That's where it gets murky. I think I passed out shortly after we arrived."

"Are you a heavy drinker?"

"I've been known to drink more than I should on occasion."

"Can you remember anything about her house?"

Jack scanned his memory. The red Chinese bed was the only thing that came to mind. The actual murder scene, from what he'd overheard from the Mutt and Jeff cops. He knew better than to place himself there. He also knew customers at the Anchor Club could identify him, as well as the highway patrolman who'd stopped to give him a speeding ticket while Lucy was in his car. "I'm afraid I don't remember much of anything."

"Do you remember what time it was?"

"It was shortly after midnight. I remember because I was having a drink in her living room and admiring all these clocks." He'd actually had the drink in Lucy's bedroom. "You want to know what I think?"

Holden stopped writing and looked up.

"I think she drugged me."

"What makes you say that?"

"Because the next thing I knew it was morning, and I was in a dumpy motel room."

"Have you ever blacked out while drinking?"

"No."

"Do you use recreational drugs?"

"Not since college. I smoked a little pot back then, but I never got involved with the hard stuff."

"Do you remember the name of the motel?"

"No."

"Or what time you checked in?"

Jack knew it would be easy enough for them to find out. "I think I may have passed out on her sofa for a while. I got up at some point and left. I remember driving for a long time. I think I was trying to figure out which highway to take to Hilton Head. Finally, I spotted this motel and pulled off." He raked his fingers through his hair. "I'm telling you, Sheriff. I think this lady put something in my drink."

"You're saying you don't remember being in Mrs. Hodges's bedroom?"

"No. I remember the sofa and the clocks."

"We found black hair on the pillow next to where the body was found, Mr. McCall. We're going to take samples of your hair, and I'll bet my ass they match."

Jack shrugged, but years prosecuting a case told him he was screwed. "Maybe she put a pillow under my head when I passed out on the couch, how the hell do I know? Look, I didn't kill her. Matter of fact, I was hoping to look her up once I finished my business in Hilton Head."

"You say your memory is sketchy, that you passed out at some point. What makes you so sure you didn't kill her?"

Jack gave a snort of disgust. "C'mon, Sheriff. A woman is mutilated and stabbed. You think someone could forget doing that sort of thing?"

"People go off the deep end all the time."

"Check the clothes I was wearing that night. You won't find a drop of blood." He made a sound of disgust. "I wouldn't have the stomach for it. I don't even hunt, for Christ's sake."

"As a prosecutor, I'd imagine you've seen your share of gore."

"I have. But I also look for motive. Tell me what mine was." He leaned forward. "Give me one reason why I'd carve up a beautiful woman, then stab her to death."

Holden looked at him. "I'm still working on it."

"Then why don't you find out who the guy was that walked out on her at the Anchor Club."

Holden was surprised. "She was with someone else?"

"An older fellow. I didn't get a good look at him because I was eyeballing her. He left, and the next thing I know she's standing next to me at the bar. Said she'd just had an argument with her boyfriend. Could be he waited in the parking lot and followed us back to her place. The reason I'm suggesting this is because I noticed she was real nervous. At first I thought it was me, because she didn't know me very well." He shook his head. "I think she knew someone was out to get her. Could be this person put something in our drinks." It was the first time Jack had considered that possibility.

"Did you hear or see anybody while you were in the house?"

"Not a soul. I think she might have mentioned having a kid, but I never saw him."

"Did you lock the door behind you when you left?"

Jack gave a snort. "Hell, I don't know. All I know for sure is I didn't touch the lady."

Holden checked his notes, then looked up at the man across the table from him. McCall was lying. He knew it as well as he knew his own name. "I'll check this out, Mr. McCall, but with the evidence we have against you, I have no choice but to hold you."

Jack glared at him. "You're going to try and pin this on me, aren't you?"

Holden stuck his pen in his shirt pocket. "I will note for the record your cooperation during questioning."

"We both know that doesn't mean jack-shit. I'd like to call my attorney now."

Ten

LEE BOLTED from the chair when Holden reentered his office. "Did you get a confession?" she asked.

"Nope." He looked at the deputy. "Tell Teresa to bring two cups of coffee in here, please, ma'am. Then I want you to get Steven Hodges ready to go. Bring him to my office." She nodded and hurried out.

Holden rounded the desk. "Mind if I sit in my own chair?"

Lee moved to the other side of the desk. "What'd he say?"

"Oh, he admitted to running into Lucy in a bar in Hilton Head. Said he took her home because she'd had too much to drink."

Lee waited for him to go on. "And?"

"That's all he remembers. When he woke up he was in a motel room."

"So he denies killing her?"

"No surprise there. The prisons are filled with innocent men. But like I said, I've got hair samples from the pillow and fingerprints on a glass. If they match up I can put him right smack in the bedroom where Lucy died. I don't have motive yet, but I'll come up with something."

"The guy's sick, Holden. He did it for the thrill of

it. We already know he's got a record of spouse abuse. Probably hates all women."

"There's usually sex involved in a crime like this. But no semen was found."

"Maybe it had nothing to do with sex. It was a crime of hate."

The door opened and Holden's secretary carried in a small tray of coffee and set his on his desk. "I shouldn't be discussing this with you, Lee," he said, once they'd sipped in silence for a moment.

"We're talking about my sister here," she said, her mouth set in annoyance. "I can help you with this. I can question people, find out information you need. Folks're going to open up to me a lot quicker than they would someone in a uniform."

He leaned back in his chair and crossed his legs. He almost looked amused. "I don't know how I got by all these years without your help, kiddo. What would you think about signing on as my top deputy?"

"I'm in no mood for jokes, Holden."

"Listen, I've been sheriff for seven years, and I haven't had any complaints. I'll investigate this case as I see fit, and you'll stay out of my way. I mean it, Lee," he said firmly.

She took another sip of coffee, undeterred by his remark. "He could have a serious accident in his cell," she said. "Think how much money you could save the taxpayers."

"Stop it." Holden pointed a finger at her. "I'm going to pretend I didn't hear any of this nonsense and you're going to go home and let me do my job."

She opened her mouth to respond, but she was interrupted when someone knocked on the door. Through the window beside it, she saw Stevie peering in. Lee quickly opened the door, and the boy rushed into her arms.

"Aunt Lee, I'm so glad to see you!" he exclaimed.

"I'm happy to see you too, Stevie," she said, her eyes immediately filling with tears. Lee hugged him tight, then stepped back to look at him. He was taller than her, but still small for his age, and pitifully thin. The brown freckles across his nose stood out against a face that was too pale, as though he spent very little time outdoors.

"What's the matter, kiddo, did you run out of comic books?" Holden was smiling.

The boy looked at him. "It got pretty boring after a while. And you guys really need to get cable on that TV."

Holden looked at Lee. "I explained to Stevie that we felt it necessary to hold him here for his own safety. You understand, don't you, son?"

Stevie shrugged. "I guess so." He looked at Lee, and the light went out of his eyes. "I suppose you heard about my mom."

She ached for him, reached up, smoothed his hair from his eyes. "Yes, and I'm so sorry, honey. I loved your mother very much." She paused. "I thought you might like to have a hand in planning her funeral. Or would that be too hard for you?"

His youthful face seemed to age as he stood there. "I guess it would be okay."

"Well, if you change your mind, just tell me. Right now, we're concerned with taking care of you."

"Am I still in danger?"

"No," she assured him. "Holden has arrested the killer. You're perfectly safe."

Stevie's eyes got big. "You found the man who killed my mom?" he asked.

Holden shot Lee a dark look. "I have someone in custody, Stevie, but he hasn't confessed. The sooner you get your Aunt Lee *out of here*, the sooner I can get back to my investigation."

* * *

"Are you hungry?" Lee asked Stevie as they climbed into her truck.

"Starving. All they had for breakfast was oatmeal, and I hate that crap."

"We'll drop by the Cozy Kitchen, how's that?"

"Yeah, okay." He was quiet while she started the engine and backed out of the parking space. "Did you hear what that guy did to my mom?" he asked, a heaviness in his voice.

Lee pulled to the main road and braked. Something squeezed her heart painfully. She looked at her nephew. "Yes."

He shook his head, and there was misery in his eyes when he looked at her. "Put a knife right through her heart."

Lee felt as though someone had put a knife through her own heart. "Does it help to talk about it, honey?"

"I dunno. They sent a shrink to see me yesterday and again this morning, but I didn't feel like talking to her."

"You might have felt better afterward if you had." She pulled out into the traffic.

He made a grimace. "I'm not going to tell some stranger a bunch of private stuff. Besides, I don't need a psychiatrist just because I got into a lot of fights at school."

"I hear one of the kids is picking on you," Lee said, hoping he would open up to her. "I wish you could just ignore him."

He made a sound of disgust. "Would you ignore it if some creep was constantly telling you your mother was the town slut?"

Lee gasped. "Is that what it's all about?"

"Yeah." He wouldn't look at her.

"Did you tell the headmaster?"

"No. I didn't even tell my mom until she threatened to send me away."

Lee reached over and patted his shoulder. "I'm sure she understood you were trying to defend her."

He leaned back in the seat and sighed heavily. "Every time I close my eyes I see her face . . . the way it was all cut up like that." His voice broke. "I don't get much sleep."

"I know, honey. I don't sleep well either. All we can do is try to support one another and hope that each day gets a little easier."

He looked at her. "Do you believe that? That each day gets a little easier?"

Lee pulled into the parking lot of the restaurant and cut the engine. "Yes, Stevie, I honestly do." Even as she said it, Lee hoped and prayed that was the case. She would not last long with the amount of pain and heartache she was carrying around.

Lee could tell Carol had something on her mind when she and Stevie walked into her stained-glass shop, but her friend quickly put on a smile and started chatting with the boy. She fished a Snickers bar out from behind the counter and handed it to him.

"Do you care if I look around in back?" he asked, tearing the paper off the candy bar and chomping on it.

Lee wondered how he could possibly eat with all that he'd just put into his stomach. "Sure. Just be careful not to disturb what's on the work table."

Carol waited till the boy had disappeared on the other side of the door. "A sheriff's deputy left here not ten minutes ago. Asked me a bunch of questions about Lucy. I answered every one of them as truthfully as I could, just like you told me to. Which was really unnecessary since I always tell the truth anyway."

Lee had finally given Carol the news in a phone call from her parents' house the day before, only to spend the next twenty minutes listening to every gory crime Carol had ever read about. "What did he ask you?" Lee asked, wanting to cut things short if at all possible.

"First he wanted to know how well I knew Lucy, and I told him I didn't know her at all. I explained everything I was about to tell him was hearsay and nothing more."

"In other words you admitted to being a gossip," Lee said, giving her a wry smile.

"Wise ass."

Lee waited. "So, what'd you tell him?"

"That I'd heard Lucy was going out with married men. And that she was having an affair with her plastic surgeon."

Lee threw up her hands in frustration. "Carol, how can you possibly know all this?"

"I hear things. And the reason I know about the plastic surgeon is because his receptionist used to be a good friend of mine. We met for lunch last month, and she told me all about Dr. Kit's star patient. She didn't mention Lucy by name, but she said the woman had been in a house fire, etcetera, etcetera, and it was obvious as hell who she was talking about."

"Is Dr. Kit married?"

"Thirty years to the same woman." She paused. "You know why Lucy only dated married guys, don't you?"

Lee sat on a stool behind the counter. Of course she knew. "Enlighten me."

" 'Cause she hated men and had no intention of ever committing to one after what she went through. Can you blame her?"

For that, Lee didn't blame her. "She's dead, Carol. What does it matter how I feel one way or the other?"

"Wouldn't surprise me if Dr. Kit's wife got wind

of the affair and decided to destroy her husband's masterpiece."

Lee had already thought of that. "It sounds good, but they've already got the murderer behind bars." Carol's mouth dropped open but nothing came out. Lee considered it a miracle of grand proportions.

Stevie came through the door, and the conversation came to a halt. "Man, that's some awesome stained glass you got back there, Aunt Lee. Did you do it?"

She smiled. "Yes, I did. It's going into the new Catholic church on Main Street. The one on my work table needs soldering. I'm waiting for this guy named Rob to come by and do it."

"Who hasn't bothered to call me back," Carol said. She suddenly snapped her fingers. "I forgot to tell you. Southern Contractors called. They wanted to know if you could finish the panels in a month."

"A month?" Lee gaped at her. "Are they crazy? I need almost twice that amount of time."

"Maybe I could help you," Stevie said. "I don't know anything about stained glass, but I could sweep or answer the phone or run errands. You wouldn't even have to pay me." Something flickered in his eyes. "Besides, it might help keep my mind off other stuff."

Lee thought it sounded like a grand idea. Not only would it take the boy's mind off his troubles, he would be close by. She definitely wanted to keep her eye on him for the time being. She forced a smile she didn't feel. "Great. When can you start?"

Eleven

HYRAM ATWELL heard the doorbell and wondered if it was Grace, his cleaning lady, coming by to check on him. She'd called the evening before after learning about the murder, and knowing her as he did, it would be just like her to show up unexpected with a bag containing something good to eat. Hyram's smile quickly died when he pulled the door open and found Detective Willis Green standing on the other side.

"Detective Green, what are you doing here?" he asked.

"I'll just take a minute of your time, Mr. Atwell. I was wondering about that little cemetery you have out back."

Hyram simply stood there for a moment, not knowing what to say. "Would you excuse me one minute?" He hurried over to the chair and put his hearing aids in, taking a little time so he could think. When he turned to the deputy he was smiling. "I'm sorry, you were saying?"

"I was asking about the little cemetery out back. I wondered if you could tell me what's buried out there?"

"Oh. Well, let's see." He scratched his head as though he were giving it a lot of thought when, in fact, he knew precisely what lay under those perfect mounds of dirt. "There's a few squirrels," he said. "Might even be a cat or two. I found one dead at the back of my property last summer. Snake probably bit him."

"When's the last time you buried something there?"

More head scratching. "My memory isn't as good as it used to be but it's been a while."

"Mind if I have a look?"

"Have a look? You mean dig them up?" Hyram wrinkled his nose at that. "I don't know, Deputy Green. That sounds pretty awful to me."

"Mr. Atwell, I don't have a search warrant, and I wouldn't normally make such a request, but I promise to put everything back like it was if you'll just let me have a quick look."

Hyram rubbed his chin and realized he hadn't shaved in two days. "I guess it'll be okay. As long as I don't have to look."

"Don't worry about a thing," Green said. "You won't even know I'm back there."

Hyram closed the door and hurried into the kitchen. Very cautiously he peered out the wooden blinds. Detective Green was already in the backyard, heading in the direction of the little graveyard with a spade. Under one arm was a roll of plastic.

A feeling of dread washed over him.

The doorbell rang and Hyram almost jumped out of his skin. He retraced his steps. When he opened the door, he found Grace standing on the other side, holding several grocery sacks. Her black forehead was wet with sweat despite the cold.

She glared at him. "If you're not going to help me with these bags, would you at least see if there's a gentleman in the house who will?"

Hyram mumbled an apology, grabbed one of the sacks, and followed her into the kitchen. She set her bag down and gave him one of her stares.

"What?" Hyram held his hands out as though sur-rendering.

"Just look at you," she exclaimed. "You haven't shaved, and your clothes are all grungy. Why aren't you wearing one of those outfits I ironed for you last time I was here?" She paused and gaped. "And since when did you start wearing a hearing aid?"

Twelve

"WHAT THE hell took you so long?" Jack demanded the minute David Hill was ushered into his cell.

Both blue-veined hands squeezed the handle of the briefcase as the old attorney looked around for a place to sit. Since the cot and toilet were his only choices, he remained standing. "I wanted to find out exactly what you were being charged with."

"I told you. Murder."

"Of a heinous nature, I might add. I saw the report. The woman's face was cut to ribbons. They found your fingerprints all over the place."

"So that makes me a killer?"

"That makes you the number-one suspect. And that chip on your shoulder isn't going to win you any popularity contests. Fact is, they can't wait to see you fry."

Jack snapped his head up and found the attorney watching him closely. "You've got real balls coming in here talking to me like that."

The lawyer's voice was syrupy, a true southern gentleman. "I'm just telling it like it is, Mr. McCall," he said, drawing the name out. "A woman has been mutilated and stabbed, and you're the only one they've placed at the scene.

"This is a tight-knit community: everybody's related to one another by birth or marriage. Baptist church on every corner, hard-working people who know the value of a dollar. You're like a big fat cockroach that has invaded their nice little town, and they want to stamp you out just as quickly as possible." On the other side of the bars, a guard nodded. "Frankly, I'm surprised they haven't already lynched you in some backwoods."

Jack gave him a withering stare. "Jesus, is this your way of trying to make me feel better?" Hill shrugged. "We'll have to arrange for a change of venue," Jack said. "I'll never get a fair trial in this one-horse town."

"We?" The lawyer laughed. "You've obviously mistaken me for someone who has an interest in your welfare—which I do not."

The guard chuckled.

"Thanks for your vote of confidence, old man. I should have my head examined for calling you in the first place. Do you think you can at least arrange for a grave plot once they strap me to the chair?"

"I am under no obligation to take your abuse, Mr. McCall," Hill said. "Especially after the way you conducted yourself in my office. The only reason I came was out of respect for your father's memory, not because I fear anything you can do to me. And if they do decide to execute you, I hope they sell tickets because it should draw a big crowd." He moved to the cell door and the guard made to let him out.

"Where the hell do you think you're going?" Jack's features were hardened with anger.

"I have no desire to stand here and watch a grown man drown in self-pity."

Jack jumped up. "Wait! You can't just walk out on me. My preliminary is tomorrow."

Hill shrugged. "I'm expected at my club."

"Fuck your club."

The attorney stepped through the door, and the guard closed and locked it, then smirked at Jack as if to say, "You're screwed."

Jack put his hands on the bars. Hill was really walking out on him. "Hey, you can't just leave me here. I need your help, man." A tense silence ensued. "Look, I'm sorry I was an SOB to you, okay? You can use the building as long as you like, and I'll keep you on retainer. Same deal you had with my old man."

"Not interested. Besides, I'm not a defense lawyer, which is precisely what you need under the circumstances."

"I don't need a damn defense lawyer; I can plan my own defense. I need somebody with a goddamn license to practice in this godforsaken place."

Hill paused. "You have an extensive vocabulary, Mr. McCall, you should go far in this world."

Jack sank onto the cot and covered his face with his hands. "I'm fucked." He looked up suddenly, a look of desperation on his face. "What if I begged?"

Hill and the guard exchanged looks. Finally, the lawyer shook his head sadly and started to walk away.

"How 'bout I get down on my knees?" Jack asked.

David Hill turned and seemed to ponder it. "I think I might like to see that."

"Me too," said the guard.

Thirteen

PERPETUAL CARE Funeral Home and Gardens was one of a dozen or more antebellum homes remaining in Comfrey. Lee suspected at one time it must have been spectacular, back when young couples courted on the wide verandah and barbecues were held in the backyard. It had gone through a few owners and just as many restorations; now, it was slightly shabby—like a favorite hat that had become worn and frayed but was still serviceable.

The McPhees did their best to keep the place up, painting whenever it needed it, seeing that the wrought iron fence surrounding the property stayed in good repair. An old black man in a red bandanna kept the lawn in order and tossed out grass seed from time to time to cover the bare spots, and cut back the fat, lavender hydrangeas that grew beside the house. Lee could remember when she and Lucy would cross the street to keep from walking in front of the funeral parlor, and to this day she couldn't look at a hydrangea bush without thinking of dead people.

Now, as she and Stevie stepped inside the gate and went up the cracked sidewalk, Albert McPhee hurried out onto the verandah and welcomed them in pronounced drawl. He was perspiring and seemed out of breath, and the single button on his dark suit strained against an oversized belly. Nevertheless, he looked tickled to see them. One would have thought they were paying a social call.

Lee dreaded going inside.

"It's so good to see you again, Lee, honey," Albert said, taking her hand in his plump one. "And this must be young Steven. I just want you to know how deeply sorry we are for your loss, and I hope you'll find comfort in knowing how much Lucy was loved in the community."

Stevie gave him an odd look. "Well, we know there was at least one person who wasn't crazy about her. How many bodies you got inside?"

Lee and McPhee just looked at him. Finally, the man gave an embarrassed cough. "Ya'll come on in the house," he said, opening the massive front door and leading them into an entryway wallpapered in magnolia blossoms. "My wife had to run out to the grocery store so it's just the three of us. Why don't we go sit in the parlor?"

He motioned them into a room with worn but serviceable furniture. Lee took a seat next to Stevie and noted right away that it was too warm. She took a deep breath and smelled flowers. Nauseatingly sweet. Probably coming from another parlor where someone else was at eternal rest. She shifted in her seat.

"Would anybody like something to drink?" McPhee asked.

Lee and Stevie both shook their heads. "I'm afraid we don't have a lot of time," Lee told him, antsy to be out of there. "Holden is expecting us back at the sheriff's office."

"Fine, then, we'll get started right away. First I need a little information." He picked up a clipboard and a pencil.

Over the next half hour, Lee and Stevie answered numerous questions about Lucy, mostly vital statistics—where she'd attended school and church, any clubs or organizations she'd belonged to. They decided on a small graveside service with family only, to be held on Friday. Finally, Albert asked if there was a particular dress they wished to have her buried in.

"She has these white satin pajamas," Stevie said. "And matching ballerina slippers. I'd like her to wear that. And I want her buried in a white coffin with lots of gardenias on it. That was her favorite flower."

Lee remembered the gardenias and felt a deep sense of loss.

Albert took notes. "You'll have to get the pajamas to me. As far as the coffin, that's no problem. But I can't promise you gardenias, son. It's too late in the season. I'll do my best, though."

"Thank you," Stevie said.

McPhee looked at Lee. "Do you have a florist you prefer using?"

"No." The only thing she preferred right now was getting the hell out of there. She could feel herself perspiring. The heat, the flowers, the knowledge that her dead sister was on the premises—it was too much. She suddenly felt she would suffocate.

"I'll have my wife call the people we deal with, see if we can get our hands on some gardenias. Where can I reach you later?"

Lee had to force herself to concentrate. "I can't say for sure. Why don't I call you back."

They went into the back to select a coffin. Lee remained at the door while Albert led Stevie around, discussing features on each casket as if they were checking out used cars. She tried to turn her thoughts elsewhere. Finally, Stevie made a selection.

"Ready to go?" Lee asked breathlessly. They started down a long hall toward the front door, with Stevie walking ahead. Albert paused and put his hand on Lee's arm. "How does he seem to be handling it?" he asked, once the boy was out of earshot.

Lee sighed. "It's hard to tell with teenagers."

"When I run your sister's obituary, there'll be no mention as to where she's being buried, only that it's a private service. I'm hoping to keep the press away."

"Thank you."

He squeezed her elbow. "You'll get those pajamas to me?" When she nodded, he went on. "Every day will get just a little bit easier."

Lee gave a weary sigh. "I'm counting on that, Albert." She turned and escaped to the car.

Fifteen minutes later, Lee and Stevie ducked past several reporters outside the sheriff's department. They arrived in Holden's office slightly out of breath.

"They've been here since early this morning," Holden said, when Lee asked about the press. "Try to avoid them if you can." He suddenly grinned, reached behind his chair, and tossed Stevie a football.

The boy managed to catch it, even with the element of surprise. "What's this for?" he asked.

"I got 'cha a little present. Thought it might lift your spirits."

Lee wondered if he was feeling guilty for having suspected Stevie in the beginning. "What'd you get me?" she asked, taking the chair in front of his desk.

"I'm going to give you a whack on the behind if you don't stop bugging me." He turned his attention to Stevie, who was tossing the ball in the air. "We need to get serious for a minute, son," he said.

"Okay." He continued to play with the ball.

Lee had noticed moments of hyperactivity in the boy, but she suspected he was just reacting to his mother's death. It seemed he got worse as the day progressed. "Stevie, you need to put down the football and listen to Holden," she said gently.

Fleeting annoyance crossed his face, then he held the ball in his hands and gave Holden his undivided attention. "Okay, shoot."

Holden leaned back in his chair. "I want to talk about the man you thought was in the house."

The boy's expression clouded, and he sounded impatient when he spoke. "You've already asked me about that. I told you, I never saw him."

"Bear with me, kiddo," Holden said. "I wouldn't be asking you again if it weren't important. Now, did you at any time hear his voice?"

"I heard a rumbling that sounded like it belonged to a man's. I couldn't make out what he was saying, but it was low-pitched, and my mom's voice was high-pitched."

"You didn't get scared or wonder what a man was doing in the house that time of night?"

Stevie's shoulders sagged, he crossed his arms as though he'd caught a sudden chill. "It wasn't the first time."

Lee bit her bottom lip and looked away. She could not bear to see the hurt on her nephew's face. What had Lucy been thinking to have brought strange men into the house? she wondered.

"I must've dozed off at some point," Stevie added, "because the next thing I know, the alarm was ringing."

"And you saw nothing."

"No. I started down the hall toward the kitchen to get some breakfast, then remembered I had to wake my mom so she could take me to school since I'd been kicked off the bus for fighting. When I opened the door, there she was. Covered with blood. At least her face and chest were. And she was staring straight up at that mirror on the ceiling. I thought she was alive, since her eyes were open. I started shaking her. She was still warm. I put my head to her chest, there was no knife in it, but I didn't hear anything. I grabbed her face and turned her so that she was looking at me; then I realized—'' He paused and shuddered, and when he spoke his voice broke. "She was dead."

Lee moved closer and put her arm around him. "Holden, is this really necessary?"

"I'm almost finished," he said. "Look, I know this is hard, Stevie," he said, his tone softening. "Are you one hundred percent sure you saw no knife?"

The boy shook his head emphatically. "No. There was nothing. I didn't even notice it at first because . . . well, because of her face. I just stared at her. I guess I musta put my hand on her chest because when I backed away it was wet with blood. Then I realized she'd been stabbed." He looked at Lee. "Can we leave now?"

"Not so fast, Stevie," Holden said. "I know you said you didn't see anybody, but sometimes people see things and forget. Your subconscious stores it. Something as insignificant as a man's shadow or the back of his head as he's leaving. You ever seen a lineup?"

"On TV."

"I'd like for you to take a look at several men. See if anything jogs your memory."

The boy suddenly looked excited. "That'd be awesome!"

Holden picked up the phone, punched a number, and chatted briefly with the person on the other end of the line. When he hung up, he smiled at Stevie. "Okay, pal, it's been arranged. After you've looked the men over, I'm going to ask them to say something, and I want you to listen carefully to their voices. I know you said you were half asleep when you heard someone, but you never know what you'll remember."

"May I go?" Lee asked. When Holden looked as

though he'd say no, she went on quickly. "I am, after all, the boy's guardian."

"I don't want any trouble."

She pretended to be insulted.

Holden led them to a small room where chairs had been placed in front of a large picture window. They could see into a room with bright fluorescent lighting and height measurements marked on the wall.

"Now, the men are going to step through that door in just a minute," Holden explained to Stevie.

"They can't see us, right?"

"Right." He patted him on the shoulder. "Just like on TV."

The door opened and six men marched through and came to a halt at a designated spot on the floor. Stevie leaned close to the window, almost pressing his nose against the glass. The men turned and faced them head on. Lee automatically leaned back in her seat when Jack McCall seemed to fix his gaze on her. She clenched her jaw, her mood veering sharply. Her eyes blazed with hate as she thought of the things he'd done to her sister; she could barely catch her breath for the fury she felt inside of her.

"I don't recognize any of them," Stevie said.

Holden spoke into a microphone. Each man was asked to step forward and count. McCall's voice was deep and self-assured, and carried a thread of sensuality that made Lee keenly aware of his masculinity. Lucy would have been immediately attracted. What woman wouldn't be? He would be able to lure his victims wherever he wanted. His stance was powerful and proud. It was obvious he'd spent a lot of time in a courtroom, because he had a presence that was sorely lacking in the other men. Another Ted Bundy, she thought.

Stevie shook his head. "Sorry, Holden. I've never seen those men before."

"Try harder," Lee hissed. "What about that man with the black hair?"

Holden pulled the curtain closed before he faced Lee, his eyes snapping with anger. "You know better than that!"

She felt thoroughly chastised. "I'm sorry. It just came out. I wasn't thinking."

"There's *no* excuse, Lee. None."

"I wish you guys wouldn't fight," Stevie said, looking from one to the other. "Open the curtain. I'll try harder this time."

Holden smiled at him, though it was strained. "I think you've had enough for one day."

Lee walked behind them as they made their way down the hall. When Stevie asked to use the bathroom, she apologized to Holden again.

"You're just lucky McCall waived his right to have his attorney present during the lineup," he said. "He could have chewed us up and spit us out after what you did." He pointed his finger in her face. "This is the last time I'm warning you, Lee. Either get a grip on your emotions or I'll see that you don't come anywhere near this building or set foot in the courthouse during McCall's trial."

Holden was in a sour mood when Deputy Willis Green knocked on the door. Scott Wall, a lanky blond and the newest man on the staff, was right behind him. Holden noticed their stained clothes and shook his head. "What Dumpster did you two crawl out of?" he asked.

Green started to sit down, then obviously decided against it because of his clothes. Instead, he placed his hands flat on the desk and leaned closer to Holden. "You won't believe what we found in the old man's backyard."

Holden regarded him. "Try me."

"Buncha' dead animals. Birds, squirrels, a raccoon, and two cats."

"And that ain't all," Scott Wall said.

"Shut up and let me tell him," Willis said.

"Sorry," Wall said, a heavy dose of sarcasm in his voice.

"Somebody better tell me," Holden snapped. "I've got work to do."

"They were all tortured, Sheriff," Willis said. "At least that's what it looked like. Every one of them had broken bones, and some had their necks twisted almost completely off."

"Really gross," Wall said.

Green nodded. "And get this. The whole time we're digging, that old buzzard is peering out the window at us."

"You didn't happen to come across a knife with a two-inch blade, did you?"

"No. And believe me, we sifted through dirt for hours. If it had been there, we'd have found it. You want me to get a search warrant and have a look inside?"

Holden shook his head. "Let's don't rush the old guy; he's had enough excitement for one day. I have an appointment with a plastic surgeon this evening. I'm hoping he can help me."

Green smiled. "You thinking about getting a tummy tuck, Sheriff?"

Holden almost smiled. "Yeah. My britches are getting tight around the middle."

"This is about the Hodges case, right?" Green said. When Holden nodded, he went on. "You got the killer sitting back there in jail right now. Why are you still looking?"

Holden arched one brow. "Same reason you're out digging up dead animals, Willis. I'm looking for the truth."

*   *   *

Wade Emmett was at her parents' house when Lee arrived with Stevie in tow. He'd obviously just cut the grass; now he was burning leaves in the backyard. "Where have you been?" he asked as soon as Lee stepped out of the truck.

"Stevie and I have had a busy day. Was there something in particular you needed?"

"The Allen brothers started putting in your furnace today. I drove over and let them in."

"I forgot to give you a key."

"Yes, but I found a spare under the front door mat. Really, Lee, don't you think that's a bit obvious?" He handed her the key.

"Thanks, Wade. Did they give me a good price?"

"Better than you'll get anywhere else. I did some checking. They'll send you a bill, said you can make monthly payments if it'll be easier on you. By the way, Carol is not real happy with me for taking over, but I figured you'd still be waiting for that furnace this time next year if you left it up to her."

"I'll talk to Carol."

He grinned at Stevie and put out his hand. "Gimme some skin, kid. Where'd you get that football? I thought your talent was baseball."

Stevie shook hands with him. "Holden gave it to me. We got to see a lineup."

"No kidding?" Wade looked impressed. "Did you pick out the bad guy?"

"Have you spoken to my parents?" Lee interrupted, not wanting to discuss what had happened.

He nodded. "Your mom seems okay. Your dad's kinda quiet, but he usually is."

"How come you're cleaning my grandparents' yard?" Stevie asked. "Are you trying to earn extra money?"

Wade smiled. "Why would I need extra money when I'm getting rich at being a football coach?" he asked. "No, just kidding. I'm helping out since your grandpa isn't up to it." He looked at Lee. "And because your aunt and I are good friends. She'd do the same for me, right?"

Lee kissed Wade on the cheek. "Hold that thought," she said, chuckling. "Why don't you finish up and come inside where it's warm. I'll have fresh coffee waiting. All this hard work deserves a reward."

Lee found her mother trying to coax her father into taking his medication when she went inside the house. Once the woman had finally managed to get him to take it, Lee greeted them each with a kiss on the cheek. "How's it going?" she asked.

"People have been bringing food all day," Shelby said. "And there've been reporters knocking on the door. Can you believe that, at a time like this?"

"I'd believe anything at this point," Lee replied sourly. "What can I do to help?"

"Help me put the food away first." Lee followed her mother inside the dining room, and Shelby closed the door. "How did it go at the funeral home?"

"We decided on a private graveside service to be held this Friday. Family only. I'll make the necessary calls if you like."

"And Stevie?"

Lee shook her head. "I'm not even sure it's sunk in yet."

"He's lucky to have you there for him," Shelby said.

Lee didn't know how to respond. She'd quit teaching school because kids got on her nerves. Now she had no choice. "We'll see."

Shelby Cates leaned her head on her daughter's shoulder. "I'm so blessed to have you. You're strong, Lee. You give me strength." But she didn't see the tears in her daughter's eyes.

Fourteen

LEE AND Stevie arrived at the courthouse early the next afternoon. It was an imposing old building, standing three stories high, its red brick exterior faded but as sturdy as the day it was built. The courthouse lawn was dotted with statues of Confederate heroes, and lush flower beds grew at their feet as if paying homage.

Lee saw several TV crews already in place. She mumbled for Stevie to hurry, but an attractive blond in a camel-colored suit caught up with them before they could reach the tall steps, and a microphone was suddenly thrust in Lee's face. She recognized Melissa Grant from the local news. Not very bright but she added color to the news set, and that must've been good enough for the producers because they kept her on. She'd planted herself on Lee's parents' doorstep the day of the murder, and that in itself was enough to make Lee dislike her. She was certain her cold stare suggested as much.

Miss Grant was obviously accustomed to a certain degree of hostility from those she interviewed, because she was not deterred by Lee's aloofness. "Ma'am, are you attending the preliminary hearing of Mr. Jack McCall?" she said in a voice thick as tree sap.

"Yes, I am." Lee's tone was crisp, no nonsense.

"It's rumored they may have arrested the wrong man. What do you think about that?"

"Since when has our local media resorted to repeating rumors?" Lee asked sharply.

The woman's smile faltered. "Oh, I didn't mean—"

"The *evidence* against Mr. McCall speaks for itself, Miss Grant." Lee glanced at Stevie, who seemed to be in awe of the attention. "His fingerprints were all over the victim's bedroom and he even confessed to being at the scene of the crime. What more do we need?"

"Yes, of course." Melissa seemed to take a moment to gather her thoughts. "Do you think McCall can get a fair trial in Comfrey?"

Lee didn't hesitate. The last thing she wanted was to see Jack McCall moved to another location. She wanted to be there when the guilty verdict was handed down and he was sentenced to death. "Why shouldn't he get a fair trial? The people in this town are intelligent, and they will take their duties very seriously if asked to serve on the jury. It is my feeling they will weigh the evidence carefully before coming to a decision as to Mr. McCall's guilt or innocence. Now, if you'll excuse us."

"Could we get your statement on tape, ma'am?" Melissa called out as Lee hurried up the steps to the courthouse entrance.

"Can't do," Lee called back. "Late for an appointment. Just quote me as an unidentified source."

"Why didn't you tell her your name?" Stevie asked, once they'd ducked inside the courthouse.

"My statement won't hold much weight if they know I'm the victim's sister," she said. "I just hope the bimbo prints what I said."

Stevie glanced over his shoulder. "I wouldn't mind going out with her."

Lee feigned a look of disgust. "All you men are

just alike, you know that?'' They entered the main courtroom where Holden had said McCall's preliminary hearing would be held, and managed to find a seat in the front row. Lee could feel the tension building inside of her as the room began to fill. By the time Jack McCall was led inside by Holden and another deputy, her anxiety level had reached a new high.

The first thing she noticed was that he wore no handcuffs or shackles, which renewed her anger. After what he'd done, he deserved to be treated no better than an animal. She watched him follow his lawyer to the defendant's table, no more than ten or fifteen feet from where she and Stevie were sitting.

He looked much different today than when she'd first seen him. They'd obviously tried to disguise the killer in him. Gone were the shaggy hair and unshaved jaw, as well as the faded jeans. His hair had been cut into a conservative style, and the navy suit he wore reeked of money. He looked like the CEO of a Fortune 500 company.

Which was exactly what they'd hoped for.

Once again, Lee could see why Lucy had been attracted to him.

McCall glanced around the room, and his eyes found hers. Their gazes locked. His stare was bold, assessing. Lee's stomach tensed, and her breathing became shallow as he searched her face, those blue eyes boring into hers. Her sister had looked into those very eyes while he'd ruined her face. Had Lucy begged for mercy? Had she pleaded with him to plunge the knife through her heart and end her suffering?

Then Lee remembered Lucy had been bound and gagged. She would have been totally defenseless against McCall.

She felt sick, and choked back the nausea. She would not give the man the satisfaction of seeing what he could do to her. Even harder to bear was the rage that was so intense it took every ounce of self-control to keep from leaping over the rail and going for him.

But Lee knew that Holden would see that she never set foot in the courtroom again. She would not get to see the look on McCall's face when they passed down his death sentence. And he *would* die. That knowledge would have to sustain her for the time being.

Finally, he looked away and sat down, and Lee realized everything had taken place in a matter of a few seconds.

She felt Stevie tug at her sleeve, and she looked at him, hoping he couldn't see how upset she was. "That's the man from the lineup," he whispered. "Do they think he's the one who killed my mom?"

She nodded. She hadn't been crazy about the idea of letting Stevie come with her, but he'd pleaded with her until she'd given in. Afterall, he was an adult be most standards and had every right to be there. "That's the one," she answered. "Are you okay?"

He nodded. "Yeah."

Stevie continued to stare at the man, but it was hard to get a fix on what the boy was thinking. "Don't look at him," Lee whispered, afraid Stevie might do something they'd both regret. She glanced at Holden, who was standing near the exit, and found him watching her. His look warned her against creating a scene, and she knew he'd have no hesitation in hauling her out of there.

The judge entered the courtroom, and Stevie turned his attention to the man in the flowing black robe. Judge Elvin Bishop was considered fair but sometimes too lenient on first-time offenders, mostly teenagers, who often went out and committed another crime as soon as they were released. Lee stood, then tapped Stevie on the shoulder and motioned for him to do the same. He seemed to be in a daze. She had to tug his sleeve when they were told to sit.

Judge Bishop briefly read the criminal case number and the charge of murder. His salt and pepper hair was slicked back, half-moon glasses perched at the end of a bulbous nose. He glanced up. "Would counsel please identify themselves for the record."

Lee listened as the prosecuting attorney gave his name and made a brief statement. The attorney representing Jack McCall stood, and identified himself as David Hill. "Your Honor, on behalf of Mr. Jack McCall, the defendant, I would request the court enter a plea of not guilty."

"Plea is entered, Mr. Hill," the judge said, making a note.

"Also, we'd like to request bail—"

"Bail is denied."

Hill didn't look deterred. "If I may address the court."

"Do so quickly, Mr. Hill."

"Your Honor, we realize the serious nature of the crime, but the accusations against my client are entirely false. My client freely admits to being at the victim's house the night of the murder, but he was in no way responsible for her demise. Mr. McCall is not a threat to this community. In fact, he spent almost ten years working as an assistant district attorney in Atlanta and made quite a name for himself."

"Yes, I know all about Mr. McCall's record, Counselor," Judge Bishop said dourly.

"Sir, I have letters in my possession, letters that were faxed to me by officials in Atlanta, and even the lieutenant governor of the state of Georgia, praising my client's good character. Those who know him best, those who worked closely with him, know he is incapable of the crime for which he's been accused. If I may approach the bench."

Judge Bishop nodded and accepted the file David Hill handed him. He read through the letters and looked up. "Okay, I've looked at Mr. McCall's character references. What is it you're requesting, Counselor?"

"Your Honor, Mr. McCall is offering to deposit one million dollars cash with the clerk of the court to insure his full cooperation in the investigation and provide surety that he make all future court appearances. Mr. McCall has vast real estate and development holdings in Hilton Head and will suffer a staggering financial loss if he is not able to attend to his business matters."

"That's not the court's problem, Mr. Hill," the judge said.

Hill went on. "Furthermore, Mr. McCall wishes to donate five hundred thousand dollars to the investigation, in hopes of hiring extra manpower and bringing in forensic experts to prove his innocence."

The prosecuting attorney stood. "Your Honor, I have never heard of something so ridiculous in my life. There's absolutely nothing wrong with the way this investigation is being handled. Besides, we are talking about a crime of a heinous nature, and a crime scene that was littered with evidence of Mr. McCall's presence on the night of the murder."

"Sit down, Counselor," Judge Bishop ordered. "Mr. McCall does not deny being at the scene of the crime." He reached for his gavel. "This court will take a fifteen-minute recess." He slammed it hard and left the room.

Lee wondered if that meant the judge was considering McCall's request for bail, and she couldn't believe it was a possibility. If the man had a million dollars to give the clerk of court and had vast real estate holdings, he had enough money to skip the country as well. She glanced at Stevie, who leaned his head back and closed his eyes. Lee watched the clock on the wall. She preferred anything to looking at the back of McCall's head. Time moved slowly.

Judge Bishop reentered the courtroom but motioned everyone to keep their seats. Lee held her breath and waited, her nerves like a fragile eggshell on the verge of cracking.

"Mr. Hill," he began somewhat brusquely. "I have called some of the distinguished people who authored these letters, including the esteemed lieutenant governor for the state of Georgia, and I've received nothing but adulation for your client."

"Thank you, Your Honor," Hill said, as though the praise had been directed at him.

"In fact, a couple of the people I spoke with were willing to put up their own money for Mr. McCall's bail. With this in mind, I will grant your client bail under the conditions you mentioned, with a few added conditions of my own. The court hereby orders Mr. McCall to surrender his passport . . ."

Lee didn't hear the rest of it because of the roaring in her ears. Her face felt as if it were sagging, as though it had lost all muscle control, as though the blood had drained out of it and exited her body completely. "Let's go," she told Stevie.

As they left, Lee turned for one last look at McCall and found him watching her. She had expected to find him gloating, or glaring at her through hostile eyes. Instead, he looked sorry for her. As though he pitied her. And that only fueled her hatred for him.

Shelby Cates listened to Lee's news quietly, but her outrage was clearly visible in her grim, tight-lipped expression. "Well, don't that beat all? They let him go. Goin' to let him run the streets so he can do the same thing to some other poor, unsuspecting woman. I don't know what this world is coming to."

Lee was past the point of trying to comfort anyone. "A person can get away with anything if he has enough money, and McCall seems to have plenty." She took a sip of her iced tea. She had already visited briefly with her father, but he hadn't had much to say. How different he was from the man she'd known growing up. Back then his word was rule, and those around him had complied, no questions asked. Now even the simplest decision, such as whether he preferred oatmeal or cold cereal, was more than he could tackle. He wept easily.

Lee realized her mother had grown quiet. "What are you thinking?" she asked.

"I'm afraid for you."

"Me? Why?"

"What if—" Shelby paused and lowered her voice to a whisper. "What if he comes after you? You and Lucy always bore a strong resemblance. Or what if he comes after Stevie, thinking he might have seen something?"

The thought made Lee shiver. Was Jack McCall sick enough to come after her simply because she and Lucy looked alike? She had no answer for that. But he had laid down a fortune to keep himself from going to jail, and if he thought Stevie might remember seeing something, *anything*, well, he might try to silence the boy. But there was no way Lee was going to admit as much to her mother.

"I think Mr. McCall would be wise to stay as far away from Stevie or me as he can," she said. "He might be out free, but you can bet Holden's not going to let him out of his sight."

"Maybe you should take your father's hunting rifle just in case. I'm sure Wade can teach you how to use it."

"I don't want guns in my house. Besides, that rifle is so big I'd just end up hurting myself." Her mother started to argue, but Lee hushed her. "Nothing is going to happen. Stevie and I are perfectly safe."

She prayed she was right.

*   *   *

Jack McCall paced the floor and listened as David Hill tried to convince him to see things his way.

"Leo Nausbaum is one of the best defense attorneys in Charleston," he said. "He's considering taking on your case, even though it means he'll have to . . . er . . . reassign several clients he presently represents."

Jack wasn't moved. Not only did he dislike most defense attorneys, he didn't think much of a lawyer who'd drop clients right in the middle of a case in order to obtain a higher-priced one. Not that lawyers didn't do it all the time. "I told you I wanted to handle my own defense," Jack said.

Hill looked peeved. "Jack, this is a capital murder case. If you lose—"

"If I lose, I fry," Jack said, waving the statement aside as though it held little meaning for him. "But who's going to work harder to prove my innocence, me or some hotshot attorney out of Charleston?" He didn't wait for Hill to respond. "I think we did pretty damn good this morning, Counselor."

"You bought your way out of jail, Jack. We did nothing spectacular."

Jack ignored him. "I have a friend in Atlanta who's a damn good private investigator. He's grabbing a plane tonight. If anybody can get information, he can."

"Fine, hire all the investigators you want. But you still need a good defense lawyer."

"I'm going to do this my way," Jack said.

Hill threw up his hands in frustration. "I give up. If you're not interested in saving your own neck, why should I worry?"

Jack regarded him. "Why? I think you know the answer better than I do."

"Oh, so we're back to that. I *owe* you." He glared at Jack, and the veins stood out in his neck. "Listen to me, boy. I did not put that noose around your mother's neck and neither did your father. *She* chose to end her life because she was a quitter."

Jack's jaw went rigid. "Be careful what you say about my mother. I've already been accused of one murder. As I see it, I have nothing to lose."

Hill pressed both hands on the table and leaned close. "Stop feeling sorry for yourself. You've already wasted two years of your life; how many more are you going to send down the toilet? And what about that law degree you busted your ass to get? Are you going to let that go down the sewer pipes too?"

Jack clenched one fist. "You've got balls talking to me like that," he said.

"Somebody needs to talk to you before you screw up the rest of your life." He shook his head. "You've got enough money to get back at that bastard in Atlanta. You could take him down. If you don't fight back, it's going to stick in your craw for the rest of your life."

Jack didn't speak right away. Finally, he looked at Hill. "I'm going to practice law again," he said. "As for that business in Atlanta, I've put it behind me. He's not worth the trouble. Like you said, I've already wasted two years of my life."

Disgruntled, Hill gathered his things together. "Let me know if you change your mind about Nausbaum."

An hour passed before Jack picked up the phone. He dialed the lieutenant governor's office in Georgia and waited another twenty minutes before his friend picked up. Gerald Beckman greeted him heartily. He and Jerry had been roommates in college. Even then, Beckman had had political aspirations.

"Sorry to bother you, Jerry," Jack said. "I would gladly have left a message."

"My secretary has orders to put you through no matter what. I've already told her you have enough information on me to see that I never make governor."

Jack laughed. Jerry had raised a lot of hell in their college days; Jack had bailed him out of more than one jam.

"How's the case going?" Jerry asked.

"Too soon to tell."

"You can beat this, McCall. And you know I'll do what I can to help. I'll fly up there personally to testify on your behalf. Hell, I'll get the governor to come with me. Whatever it takes, man. I owe you."

"Thanks, Jerry." Jack took a deep breath. "I need one more favor, if you don't mind."

"Name it, and it's yours."

"I want to practice law again."

Lee and Stevie arrived home to a warm house, thanks to Wade seeing that the furnace was installed in record time. As Lee led Stevie to the guest room she'd prepared for him, he pointed to the stairs leading to the third floor.

"What's that?"

"Oh, it's just a small apartment."

"Can I see it?"

"You mean now?" He nodded and Lee couldn't help smiling. She remembered how much she'd enjoyed exploring the big Victorian house as a child. She and her cousins had never been allowed in the apartment, but that hadn't stopped them from snooping when nobody was looking. "Sure. I'll make hot cocoa while you look around. Oh, and remind me to call Holden. We've got to get your clothes."

"Yeah, okay."

Lee went down to the kitchen. It was her favorite room. The solid oak cabinets were old, but she'd refinished them the year before, and although the yellow counter tops had just as much age on them, they'd been well cared for. She'd wallpapered the room in yellow gingham, hoping to match the counters. It wasn't exact but it was close. The turret had window seats that matched the curtains her mother had made for her, so the room had a cozy feel to it.

She was setting the cups of cocoa and cookies on the table when Stevie walked into the room. She could not imagine wanting anything else to eat after the spread at her parents' house, but she knew Stevie would. The fact that he could eat so much and stay so thin amazed her.

"I looked around," he said, taking a seat at the table and grabbing a cookie. "That apartment is awesome. That's where I want to stay."

Lee glanced up quickly. "Oh, Stevie, you don't want to sleep up there. It's probably freezing."

"I opened the vents so the heat could get in. Besides, that way, I won't feel like I'm in your way."

"You're *not* in my way. Whatever gave you that idea? I'm more than happy to have you. I just don't think—"

"And there's a stove up there. I could cook my own food. Please let me stay up there, Aunt Lee."

She could see from the look on his face how much he wanted it, and with all he'd been through, she knew she couldn't deny him anything. Even though he didn't look it, he was seventeen years old, a man by most standards, and he would naturally crave independence. "I'll agree to let you stay up there *temporarily* under one condition," she said. "You take your meals down here with me. I don't want you cooking. You have to promise me."

"Can I keep a few snacks up there?"

She smiled. "Yes. We'll buy them when we go grocery shopping. So, it'll be like you have your own little bachelor pad. You can take the TV set from the guest room."

"Wow!"

"One more thing," she added quickly. "It'll be up to you to clean it and bring your dirty laundry down. I'll show you where the cleaning supplies are."

"And you won't come up there and bother me?"

She wouldn't go up there if he begged her, but she wasn't about to tell him that. "Not if you'll agree to those conditions."

"I'll keep it clean, don't worry." He grabbed another cookie, inhaled it.

Lee tried not to let her disappointment show. She had hoped they could get close, that perhaps she could be a friend and mother substitute to him. His living on the third floor would distance them physically and emotionally, she feared. There would also be the added expense of heating the apartment, something she didn't relish on her tight budget. Hopefully, Stevie would grow bored with the whole thing in a few days and decide to move into the guest room.

Lee joined him at the table and sipped her hot chocolate as he told her how he planned to decorate his new place. "I have my own bank account," he said proudly.

"Good. You can give me a loan."

He smiled. "How much do you need?"

"A hundred thou would catch me up on my credit cards."

He laughed. "You must shop like my mother. Do you take checks?"

"I gotta have cold hard cash or nothing."

"Aunt Lee, could you teach me to drive?"

The abrupt subject change took her by surprise. "Teach you to drive?"

"All my friends have their driver's license, but I don't even have a permit. I asked my mom to teach me, but she never had time. Besides, she didn't want me practicing in her Jaguar."

Lee didn't blame Lucy for that one. "Honey, all I have is my bomb, and it's a stick shift."

"That's okay."

"Maybe Wade will teach you."

He shoved his chair back from the table so hard it made a nasty scraping sound on the wood floor. "If you don't want to teach me, just say so," he blurted.

Lee was stunned by the outburst. "Stevie, I didn't say I wouldn't."

He put his dishes in the sink and faced her. "Nobody ever has time for anything."

She stood as well. The look on her nephew's face was more hurt than angry. "Of course I have time for you. It's just, well, I've never taught anyone to drive, and I thought it would be easier if you learned on an automatic, which Wade has." His eyes were glistening. "If you don't mind learning the hard way, I'll teach you," she added.

"It doesn't matter. I'm tired. I want to go to bed." He left without another word.

Lee heard his footsteps on the stairs and reclaimed her seat at the table, feeling more than a little shaken. As she sat there, sifting through her perplexing emotions, it hit her. The conversation hadn't really been about learning to drive. Stevie had been testing her, to see if she cared. To see if she really wanted him there.

She wondered how much time Lucy had spent with her son before her death. She knew the changes in her sister had been dramatic, that Lucy had literally become a different woman. Had she ignored her child as well?

Somehow Lee had to make him understand that she loved him, that he wasn't a burden to her. She left the kitchen and went upstairs, then climbed the short flight leading to the third-floor apartment. She tried the doorknob. Locked. She knocked on the door. "Stevie, let me in." She waited. No answer. This time she knocked louder. "Stevie, please open the door. We need to talk."

After several attempts, Lee gave up. She knew she could probably pick the lock, but she decided against it. The boy wanted his privacy. And there was probably a good chance he was sitting in there crying over his mother, which she knew was healthy. Perhaps that's why he'd gotten angry in the first place—he'd felt a need to vent his feelings. She preferred being there to comfort him, but he'd obviously taken that decision away from her.

Lee descended the stairs. She, too, felt like crying. Would there ever come a time when she would find peace?

Holden arrived at Dr. Kit Jones's office promptly at nine that night. The doctor greeted him at the front door, and while he was polite enough, Holden got the distinct impression he didn't appreciate the intrusion on his time.

"You didn't come in your patrol car, I hope," he said.

Holden shook his head. The doctor's waiting room looked like the lobby of a plush hotel. "No, I brought my personal car."

Jones motioned him to follow. "The last thing I need is for my patients to see the sheriff's department outside my door." He managed a tight smile.

If Holden had thought the waiting area nice, it was nothing compared to the good doctor's private office. The art on his walls had to be worth a cool million; the furnishings and antiques would've brought a king's ransom. Holden found himself wondering, once again, why he put in twelve- and fourteen-hour work days for the kind of money he made.

"I hope you have a good security system, Dr. Jones," he said.

"Yes, I do. There's also a security guard on the premises." Jones led him inside. "Please sit down. I'm afraid I can only spare a few minutes; my wife is expecting me home."

Holden sat in a comfortable chair and Jones took a seat opposite him. Holden had the stats on Dr. Kit Jones, knew he pulled in a couple of million a year doing what he did, and lived in a grand style. The man was in his fifties but didn't look a day over forty-five. His face was free of lines, his hair contained only enough gray to be flattering. His body appeared hard and solid, as though he worked out regularly.

"Well, you've had a good look at me, Sheriff," the man said. "Do I look like a cold-blooded murderer?"

"Unfortunately, murderers don't carry signs, Doctor. But you're not a suspect at this time. However, I am interested in your relationship with Lucy Hodges."

"She was my patient, of course. That's no secret."

"So you knew her on a professional basis only?"

"I didn't say that. Lucy and I had an affair. Not just a simple fling, mind you. I was prepared to leave my wife for her." He paused. "You said this would be confidential."

"As long as you haven't broken any laws. I'm not out to hurt your reputation." Holden sat forward, placing his elbows on his knees. It was meant to inspire confidence. "Do you make a habit of sleeping with your patients, Doctor?"

The man's mouth grew tight. "I'm offended that you would even ask me that question, Sheriff. The answer is no."

"So Lucy Hodges was your first."

"Not my first affair, but the first with a patient." He sighed. "I didn't come on to Lucy, she came on to me, and I simply couldn't resist her."

"Why was she different from your other patients?"

He paused as though remembering. "She came into my office scarred from a fire that almost took her life, and from constant battering. I felt sorry for her. Her self-esteem was so low at the time it broke my heart. She was nothing like the spoiled bitches I deal with on a regular basis," he added cynically. "I knew I was going to do everything in my power to make her beautiful. She was already beautiful inside—or so I thought at the time. I fell in love with her."

"So you proposed marriage?"

The doctor gave a short laugh. "Hardly. When I told my wife I wanted out of our relationship, she pulled out several letters Lucy had written her. It gave detailed accounts of our time together, even what we did in bed, for God's sake."

Holden had to work at keeping his expression closed. "Do you have those letters?"

"They are in a safety deposit box in my wife's name, and she has no intention of giving them to me. You see, she enjoys a very privileged lifestyle. She enjoys being the wife of a successful surgeon and has no desire to get divorced. As for me, I've seen the copies of Lucy's letters, and I have no wish for them to be made public."

"So your wife is blackmailing you to stay married to her."

"She refers to the letters as her insurance policy."

"Did you see Lucy Hodges on the day she was murdered?"

"You know I did; otherwise you wouldn't be here. I met her for a drink at the Anchor Club and told her what I thought of her sick little game. Told her it was over."

"How did she react?"

"She dumped a drink in my lap and went to the bar to sink her claws into some other poor sucker."

"What did you do?"

"I left. Actually, I was relieved it was over. The whole relationship was too intense." He sighed. "I know this is going to sound self-serving, but I shudder when I think of some madman destroying her face like that. At least that's what the papers say happened." He checked his wristwatch. "If there's nothing more—"

"One more question, Doctor. Where were you Monday morning between the hours of one and six a.m.?"

Dr. Kit Jones gave him a sad smile. "My wife has those letters, Sheriff Cates. She could leave me in financial ruin. I was in bed next to her, naturally."

Fifteen

STEVIE WAS quiet the following morning as Lee parked behind Holden's patrol car in front of Lucy's house. In fact, the boy had said very little since waking up, despite her attempts to draw him into conversation. She knew he was grieving his mother's death, as were they all, but she longed for him to reach out to her. She wanted to comfort him, but she wouldn't push and risk scaring him off. She deeply regretted that they had not been closer when he was growing up.

Holden was already at the front door, unlocking it, several boxes stacked beside him. Lee was glad he'd remembered to bring them because it had slipped her mind completely. She had to struggle to remember even the most significant details; as a result, she found herself writing notes to herself constantly. She was certain it was due to exhaustion and stress, neither of which she could control at the moment.

The crime scene tape was still in place, and Lee thought it looked garish against the perfectly manicured lawns and luxury homes. No doubt the neighbors shared her opinion. Besides, who wanted to be reminded what had occurred in the Hodges' house every time they stepped out their door?

Holden greeted Stevie warmly, but all he had for

Lee was a curt nod. She figured she deserved it and let it pass, but it hurt her feelings regardless.

"You doing okay today, son?" Holden asked, his voice sounding tight with tension. He looked weary.

"I'm okay," Stevie mumbled.

Lee thought Holden seemed reluctant to enter the house. She didn't blame him; she felt momentary panic at the thought of going inside the place where her sister had been violently murdered. She was only there to support Stevie. And if she was having a problem with it, the kid was probably struggling a whole lot more.

Holden cleared his throat. "Now, remember, Stevie, this is still a crime scene so I'll have to stay beside you at all times. Don't touch anything unless I give you the go ahead." He paused. "And if you change your mind and want to leave at any time, I'll try to grab the things you need. How's that?"

"Yeah, okay," Stevie said.

Lee entered behind them. The house was cold and smelled of gardenia. She'd never be able to smell that scent now without thinking of her sister and how she must have looked that night, once Jack McCall had finished with her. And that monster was still walking the streets. She took a deep, shaky breath as fear and anger began tying knots in her stomach. She didn't need to think about the murder *or* McCall right now; she had to stay calm and cool-headed for Stevie.

Lee paused in the living room, still dusty with fingerprint powder, the champagne-colored carpet trampled. She forced herself to swallow back her indignation at having her sister's home treated with such blatant disregard, reminding herself it had all been necessary. Whatever it took, she told herself, to prove McCall a cold-blooded killer. Even if it meant tearing down the walls in the process.

Lee looked up at her sister's portrait over the fireplace. Lucy gazed down at them majestically from her perch, looking so real that Lee could almost imagine her stepping out of the painting and greeting them warmly. The expression on her face was one of mild amusement and maybe a tinge of curiosity, as though she was wondering what all the fuss was about.

Lee glanced away quickly, her emotions too fragile to look at the picture. Perhaps later, once she'd healed. If healing was really possible under these circumstances.

"Where do you want to go first, Stevie?" Holden asked.

"My room."

They followed the boy down the hall and into a room where angry-looking rock stars peered down from posters like a wrathful God on Judgment Day. Lee didn't recognize any of them and decided she was better off. She looked around. More fingerprint powder. The bed had been stripped; the mattress lay at an odd angle, and someone had ripped up areas of carpeting. Dresser drawers stood open from having been searched, books and videos and CDs pulled from their shelves, stereo speakers sliced open. Nothing had been left untouched. Lee glowered at the mess, wondering why Holden's deputies felt it necessary to cause such destruction. But she remained quiet, not wanting to upset Stevie by having it out with Holden.

"I need to get clothes out of this dresser," Stevie said, his voice relatively calm as he observed the damage. Holden set the boxes down, pulled a pair of rubber gloves from his pocket, and slipped them on. He held out each of the drawers so Stevie could take what he needed, and the boy's hands trembled so badly he dropped a number of items. Feeling sorry for him, Lee assisted. They filled one box quickly.

"Don't forget to take a suit, honey," Lee reminded, knowing he would need it for the funeral. "And nice shoes."

Stevie pointed to the closet, and Holden brought out what he needed. "Is it okay if I take some of my CDs and videos?" the boy asked.

"I don't have a CD player at my house," Lee told him, "but I've got a VCR."

"Put on these gloves," Holden said, pulling a second pair from his pocket. "I need to have a look at what you take."

The boy began pulling out videos from the cabinet. "Most of these are just shows I've recorded. Like 'The Simpsons' and 'Beevis and Butthead.' "

"Oh, yes," Holden said dryly, "what did we do before 'Beevis and Butthead' came along?"

Stevie searched through his vast collection. "Some of these I haven't seen in years." He put several more in the box, then glanced around. "I guess I ought to take my book bag."

"Good idea," Lee said. "You probably won't feel like going to school right away, but you're going to need them eventually."

"I'd like to grab a couple of things from my mom's room."

When Holden hesitated, Lee explained, "Stevie needs to get something for his mother to be buried in."

Holden seemed to soften. "Okay. Let's carry these boxes to the living room first." They did so. Finally, he led the way to Lucy's bedroom.

Lee stepped inside with dread, and her eyes automatically found the bed. The linens had been stripped away, revealing the blood-stained mattress. She stopped breathing; it felt as though invisible hands had closed around her throat. The room spun wildly out of control, and she thought her legs would give beneath her. She reached for a bed post to steady herself.

"You okay?" Holden looked concerned.

Lee nodded quickly, found enough air to fill her lungs, and her dizziness passed. She noted the bed post, a red lacquered piece with a brass lion's head on top. She released it and backed away, wondering what her sister could have been thinking when she bought it. The ornate mirror on the ceiling left a sick feeling in the pit of her stomach. She glanced at Holden, who shook his head in response. And Stevie, who was staring at the stained mattress as if in a daze.

Trying to bring herself under control, Lee stepped closer to her nephew. "Let's get what we need, honey," she said, trying to hurry him along. "I'm sure Holden has things to do."

The boy found the pajamas right away and handed them to Lee. She could see they were of excellent quality. Lucy had undoubtedly purchased them in an exclusive Hilton Head store because Comfrey didn't offer such finery.

"The slippers should be in this closet," Stevie said, moving toward a set of French doors that opened into a walk-in closet that could have easily served as a sitting room.

Stevie located the satin slippers, then reached for a dress. "Is it okay if I take this, too?" he asked Holden. "I bought it for my mom's birthday. It was my favorite."

Lee didn't think the simple cotton print with its lace-trimmed collar and quarter-length sleeves looked like Lucy at all; it looked like something a farm wife or young mother would wear. She wondered if her sister had worn it for her son, knowing he'd bought it with his own money.

"That'll be fine," Holden said, and patted Stevie on the shoulder.

"There's a photo album I want, too," the boy said. "I took most of the pictures myself with my new camera."

"Where is it?" Holden asked.

"In the hall closet. It's a blue album."

They left the room so Holden could retrieve it, then they started for the front door.

"Mind if I ask you something, Stevie?" Holden asked. "Why'd your mama have so many clocks?"

"She liked collecting them. Said it reminded her that time was short, and she had to make the best of it. She felt like she wasted so much of it living with my dad," he added.

They exited the house, each carrying a load. Lee was thankful to be out in the fresh air. The boxes were placed in the back of her pickup; Stevie carried his mother's things and his suit up front with him. On the way home, Lee stopped by the funeral home to give Albert McPhee Lucy's satin pajamas and slippers. Stevie stayed in the truck.

"I'm glad you stopped by," McPhee said. "My wife has tried all her sources, but she can't find gardenias anywhere. She did manage to find white tea roses, though."

"I'm sure that'll be okay," Lee said, "but if my nephew has a problem with it, I'll call you right away."

On the drive home, Lee explained the situation to Stevie, and he shrugged as though he couldn't care less about the selection of flowers. Lee wondered why it had been so important before, when he obviously didn't much care one way or the other now. She tried to start a conversation with him but he was quiet. When they arrived home, Stevie carried his things upstairs while she prepared lunch.

He came into the kitchen a few minutes later holding the dress. "I want you to have this," he said.

"Oh, honey, no," she protested. "That belonged to your mom."

"She never even tried it on," he said. "I don't think she liked it. Maybe you'll wear it some time."

Lee could see it meant a lot to him. "I would consider it an honor," she said. "But if you ever change your mind and want it back, all you have to do is ask."

He shrugged. "Maybe it'll make up for the way I've been acting. I'm sorry I was rude to you last night."

Lee was touched. "Honey, if I'd been through what you had, I would have acted a lot worse, believe me. I just want to help you if I can. I want you to be happy here. And if you still want to take driving lessons, we'll use my old bomb."

"You're really okay, Aunt Lee. How come you never had children?"

"Well, I've never had a husband, for one thing."

"Are you going to marry Wade?"

She couldn't hide her surprise. "Wade and I are just friends. We've been friends since our school days."

"I think he likes you, though." He looked at his feet as though unsure what to say next. Finally, he looked up. "Do you care if I watch a video in the living room?"

"Be my guest." Lee watched him go and hoped they'd made some progress. When she called him in for lunch, he was talkative but kept yawning.

"Are you tired?"

He nodded as he bit into his second ham and cheese sandwich. "I didn't sleep much last night."

"Tell you what," she said. "I've got to check on my parents, then run by the shop for a couple of hours. I've got a big job coming up, and I have to order supplies. Why don't you hang out here and watch videos? You can bring a blanket to the sofa and take a nap there if you like."

"Okay."

Lee went out to her truck twenty minutes later, comfortable that her nephew would be okay while she was gone. She paused when she heard an approaching vehicle. A black stretch limo moved slowly down the dirt road in front of her house. She eyed the car suspiciously, wondering who it could belong to. It passed, as did her moment of unease, and she climbed into her truck and drove away.

Inside the limo, David Hill regarded Jack. "That wasn't very smart."

"All we did was drive by her house," Jack replied. "No harm in that."

"She could say you're harassing her."

"She didn't see me. How's she going to know?"

"How many black limos you think you'll find in this town? Why take a chance?"

Jack shrugged. "I just wanted to see what kind of place she lived in and if she was doing okay. She just lost her sister."

"And you've been accused of murdering that sister," Hill said. "Take it from me, kid. You need to stay as far away from Lee Cates as you can."

The funeral was held at ten o'clock the following morning, a simple graveside service in the little cemetery beside Grace Baptist Church. A spray of white tea roses adorned the coffin. They appeared surreal against the misty, gunmetal-gray sky. As the minister read from the book of Psalms, his breath steamed the chilled air.

Lee gripped her mother's cold hand as Shelby wept quietly into a wad of tissue, trying to grieve with as much dignity as possible. On the other side of Lee, Stevie sat stone-faced, staring at the shiny brass handles on his mother's coffin. Wade had the chair on the other side of the boy, and it was obvious he was trying to offer as much comfort as he could.

Lee could not give in to the overwhelming sadness at losing her only sibling, not when so many people were counting on her. She sat frozen and dry-eyed while her heart broke all over again. And the anger. It was still there, almost more than she could bear. She could not chase away the rage that blazed in the pit of her stomach like a hot coal, and she didn't want to. She wanted to stay mad—so that she never forgot for one minute what Jack McCall had done to her sister. She would not let herself forget or be happy again until he paid with his life. The system had failed her, just as it had so many victims. It was up to her to see that he got his due.

When the service was over, the small group walked toward the parking area in silence. Holden was there, as well as his wife. A couple of elderly aunts had attended, both of whom had no business being out in the cold, as far as Lee was concerned. But tragedy brought out the best in people. Stevie helped his grandmother into one of the cars from the funeral home, then climbed in and closed the door. As Albert McPhee helped Lee into the opposite side, she caught a reflection in the glass. The black limousine, parked at a discreet distance.

Lee's scalp tingled.

"Excuse me, Mr. McPhee," she said. "I'll be right back." Lee strode purposefully toward the limo, even as Wade called out to her. As she approached the vehicle, the back door opened and Jack McCall stepped out. He wore a charcoal suit, white shirt, and burgundy tie.

"Miss Cates," he said softly. "I'd like to offer my sincere condolences."

"You sonofabitch." Her anger was quick and furious, but she kept her voice low because she knew her family was watching. "You have some nerve showing your face here. Haven't you caused enough suffering? You're lucky I don't have a weapon on me, because I wouldn't hesitate to take you out and end your miserable life."

"I did not kill your sister," he said. "I might be a lot of things, but I'm not a killer. I liked Lucy."

"You're not fit to say her name."

"You're not listening," he snapped. "You can think what you like, but I'm innocent. And while we're having this conversation, the real murderer is running loose. What makes you think he won't come after you?"

Lee's blood chilled. She stepped closer. It would take little provocation to claw his eyes right out of their sockets. "Are you threatening me?"

"I'm trying to save your ass. I've seen enough cases like this to know the killer usually follows a pattern. He's likely to kill again."

"You're slick, McCall—but I've got your number. You may very well be the next Ted Bundy, for all we know. And I'm going to take great pleasure in watching your execution. And you *will* be executed, because I'm going to fight until my last breath to see that you are." She turned to go.

"You're making a mistake."

Lee whipped around and glared at him, the hate in her eyes startling. "Stay the hell away from me and my family or I swear to God I'll kill you before the state gets a chance."

Jack climbed into the car and closed the door, then leaned his head against the seat. "Dammit!" he said.

David Hill sat across from him. "Happy now? I warned you that coming here would only make things worse. But you refused to listen."

Jack bit back the hateful reply on the tip of his tongue. "Let's get the hell out of here," he snapped to the driver.

Sixteen

LEE WAS glad when Stevie wanted to go back to school the following Monday, because it meant they could regain some sense of normalcy—if only as a facade. As she dropped him off in front of the high school, she hoped the other students would remember to be kind.

The boy needed kindness right now. She saw the haunted look in his eyes, and she wondered if he ever cried. She allowed herself to grieve when she was alone in her bedroom at night, allowed those tortuous thoughts to surface—how Lucy had spent her last hour, her last fifteen minutes. What had gone through her sister's mind as her face was carved into something unrecognizable? Was it truly possible she'd been unconscious or had she been awake throughout the ordeal? And in the end, had she welcomed the butcher knife? These were the thoughts that intruded constantly, whether she was awake or asleep, so that she was forever pushing them back, stuffing them under so she could concentrate on what needed to be done. Sometimes, she thought she'd go crazy.

Wade was being an absolute gem. He'd brought a bucket of chicken over the night before, and a new Arnold Schwartzenegger video. Though she'd had little interest in watching an action adventure movie, Stevie was absorbed by it.

Wade had walked into the kitchen while she was struggling to get the cap off a childproof container of aspirin. "Here, let a grownup handle this," he said with a grin. She popped two in her mouth and drank a glass of water.

"You eat those things like candy," he said. "You know that can be habit forming."

"Promise you'll visit me when I'm in drug rehab." She kissed him on the lips and caught his look of surprise.

"What was that for?"

"For being such a nice guy."

"Nice guy?" he repeated. "That doesn't sound very exciting. Maybe that's my problem."

"You have a problem with nice?"

Wade smiled and stepped closer, slipping his arms around her waist, and it was Lee's turn to be surprised. "Face it. Women are more attracted to dangerous men."

"Oh, really?" Lee arched one brow. This was a side to Wade she had never seen before. "There are plenty of bad men out there. It's nice to know there are a few good ones left."

He gazed down at her. "I can be naughty if the occasion rises," he said. "I know this isn't a good time, but maybe you ought to give that some thought. Lord knows we've nursed each other through enough broken hearts over the years. Maybe what we were really looking for was each other."

Lee wondered why she hadn't seen it coming. Perhaps because she'd been so busy trying to keep her business afloat. But she had to admit it felt nice being held by a man again. She finally found her voice. "I don't know what to say, Wade."

"You don't have to say anything right now,

honey. Just know that I'm here for you."

"You've always been there for me," she said. Which was true. Who else would find time in his busy schedule to take care of her parents' yard because he knew they couldn't afford to hire someone? "Don't think I don't appreciate it."

"I know you do, but you've always been there for me too, kiddo, so don't go trying to give me all the credit. We know we like each other as friends; perhaps it's time to see if there could be more between us."

He kissed her on the nose and let himself out the back door, and Lee had spent much of the evening pondering the whole thing. For a while, just a little while, her thoughts had not been on her sister.

Now, as Lee parked behind her stained-glass studio, she wondered if maybe Wade wasn't on to something. He was good and kind and gentle, and she hadn't been real lucky where the opposite sex was concerned. Her last relationship had crumbled when the man she was dating had up and remarried his ex-wife. She'd been stunned, even though Wade had mentioned seeing the couple together at various functions. He'd even put her in his car late one night and drove to the ex-wife's house so that she could see for herself the second car parked in the driveway. *His* car. They'd ended up in a bar, where Lee drank too much cheap wine and spent the night throwing up and crying on Wade's shoulder. She figured any man who'd sit through that had to be okay.

But could she love him the way a woman was supposed to love a man? she wondered as she climbed out of her truck. She picked up an armload of supplies from the back. Sure, she loved him, had always loved him, but it wasn't the kind of love she'd dreamed about.

Lee paused at the back door. Who the hell was

she kidding? Any dreams she might have had about how life was supposed to be had been snuffed out with her sister's murder. Life was not the same as it had been when she was growing up, when you played hopscotch on the sidewalk in front of the house without fear of abduction, or walked home at night after studying with a girlfriend without being afraid of rape or murder. Today's world was a war zone, and there was no place left to go where one could feel safe. Perhaps a relationship based on trust and deep friendship was enough. In time, it could blossom into something more.

Lee unlocked the door and shoved it open with her hip. The building was cold, and there were few windows to let in the light. She shivered and kicked the door closed, then, freeing one hand, groped for the light switch.

Her heart jumped in her chest as another hand closed over hers. Her supplies clattered to the floor and she opened her mouth to scream, but the sound was blocked by a large hand. Ice-cold fear shot through her veins, and she struggled. And found herself pressed tight against a solid male body.

"Don't scream," he whispered. "I'm not going to hurt you."

She recognized the voice, and her fear suddenly took on a life of its own. Carol wouldn't arrive for a couple of hours. He knew this, or he wouldn't be there. That could only mean he'd been watching her. She heard him fumble with the lock on the back door, and her knees almost gave way beneath her.

Jack McCall's voice was steady when he spoke. "Miss Cates, I just want you to hear me out. Then I'll be on my way." He paused as if giving her time to process the information. "If I let you go, would you promise to keep quiet?"

Lee knew he would never let her go. Not when he knew damn good and well she'd run to Holden first chance she got. He was a killer. She had humiliated him, shunned him, and done everything she could to make life harder for him. And now she would pay. He had killed her sister and he would kill her.

Lee cringed in horror. There were enough cutting objects in the room, not to mention jagged pieces of glass, so that her own mother wouldn't recognize her when he was finished. Her mother would have to deal with another murdered daughter; Stevie would have to live in foster care.

"Miss Cates?" Jack feared the woman had gone into shock. He was disturbed by the pleasure he felt at her slender body being pressed against his, when it was obvious she was terrified of him. "Miss Cates? Lee? Will you cooperate with me for a few minutes?" he asked.

Lee managed to nod. She would promise him anything, *anything*. But she would search for an opportunity to escape or a way to defend herself. He removed his hand from her mouth, and Lee gulped in air. Jack turned on the light.

"Sit down." He motioned to a chair. When she didn't make a move to do as he said, he added, "Please."

Lee moved woodenly to a metal folding chair. She sat. And waited. She noticed he wasn't wearing one of his expensive suits today. He was dressed in faded jeans and a navy tee-shirt.

The clothes he did his killing in.

She shivered.

Jack pulled a chair close to her and sat down. He saw the fear glittering in her eyes. "Settle down," he said softly. "I swear I won't lay a hand on you. I just want to talk."

Lee looked at him, saw that he was unshaven. "How did you get in?"

"There was a key under the mat."

"Shit." She shouldn't have left the key for Rob,

her assistant, in such a conspicuous place. But she'd never had to take precautions before. Comfrey had always been a safe place.

"Not a good idea when there's a killer on the loose," he said, echoing her own thoughts. He leaned back in the chair. "I suppose now they'll add breaking and entering to my list of crimes." He offered a grim smile. "But once you've been slapped with a murder charge, it doesn't seem like such a big deal."

Lee met his gaze. A chill black silence loomed between them. "Well, what are you waiting for?" she snapped. "Go ahead and kill me." He remained still. "Oh, I get it, you'd rather I cry and plead for my life first, is that it? Is that what gets you off? Well, you can kiss my ass, McCall, 'cause I'm going to laugh in your face the whole time you're doing it."

He looked amused. "And I had you pegged for a nice girl." He glanced around. "Mind if I smoke?" he asked. "Or is there flammable material in here?"

"I don't care if you send the whole fucking building up in flames."

"I'll take that as a yes." He put a cigarette in his mouth and lit it. "I gave it up a few years ago, but why worry about health risks when there's a good chance the state is going to kill me anyway. Hope you don't mind a little gallows humor this morning, Lee."

Lee glared at him. "I'm glad you're able to find so much humor in the subject of death. Perhaps you'll find your own equally entertaining."

He leaned forward, elbows on knees, hands clasped together, cigarette dangling between two fingers. "Okay, you've had your say; now I'm going to have mine. I did *not* kill Lucy. I had no reason to kill her." He took a puff of the cigarette. "I know the evidence against me is bad, but I swear to God she was alive when I left her. Somebody came in after me, Lee."

"You're very convincing, Mr. McCall," she said. "But you're right; the evidence speaks for itself."

If her words angered him, it didn't show. He looked more determined than ever to prove himself innocent. "Your sister wasn't afraid of me. She invited me into her house without a second thought."

"And died as a result."

He put his cigarette out on the concrete floor. "Miss Cates, I'm not trying to make you believe I'm a boy scout, because I'm not. I've pretty much screwed up my life the past couple of years, haven't really given a damn about much of anything or anybody, including myself. But I'm not a killer. I spent ten years as an assistant district attorney, *prosecuting* murderers. And I was damn good at it. Why would I suddenly turn into one?"

"So where do you hang your shingle these days, Mr. McCall?" she asked, her voice heavy with sarcasm.

He grimaced. "You've got a razor-sharp tongue, lady. You ever thought of practicing law?" When she didn't answer, he went on. "You're right. I was disbarred. But not for killing anyone." He sat back in his chair. "Your sister was scared of someone," he said, "but it wasn't me."

Lee decided to play along. "How do you know she was scared?"

"It was obvious by the way she was acting. I told the sheriff, but I don't know if he believed me. Lucy insisted I enter her house first that night and turn the lights on. She was antsy as hell."

"Did she say why she was scared?" Lee asked, hoping to buy some time. Carol or Rob might decide to come in early. It was a long shot, but the only one she had.

"She just laughed it off and said she was always

like that when she entered her house at night. Said something about having a mean husband who'd taught her to be afraid. I've worked with battered women in the past so I know what they're like."

Lee wondered if McCall knew his own history of battering had been made public.

"Anyway, we shared a couple of Scotches, and I was out like a light. I only vaguely remember waking up sometime later and going to my car. Lucy mentioned she had a kid, and I didn't think I should be there when he woke up. When I opened my eyes again I was in some cheap motel. I now know the Scotch was tainted. Sheriff Cates sent someone in to draw blood from me as soon as I'd been arrested. He confirmed my suspicions."

Lee didn't believe him, but as long as he was talking his mind wasn't on hurting her. Still, there was a ring of sincerity in his voice. "You say you liked my sister. Had you planned on seeing her again?"

"I tossed it around in my head a bit. But I sort of got the feeling Lucy had problems, and I had enough of my own at the moment."

"What problems?"

"I don't think she liked men very much. Oh, she was nice enough to me at the time, but earlier in the evening she'd made comments that hinted to me she didn't hold the opposite sex in high esteem. Not that I blamed her, once I heard what she'd been through."

His answer caught her off guard. "So, if my sister wasn't afraid of you, who was she afraid of?"

"An ex-lover, maybe." He paused. "Or the kid."

"My nephew?"

He nodded. "Lucy mentioned she was sending him away and that he wasn't taking it well. I understand he's staying with you now. That's why I had to come."

Lee was quick to anger. "Are you trying to insin-

uate that my seventeen-year-old nephew is dangerous, Mr. McCall? That he was capable of cutting his
mother's face to shreds before he put a butcher knife
through her heart?"

"He has problems."

"How do you know that?"

"I have my own investigator working this case.
It's in my best interest to clear my name as quickly
as possible. And I will. I just want to make sure no
harm comes to you in the meantime."

"Why the hell should you care what happens to
me one way or the other?" Lee asked, annoyed for
wondering if he might indeed be innocent of the
crime for which he'd been charged. It had been easier hating him.

Once again, his eyes locked with hers. "I've seen
the hate and contempt you have for me. It haunts
me." He sighed. "And I have personal reasons, of
course. Two years ago I was framed for something
I didn't do, and it destroyed my career. I'm not going to take the rap for this, too."

He stood. "I've kept you from your work long
enough. All I wanted was for you to hear my side
of the story, straight from me. I'm sorry that I had
to scare you in order to accomplish it." He turned
and started for the door.

Lee watched in disbelief. He was leaving! He had
no intention of hurting her! She was weak-kneed
with relief. Her legs trembled as she stood and followed, wanting nothing more than to get him out
and lock the door between them.

They had reached the door when someone
knocked. Lee prayed it was Rob.

Jack paused and looked at her. "One word of advice," he said quickly. "Watch your back."

His words sent a shiver of alarm through her, but
she didn't answer. She opened the door. Wade stood
on the other side, holding a white sack bearing the

name of a local donut place. His eyes fell on McCall, and they became hard as stone.

"What the hell are you doing here?" he demanded, stepping inside. He handed Lee the bag and grabbed McCall by the collar of his shirt. "I asked you a question, goddammit."

"Take your hands off me," Jack said, shrugging free. "I came by to speak to the lady. As you can see, no harm has come to her."

"Did he touch you, Lee?" Wade snapped over his shoulder.

"No. Let him go, Wade."

Wade didn't seem to be listening. "I ought to haul your sorry ass right up to the sheriff's office," he snarled at Jack.

"Wade, please!"

He wasn't listening. "You stay away from her, do you hear me?" he said. "If you so much as come near her—"

"You're way out of your league, schoolteacher," Jack said coldly.

"I'm not scared of you, McCall. Why should I be afraid of a man who mutilates and kills helpless women?" He sneered. "Why don't you take on a man for a change?"

Jack stepped closer, ready to take up the challenge.

"Mr. McCall, please go now," Lee said. "Please, just go."

Ignoring Wade, Jack gave her one last look. "Thank you for hearing me out," he said, then disappeared out the door.

Wade walked over to the wall phone and snatched it up.

"What are you doing?" Lee asked.

"Calling Holden. He'll throw McCall's ass back in jail so fast—"

Lee grabbed the phone from him and hung it up. "Have you lost your mind? You can't have Jack McCall arrested just for speaking to me. Besides, he didn't lay a hand on me."

Wade looked at her. "How do you know he wasn't here to do the same thing to you he did to Lucy? If I hadn't shown up when I did there's no telling what would have happened."

"He just wanted to tell me his side of the story."

He looked incredulous. "*His* side of the story? Oh, that's a good one. Who's supposed to tell Lucy's side? And why are you defending him?"

"I'm not defending him. I'm merely trying to explain that you can't have McCall arrested for doing absolutely nothing."

"I hope you didn't believe a word he said."

Lee hesitated. She didn't know what she believed. "He was convincing, I'll have to give him that."

"Jesus Christ, Lee! Have you ever met a killer who wasn't convincing when it came to claiming his innocence? You are so naive sometimes."

"I am not!"

"Next thing I know you'll be inviting him over for dinner. We can bring out pictures of Lucy before he took off her face." He winced and put a hand to his forehead. "Damn, I didn't mean to say that."

Lee was trembling, and she didn't know if it was because of Wade or Jack McCall. There was something very appealing in those dark features and the stark blue eyes. At one point she'd truly felt he was telling her the truth. Had he simply been reeling her in like he had her sister?

"I can't believe you'd risk putting yourself in danger like that," Wade said as he paced.

Lee shook her head. She had never seen him so agitated. "Aren't you overreacting?"

"Or that you even let him in to begin with! Don't you have locks on those doors? Or do you keep the key under the mat like you do at home?" He glanced up sharply.

Lee wasn't about to tell him Jack McCall had been waiting for her when she got there; then Wade would have every reason to call Holden. And she would bite her tongue off before admitting that, yes, she had left the key under her mat again. Why she was protecting Jack McCall was beyond her. Perhaps because his story sounded so convincing. But then, he'd been a prosecutor for ten years; he'd obviously seen and heard it all. He knew what worked and what didn't.

"You need a security system," Wade said. "Both here *and* at home."

Lee shot him a look of disbelief. "Are you crazy? Do you have any idea how much that would cost? I can't afford it. I just had a new furnace put in, for God's sake."

"Then I'll pay for it."

"Absolutely not."

"You can pay me back when you're able."

"The subject is closed. You're not paying to have security systems installed. This is my problem, and I'll deal with it."

"You've always come to me before," he said, sounding hurt. When she didn't answer, he walked over and put his hands on her shoulders. "I'm worried about you, Lee. Your sister's killer just walked out the door, for Pete's sake. How can I not worry? And now that he's had a chance to get to you, he'll be back. Mark my word. He knows you're gullible."

"I'm not gullible." Was she?

"It wouldn't surprise me if he started sending you flowers. Think about it: every single person in this town is a potential juror. If they see the defendant consorting with the victim's sister, they'll automatically assume he's not guilty. Oh, he's a smart one, kiddo. He knows exactly what he's doing."

Lee was getting irritated. The man talked like she didn't have a brain in her head. "Are you finished? Because if you are, I have work to do. I'm going to assume that you're being overly protective because you're worried about me, but I'm a big girl, and I can take care of myself."

The doorknob rattled, and they both jumped. Rob Hess walked in carrying his boom box. He was blond and good-looking, but a pain in the ass as far as Lee was concerned because she never knew when he'd show up. He was jealous of her and Carol's friendship; he'd even started a rumor a couple of months back that they were lesbians. He'd denied it, of course, when Lee confronted him, and the only reason she hadn't fired him on the spot was because she needed him.

"Did I come at a bad time?" he asked. "Should I split and come back later?"

Lee knew if Rob split he wouldn't return for a month, and she had work for him. "No, stay," she said. "Wade was just leaving."

"What about breakfast?" Wade asked, motioning to the sack in her hand.

"I'm not hungry." She thrust it at him, but he refused to take it.

"I'll eat it," Rob said, snatching it from her.

"Do me a favor, Rob," Wade said. "Keep this back door locked at all times."

Rob shrugged. "Sure."

"I mean it."

Rob frowned. "Hey, I said I would."

Lee followed Wade out to his car. She could tell he wasn't happy with her. Perhaps she'd hurt his feelings by insisting she didn't need his help. "Will I see you this evening?"

He paused before opening the door. He refused to meet her gaze. "I've got a meeting. Don't know how late I'll be. I'll call you."

Lee stood there for several minutes after he drove away, wondering how the day had managed to get started on such a bad note.

She walked to her back door and turned the knob. It was locked. She pounded. "Rob, it's me. Let me in." No answer. She could hear his music blaring. How many times had she told him not to play it so loud?

He would never hear her. She checked beneath the mat, but the key was missing. Of course it was—Jack McCall had it.

"Asshole," she muttered, not knowing if she was referring to Rob or Jack or Wade or all of them. She amended her statement. "Just a bunch of assholes."

She climbed inside her truck and waited for Carol to arrive.

Seventeen

HYRAM COULD tell when something was wrong with Grace. She sniffed around like she smelled something bad, and she shoved her glasses high on her nose until the thick frames blocked her eyebrows completely. He knew he was in trouble when he saw the robe in her arms.

"Mr. Atwell, would you kindly tell me what you did to this bathrobe I gave you last Christmas? There's a couple of stains on it that won't come out. Looks like blood stains."

"I cut myself shaving, Grace," he mumbled, peering at her from over the newspaper.

"Now, I know that's a lie. You'd have to cut your own throat to get this much blood on it."

He chuckled and folded the paper. He had prepared himself for the questions. It would have been easier to just throw away the robe, but he knew the woman would have searched the place until her dying day if it had disappeared. "It's tomato juice, Grace. I washed it right away, but I couldn't get the stain out."

"Did you try spraying it with a stain remover first?"

"I don't know anything about stain removers."

She gave a huff. "You are always spillin' stuff," she said, clearly miffed. "Spillin' stuff on the carpet

149

and the furniture and the front of your shirts. I don't know why you don't pay closer attention to what you're doing." She sniffed again. "Well, it's ruined now," she said. "Might as well drop it off at one of those Salvation Army bins."

He could see she was hurt. "I'm sorry, Grace. It was an accident. But I don't want you to get rid of it. I'll wear it whether it's stained or not, just because you gave it to me." Wearing the robe was the absolute last thing he wanted to do. It would serve as a reminder of something he'd rather forget. But he didn't want Grace angry with him. Who else would look after him?

She gave it to him, looking mollified. "I have to go now, Mr. Atwell. Your dinner is on the stove. All's you have to do is warm it in the microwave. I'll check in on you tomorrow."

"Thank you, Gracie," Hyram said, falling back on the name he used when he teased her. What would he do without her?

Grace left the house a few minutes later, running over the mental list of things she had to do before returning home. She was irritated with Hyram Atwell. She knew the man was old, but sometimes he acted as helpless as an infant. She often wished she could have a word with the wife who had spoiled him so bad.

"Grace Jackson?"

Grace jumped at the sound of a male voice. She hadn't even noticed the young deputy leaning against her car. "Heavenly days, you scared me!" she exclaimed.

"I'm sorry, ma'am." He stepped forward and took off his cap. "I'm Deputy Willis Green from the sheriff's department. I'd like to ask you a couple of questions if you don't mind."

"What kind of questions?"

"I want to talk to you about your boss, Mr. Atwell."

Grace thought about the bathrobe and was scared.

Eighteen

LEE WAS scoring a design from a sheet of antique glass when Carol announced she had a phone call. She grabbed the phone next to her work table.

"Miss Cates, this is Jack McCall."

Lee shivered as a wave of apprehension coursed through her. She glanced at Rob. He was intent on soldering a panel of glass on the other work table. "Yes?" she said.

"I'm sorry if I caused trouble for you this morning. That wasn't my intent. The last thing you need in your life right now are more problems."

"Which explains why you're contacting me again, right?" There was an edge to her voice. "Is there something specific you needed to discuss with me? I'm very busy at the moment."

"I just want to know if you still think I'm guilty of killing your sister."

"It's not important what I think. You'll have to convince a jury." She saw Rob glance up at that one.

"What you think is very important to me," he said.

Lee thought of what Wade had told her. If McCall won her over, he'd have no problem doing the same to the town and a twelve-member jury. "Why should you care one way or the other what I think?"

He didn't hesitate. "I sense you're a decent human

being. You're warm and caring. I used to be like that. Don't get me wrong—I was a tough prosecutor, a real SOB in the courtroom, but I had to be. When you see how people are victimized day after day, it changes you. I guess I began to think of myself as a crusader," he added with a short laugh.

She didn't know how to respond to that. "I have to go now."

"Lee, I don't want anything to happen to you."

The remark chilled her. Was he trying to warn her or was he threatening her? "What makes you think something's *going* to happen to me?" she asked. Rob looked up for the second time. Lee turned and faced the wall.

"I told you, Lucy was afraid of somebody," Jack said. "If it was just somebody she jilted, then you're probably safe." He paused. "You bear a strong resemblance to your sister, you know."

Lee felt her stomach tense. "What's that got to do with anything?"

"Maybe nothing. Maybe everything. Look, could you meet me for a cup of coffee?"

Wade's warning rang loud in her ears. "Absolutely not."

"You'd rather not be seen in public with me," he said knowingly. "I just assumed you wouldn't want to meet me in a private place."

"I have no desire to meet with you at any location," Lee said. "And I'd appreciate it if you didn't contact me again. You have enough problems of your own without worrying about my safety. Now, I have work to do." She started to hang up, but his voice stopped her.

"Get some protection, Lee."

"I beg your pardon?"

"The sheriff's your cousin. He could assign a deputy to be with you around the clock. Or let me arrange for someone—"

"You? You must be out of your mind."

"I care what happens to you."

"You don't even know me," she snapped. "Don't call me again. If you do I'll report you." Lee hung up and went back to work. She was aware that Rob was watching her curiously, but she ignored him.

Lee was still thinking about the phone call as she waited to pick up Stevie from school. She felt self-conscious as hell in her battered pickup, sitting in a long line of BMWs, Volvos, and a slew of expensive four-wheel-drive vehicles. She hoped Stevie wouldn't be embarrassed, but as he climbed in the passenger's side wearing a grim face, he looked as though he had other things on his mind.

"Bad day?" she asked, weaving in and out of the waiting vehicles toward the main road.

"Some of the kids think I did it."

"What?" Lee looked at him.

"Some of the kids think I killed my own mother."

"Oh, for God's sake!" She pulled off the road. He looked at her, and the expression on his face made her want to cry. She thought of the kid Wade claimed liked to bully her nephew, and her temper flared. "Do you want me to talk to the headmaster?"

"No!" He shook his head emphatically. "It'll only make things worse if they see my aunt coming in to fight my battles. I have to take care of it myself."

"You don't have to go to school there, Stevie. I could have you transferred to the public high school. Wade would be there for you."

He gave a grunt of disgust. "What the hell good would that do? Everybody in town knows about my mom. They know I've been in trouble before, and that she planned to send me away. They're automatically going to suspect me. Besides, I don't need Wade fighting my battles." He glanced at the passing cars. "Can we just go?"

Lee pulled back into the traffic. "Stevie, the kids are just giving you a hard time because you're so smart. If they read the newspaper, which I'm sure they don't, they'd know someone has already been arrested for your mother's murder."

"If people really thought he did it, he'd be behind bars now."

"That was the judge's decision. Not the people in this town."

"I wish the person who'd killed my mom had killed me, too," Stevie mumbled.

Lee's blood chilled at the thought. "Oh, no, you don't!" she all but shouted. "I don't ever want to hear you talk like that again."

"Why *didn't* he kill me too?" Stevie asked, wiping tears from his eyes. "Haven't you wondered? I know I have."

"He wasn't after you, that's why. He had something personal against your mother, probably against women in general." She thought of McCall with his history of spouse abuse, and almost shuddered. The fact that she had listened to him, almost believed him, made her wonder if Wade was right in calling her gullible. Perhaps stupid was a better word. "The crime had nothing to do with you, Stevie."

"I was just down the hall. I heard a voice. I should have gotten up. I don't know why I was so tired that night. I could barely raise my head from my pillow."

Lee remembered the tainted Scotch and wondered if her nephew had ingested something that evening that'd been laced with the same tranquilizers. She needed to tell Holden what she suspected. Of course, it would probably mean another lecture on how she was poking her nose into his business and getting in the way.

"If I had gotten up when I heard him, I maybe could have stopped it. My mom might still be alive."

Lee looked at him. "Do you really believe that?" When he didn't answer, she went on. "He would have killed both of you had you walked in on him. A man like that wouldn't have thought twice about killing a kid to protect his identity."

Stevie didn't respond, but he hugged his book bag close, as though he needed to hold on to something. He looked resigned.

Resigned to what? she wondered. Resigned to believing he'd let his mom down in a big way? Resigned to feeling guilty for the rest of his life?

"Stevie, you can't blame yourself for something you had no control over."

"Let's just drop it, okay?"

She could see that he really didn't want to talk about it anymore, so she clamped her mouth shut. But she didn't consider the subject closed. First, she planned to tell Wade. He would know how to handle the situation—if he was still speaking to her, she reminded herself.

"Remember when you offered to help me at the shop?" she said, hoping to lighten the mood.

He was staring out the window. "Yeah."

"I was thinking maybe I could teach you how to make sun-catchers."

This time he looked at her. "What's that?"

"They're small stained-glass designs that hang in a window. You've seen them before; they're suspended from a small suction cup that's attached to a window pane or sliding glass door. I have a ton of designs you could choose from. I'd even pay you. You could choose something you like and practice scoring from scrap glass that I keep on hand. I'll teach you all the steps involved."

"What's scoring?"

"That's what it's called when you cut glass. What do you say? Are you interested?"

"Sure, no problem," he said. "Everybody in town

knows how good I am at cutting things."

Lee shot him a dark look as a chill raced up her spine. "That's not funny, Stevie."

Once again, he looked out the window. "I wasn't trying to be funny."

Lee had put off meeting with her sister's attorney as long as she could, but James Harrison had insisted. "It'll just be you and me," he'd promised. "You can come in for coffee, and I'll tell you what you need to know. Nothing formal."

Now, as Lee sat across the desk from the forty-something man with thinning sandy hair that'd gone gray at both temples, she sipped coffee and listened as he gave her the sad facts of her sister's estate. He looked nervous, and as he raised his cup to his lips, Lee noticed he was trembling.

"Let's see if I can put this nicely," he began, shuffling through papers. "Your sister spent money like there was no tomorrow. The woman had something like twenty credit cards, believe it or not, and they were all maxed out. I advised her to invest a portion of the insurance money, and she always said she'd get around to it one day—but sadly enough, that day never arrived. She paid cash for her house and car, but the IRS plans to seize them for unpaid taxes. I have the notice right here. Received it yesterday, although this has been in the works for months." He handed Lee the notice. "Lucy never understood about taxes," he added wryly.

"How can someone go through that kind of money so fast?" Lee asked, reading the form. She was angry that her sister hadn't considered her son's welfare.

"Her plastic surgery wasn't free," the man replied, "and she and her son stayed in an oceanfront villa on Hilton Head for a number of months while she was undergoing those surgeries. She employed a housekeeper, a chef, a masseuse, a personal trainer, and a private teacher for Stevie." He paused and shook his head sadly. "All to the tune of about twenty grand per month."

"Good God!" Lee felt dizzy.

"There was no talking to her. Believe me, I tried. I even drove to Hilton Head several times to discuss her finances, but she was hell-bent on living the good life. Said she'd earned it."

He clasped his fingers together. "The only good news is that she agreed to set up a trust for her son's education. There's one hundred fifty thousand dollars in it. I've made sure the IRS can't touch it."

"Well, that's a relief. I certainly want my nephew to go to a good college. What about your bill?"

He looked embarrassed. "I'm not even going to worry about that at this point. By the time the government takes their cut, which I'm sure will include an exorbitant amount of interest and penalties, you'll be lucky to have enough left over to pay off her funeral expenses."

"I'm surprised you continued to handle my sister's affairs, Mr. Harrison. Thank you."

His right eye twitched. "Actually, I'd written a letter asking Lucy to find other representation. I know she received it because I sent it certified mail. She ignored it. Just as she ignored the mounting debts and threats from the IRS."

"You'll keep me abreast of what's happening with my sister's estate?"

"Of course. I've notified the IRS that your sister's house is presently regarded as a crime scene. They won't make a move while the investigation is going on."

"Will I be able to collect the rest of my nephew's belongings before they take possession?"

"I'll have to notify them in writing of your request to enter, and you'll have to wait their approval.

Have the boy make a list of what he wants. I can't imagine the IRS being interested in your nephew's clothes and personal belongings; they're going after the house and furnishings. I haven't been out there, but I'd imagine they've already posted something on the door. And that should wrap things up—unless you have any further questions."

Lee shook her head. As she stood to leave she noticed a group of pictures on the credenza. One was of an elderly couple that she assumed were his parents, another was of Harrison himself and another man, each holding a stringer of fish. A third picture had been turned facedown.

"Excuse me for changing the subject, Mr. Harrison, but your wife ordered a specialty item from me some months back and still hasn't picked it up. I've left a number of messages. Would you please be kind enough to tell her the Tiffany lamp is ready?"

His pale face reddened. "Yes, of course."

"It's a five-hundred-dollar lamp," Lee went on. "I have another buyer for it, but I can't very well sell it since it was your wife who ordered it in the first place. It's just sitting in my store gathering dust. Should I deliver it to your house?"

He shifted in his seat. "You'd be wasting your time, Miss Cates. Leanne is in Alabama with her parents. Her mother is gravely ill."

"Do you have any idea how long she'll be gone?"

"No. It's a chronic condition. Leanne enrolled the children in school down there temporarily. If you have a buyer for that lamp, I'd go ahead and sell it. My wife would certainly understand."

Lee thanked him and left. Instead of getting into her truck, she crossed the street to the courthouse and entered the sheriff's office. "Is Sheriff Cates in?" she asked the woman at the front desk.

Holden was doing paperwork. "I can only give you five minutes, Lee," he said. "What's up?"

"I think you should run a check on James Harrison, the attorney."

He looked up. "And why is that?"

"I think he was having an affair with Lucy. I also think his wife left him. He gave me some cock-and-bull story about an illness in the family, but I think she found out he was sleeping with a client. I also think he might have extorted funds from my sister's estate. I'd like to have an auditor go over everything." He'd gone back to writing. "Holden, are you even listening to me?"

He sat back in his chair and regarded her. "I questioned Mr. Harrison three days ago, Lee, and, yes, I'm having the files subpoenaed as a formality. I don't expect to find anything amiss. Harrison might've had trouble keeping his pants zipped around Lucy, but he's not a shyster. Lucy simply blew her wad as quickly as she could, despite his advice."

Lee considered it, downcast. "One more thing. Has it occurred to you that Lucy might have been killed by a woman? A jealous wife, maybe?"

Holden tapped his pen against his desk. "Why are you suddenly so interested in the possibility of another suspect?" he asked. "I thought you were one hundred percent convinced Jack McCall did it. Or has something happened to change your mind?"

"Wade called you, didn't he? Good Lord, I can't make a move without everybody in town knowing about it."

"Settle down," Holden said. "He was just concerned for you. What did McCall want?"

"To convince me he didn't kill Lucy."

"Do you believe him?"

"I don't know what to believe."

"Stay away from him, Lee."

She was annoyed. "He came to me, Holden, I didn't go looking for him. Besides, I'm a big girl, and

I don't need Wade calling you every time I take a leak. I told McCall to stay away from me."

"Good. How's Stevie?"

She shrugged. "Who can tell with teenagers? Some of the kids at school are giving him a hard time, but he won't let me help him. He spends a lot of time alone, up in the third-floor apartment. He likes to read."

"What's he read?"

"Books."

"Wise ass. Get out of here so I can work." He pointed a finger. "And no more investigative tips. Between my deputies and Jack McCall's private investigator, I've got my hands full."

She opened the door, stepped out, then stuck her head back in. "Did you know the IRS is going to seize Lucy's property?"

He looked up. "Yeah, I didn't want to have to tell you. Lucy knew it was coming, though."

"I'd like to know what the IRS plans to do with that damn red bed," she mumbled, closing the door behind her.

Nineteen

ON WEDNESDAY morning, Stevie announced he had a date the following weekend. Lee regarded him quizzically. "So who's the lucky girl?"

He set his book bag on the table and pulled out a chair. His toaster pastry and milk were waiting for him. "Myra Bruckenthall. She's the new girl. Obviously hasn't found out I'm a cold-blooded murderer."

Lee didn't respond. She'd quickly discovered her nephew enjoyed shocking her, and she refused to buy into it.

"Anyway, she asked me to the school dance for Saturday night. I said yes, *if* there is a dance."

"Why wouldn't there be a dance? Is Herb Henderson afraid to spend the fifty bucks on punch?"

"We only have two chaperones. He's going to cancel if we don't get more."

"So, why didn't you ask me?"

"You?" He looked her up and down.

Lee placed her hands on her hips. "What's wrong with me?"

"These people are real uppity, Aunt Lee. You know, doctors and lawyers and—"

"You're afraid I'll embarrass you, is that it?" she said, slightly offended.

He hesitated. "Well, you don't really dress all that nice."

Lee glanced down at her jeans and sweatshirt. "These are my work clothes, Stevie. My linen suit and pillbox hat don't exactly blend with my blow torch and safety glasses."

"We'd have to take your old truck."

"Hey, I can't buy a new vehicle just so you've got enough chaperones at your dance." She looked thoughtful. "We could park it at the Exxon station down the road and walk the rest of the way."

He nodded. "That'll work. You must really want to be a chaperone."

"Not especially. I just hate to see Myra what's-her-face get away. I mean, what's the chance of a girl ever asking you out again?" She grinned.

He chuckled. "I don't see the guys banging your door down to get in, Aunt Lee. Folks must believe that rumor Rob started about you and Carol."

Lee pursed her lips. "Sour grapes, my friend. Rob hit on me and I shot him down. There just aren't enough eligible bachelors in this town."

"How about Wade? You could ask him to go to the dance with you."

"Wade and I have been friends way too long. I'd hate to ruin that. Most couples I know aren't good friends."

"You wouldn't have so much trouble finding a man if you started dressing more like a girl."

She arched one brown. "Excuse me?" She knew he was teasing and was glad he finally felt comfortable enough with her.

"Speaking of clothes, I'll have to go back out to the house for something to wear."

Lee didn't want to have to tell him about the IRS. "Why don't we just go buy something? We can go this afternoon when you get out of school."

"I need a haircut, too."

"So, we'll get you a haircut."

He drank his milk in one long gulp. "I'm ready when you are. And yes, I turned everything off upstairs, and no, I didn't use the stove. I put the thermostat at sixty-five. Anything else?"

"You have a milk mustache." She wiped it off with a napkin and was surprised he let her.

They hurried out the door, her with her purse and coffee cup, him with his book bag. "Tell me about Myra," Lee said, once they were in her truck and on their way.

He shrugged. "She's okay."

"Wow, I can tell I'm going to be crazy about her," Lee joked, suspecting that was all she was going to get out of him for the morning.

At least it was a start.

Lee asked Carol to screen her calls so she wouldn't have to deal with interruptions. She was eager to finish the sixth panel for the Catholic church. She considered it her best work ever, but she'd spent an inordinate amount of time on the project. Each four-by-eight panel contained a large oval medallion in the center with a religious motif: a lamb or cross, Christ with his head bowed prayerfully, a nimbus at his crown. The medallion was fixed in lead, and surrounded by glass chips that were individually leaded. The chips had consumed most of her time.

Rob had wanted to assist her on the project, accusing her of giving him only the crap jobs, but she'd balked. Although she'd trained him in every aspect of working with glass, he sometimes rushed through projects, and his work could be sloppy at times, forcing her to redo much of it. When she mentioned it to him, he'd call her a perfectionist and pout for days. She had allowed him to solder the panels, though, and she was surprised what a good job he'd done.

Perhaps she should give him more freedom. She, too, would be bored with some of the menial tasks she'd given him, mostly making repairs. He'd accused her of hiring him for his back, and that was partially true. She needed him for the bigger jobs, to carry and lift what she was unable to. She'd have to give him more responsibility if she expected him to stay. If he quit on her it would mean training a new person, and she didn't have time for it.

If only his attitude weren't so crappy.

The morning passed quickly. At lunch Carol went for sandwiches, and they ate in the workroom while listening for the bell over the door out front which would announce a customer. "I'm leaving early today," Lee told her friend. "Stevie's been invited to the school dance Saturday night. He needs clothes and a haircut."

"How's he doing?" Carol asked, munching on a pickle.

"As well as can be expected, I suppose."

Carol looked up from her lunch. "I guess you heard what Jack McCall has gone and done."

Lee felt a sense of dread wash over her. Had there been another murder? She hated to ask. "What?"

"It was in today's paper. Front page. He went to Stevie's school and paid his tuition until he graduates." When Lee's mouth fell open, she went on. "And that's not all. He donated fifty thousand dollars toward the new library. The donation was made in your sister's name."

"Tell me you're not serious," Lee said, feeling as though vinegar had just been poured into an open wound.

"Frankly, I'm surprised the headmaster would take his money."

Lee was trembling. "I'm not," she said. "I hear he's a greedy SOB. I may just tell him that when I see him Saturday night at the dance. As a matter of fact, I probably should write a letter to the newspaper."

Rob came in, having finished his classes for the day, and he began soldering the panel on the work table. Lee complimented him on his work, and he looked surprised. "You're really getting the hang of this," she said.

He regarded her quizzically. "Does this mean I get a raise?"

"As soon as I pay off my new furnace," she promised.

"Oh. In other words, don't hold my breath." His scowl was firmly in place once more.

At ten minutes till three, Lee drove to Stevie's school and found herself, once again, surrounded by luxury cars. She spotted her nephew standing beside the administration building talking to a girl. She assumed it was Myra. Once again, she felt self-conscious about her truck. She pulled out of line and parked beneath a tree.

Stevie opened the door a few minutes later and climbed in. "Why are you waiting over here?" he asked.

"I saw you talking to someone and figured I'd get out of line." She started the engine. "Is that Myra?"

"Yeah. She's having trouble with chemistry. I told her I'd call her later and go through some of it with her."

"That's nice of you."

"I'm just a nice guy, what can I say?"

"Any problems today?"

"Nothing I can't handle. Are we still going shopping?"

"Unless you've changed your mind."

"No way. I know exactly what I want to buy for the dance."

Lee discovered he truly did know what he wanted when they walked into the men's department at the local Belk Simpson. Khaki-colored twill pants and a navy sports shirt. In the shoe department, he picked out a pair of loafers. As they headed for the door Lee spotted the clearance rack, where she found a stylish black suit that'd been marked down twice.

"Try it on," Stevie urged her.

She put the suit back on the rack. "Better not. I've got enough to pay for this month."

He checked the ticket. "It's a ninety-dollar suit," he said. "You can get it for thirty. You want to look good at the school dance, don't you? It'll be your big chance to prove you're not a lesbian."

"Stevie!" she hissed, when she saw the sales clerk look up. "Why don't you announce it on the PA system? I am *not* a lesbian, and I'm tired of defending myself against a vicious rumor. I happen to like men very much."

The clerk came over and smiled. "Are you finding what you need, miss? Oh, isn't that a beautiful outfit? And it's been marked down. Very stylish, I think. Stylish *and* feminine."

Lee glared at Stevie as she handed the suit to the clerk. "I'll take it."

"Perhaps you'd like to select a pair of heels from the shoe department," the woman said as she carried the garment toward the counter. "We're having a sale."

"No, I'll just wear my army boots with it," Lee replied and saw Stevie grin.

They left the store a few minutes later and headed to the salon a couple of doors down, where Stevie was told there'd be a short wait. He picked up a hairstyle magazine and looked through it.

"Aunt Lee, look at this," he said, showing her a chic chin-length cut. "This is what you need."

Lee was skimming the latest issue of *People* magazine. "And why is that?"

"You know how you're always complaining because your hair falls in your work. You keep it tied back most of the time anyway. Besides, my mom always said a woman shouldn't try to wear her hair long after a certain age."

"And you think I've reached that age?" she asked, studying the hairstyle. "Boy, you've done wonders for my ego." She handed him the magazine. "I'm not sure my hair would look good this way."

One of the stylists walked over and Stevie pulled her into the conversation. "Do you think this would look good on my aunt?"

The woman took the book, glanced at the photo, then at Lee. "Oh, yes. It would definitely be a good style for you, ma'am. Take ten years off your looks."

"Ten years? Well, that's certainly cheaper than a face lift. Tell you what, I'll think about it and call for an appointment."

"You can have my appointment," Stevie offered. "I'm good for another week."

"Why are you so insistent on me having a haircut?" Lee asked, laughing. He shrugged as if it didn't matter one way or the other, but she suddenly thought about the dance. She did want to look her best for her nephew and his girlfriend.

And it wasn't as if she hadn't been thinking about getting her hair cut for some time now. She'd just been too busy. And she did like the style he'd chosen. "You sure you don't mind giving up your appointment?"

"Hey, you need this more than I do."

"Thanks, kid."

"Just teasing, Aunt Lee."

She allowed herself to be led to the back of the salon, where her hair was shampooed. Then the stylist put her in a chair, draped her in plastic and started cutting. Lee didn't get nervous until she saw how much hair was on the floor. Stevie had gone back up front to read magazines.

"Do you use mousse or gel?" the girl asked, once she'd finished with Lee's hair. "I suggest the mousse."

Lee nodded resignedly. She was missing half her hair; why squabble over hair dressings? Next came the blow dryer. When it was over, Lee didn't recognize herself—and she didn't know if that was good or bad. She was beginning to think she'd made a big mistake until Stevie saw it as she paid at the front of the shop.

"Wow, you look awesome!" he said.

"You think so?" Lee pulled on her hair as if to make it longer. "The back of my neck feels naked."

"It's great. Now, do you think we could get something to eat?" he asked. "I'm starving."

"Isn't that just like a man," she said, following him out the door. "Here I am trying to deal with a significant change in my life, and you're thinking of your stomach. Did you eat lunch today?"

"I tried. But some asshole took off his shoe and dumped sand in my plate."

"What!" Lee stopped, so appalled that she didn't bother to correct his language. "Did you report it?"

He stopped and turned. "Don't make a big deal out of it, Aunt Lee. If it upsets you that much, I won't tell you anymore."

He turned and strode purposefully toward the truck. Lee wondered why he told her his problems if he didn't want her to do anything about them. She wondered if she'd ever understand him at all.

Wade's car was parked in front of Lee's house when she pulled into the driveway shortly before seven that evening. She found him grading papers at her kitchen table and sipping coffee. It warmed her to know he felt easy enough in their relationship to enter her house without her being there. He glanced up the minute she entered, but the smile on his face faltered when he saw her hair.

"I'm going to hang up my new clothes," Stevie said, hurrying to his room.

Wade was still staring at her.

"You don't like it, do you?" Lee asked.

"No, it's very flattering. I just wasn't expecting it."

"It was sort of a last-minute thing."

He stood and approached her, then surprised her by grabbing her from behind. He sniffed. "Mmm, you smell great, too."

Lee laughed but shivered as his nose nuzzled the nape of her neck. "I tested a couple of perfumes at the cosmetic counter."

"Whatever you're wearing, I intend to buy stock in the company." He pulled her tighter against him. "I think it's time we advanced past friendship, if you know what I mean."

Lee wriggled free. "Not with Stevie in the house."

"How 'bout I nail his door shut so he can't get out of his room? He'll never suspect a thing."

Lee could feel her body warming up, but she didn't know if it was due to Wade or the fact she hadn't had sex since they'd put a Democrat in office. "Does this mean you're not mad at me anymore?"

His smile faded. "I wasn't really mad at you. But I did want to punch McCall's face in. I guess you saw that writeup in the paper about him giving money to the Academy."

"Carol told me about it. I have no desire to read about it."

"You can bet Henderson is kissing his ass over it. Wonder how much McCall had to pay to get the story on the front page of the newspaper. The man might be a murderer, but he's a smart one."

"That's a lot of money," Lee said.

Wade gave a grunt. "What's fifty grand to someone with eight million? Besides, he's just buying insurance on his life by buttering up everybody. By the time he gets to trial, this whole town is going to think he's a big hero. And believe me, it would be a feather in his cap if he could convince you and Stevie he was innocent."

"Wade, what if he really is innocent?"

He snorted. "You're kidding, right?"

She told him about James Harrison, Lucy's attorney. "I think he may have extorted money from her estate. The IRS had been threatening Lucy for months. Now, her property is being seized."

"I'd heard about that," Wade said. "But I know Harrison personally, and he's not a killer. That doesn't mean he wouldn't try to line his own pockets now that Lucy's dead. There's probably money hidden in an account somewhere so the IRS can't touch it."

"That only Harrison knows about?" she asked.

"Of course."

"Well, Holden's ordered an investigation."

"Good." He reached for her, nuzzled his face against her neck once more. "You're turning me on," he said. "Let's go rent a motel room. We'll tell Stevie we're going to a revival or something."

Lee laughed and slapped his arm playfully. "I've never seen you like this."

"I just can't believe that in all this time we never got together."

"I figured you weren't attracted to me."

He turned her around in his arms. "I guess I was afraid how you'd react. That maybe you'd slug me if I put the moves on you."

"Our timing was always off," Lee said. "If I wasn't dating someone, you were, and vice versa."

"Is Stevie going to the school dance Saturday night?"

"Yes."

"We'll have the whole house to ourselves."

"I'm a chaperone," Lee told him and saw the disappointment in his eyes. "You could come with me."

"Do you know what a boring job that is?"

"I suspect it's one of the reasons they have a shortage."

"You could come by my place afterward," he suggested.

"It'll be late."

"I'll prepare a romantic midnight dinner for us. Candlelight, a good bottle of white wine, and a couple of Lean Cuisines."

She chuckled. "It's tempting. Let me think about it."

He tweaked her nose. "I have to run now. Football game starts in twenty minutes. I've got five bucks riding on it."

She smiled. "We should probably discuss your gambling problem."

He went to the table, scooped up his papers, and stacked them together neatly before slipping them into his grade book. "Talk to your cousin, the sheriff. He's the one who made the bet."

"So, you're still in the denial stage."

"Denial is a good thing. Keeps you from feeling guilty." He kissed her lightly on the lips and made for the door. "Don't wash that perfume off before Saturday night. It drives me crazy."

Twenty

GRACE JACKSON pulled the fitted sheet free, then raised the mattress high to see if anything had been tucked beneath it. Nothing. She sighed her relief, then felt as though she'd jump out of her skin when Hyram stuck his head in the doorway.

"Grace, what in the world are you doing?"

"I'm trying to turn this mattress, Mr. Hyram, and I'd appreciate your help."

"All you had to do was call me." Hyram grabbed one side of the mattress and together they managed to flip it over. "There now." He studied her. "What's wrong with you today, Gracie? You're as jittery as a long-tailed cat on a porch full of rocking chairs."

"Oh, I got things on my mind, is all. I do have a life outside this house, you know."

"Of course, I know that," he said, wondering if Grace was beginning to feel as though she were being taken for granted. Women went through that from time to time. "Is there anything I can help you with?"

"No, I have to take care of my own problems."

"Your husband doing okay?"

"Nothing like that. Just some things worryin' me is all. Did you need something?"

"Oh, yeah. My reading glasses. I'm always losing them."

"Right here." She took them from the bedside table and handed them to him. He thanked her and
left the room.

Grace sat on the bed and covered her heart, which
felt like it would fly out of her chest. She was no
good at this sort of thing, and she still didn't understand why the sheriff didn't just get a search warrant and go through the house himself. That nice
deputy had tried to explain it to her—that Mr.
Atwell wasn't a suspect, but they still had a duty to
check out anything that looked suspicious. Grace figured the sheriff didn't want people to think he might
have arrested the wrong man.

She knew Hyram Atwell had nothing to do with
what had happened next door. The man wouldn't
swat a fly if it landed on his last piece of chocolate
cake. So why was she searching his bedroom? Just
because Deputy Green had said it was her civic duty
didn't make it so. She knew why. She was bent on
proving to that wet-behind-the-ears Deputy Green
that Hyram Atwell had nothing to do with that poor
lady dying next door.

She thought of the stained bathrobe. If only Mr.
Hyram hadn't lied to her about that. And she knew
it was a lie, because there wasn't a drop of tomato
juice in the house. She should know, because she
bought his groceries. Besides, she knew his likes and
dislikes, and tomato juice was at the top of his list
of dislikes. As was buttermilk. Said he couldn't
abide drinking anything thick 'cept maybe a milk-
shake now and then.

And Grace knew what a bloodstain looked like,
even after it had set into the fabric and been washed.
She'd been cleaning and doing folks' laundry since
she was fifteen years old, and she knew how to treat
most every stain there was. She would have been
able to get tomato juice out even after it had set.

Now, blood—that was a different matter.

Grace shook her head. With a heavy heart, she went into the bathroom and began searching the linen cabinet.

Twenty-one

LEE HAD to admit she felt a little sexy as she walked into the Academy's gymnasium in her new black suit and heels. Not only did it feel good to dress up for a change, she liked knowing she could still turn a man's head. And she had definitely turned a few heads as she and Stevie had made the two-block trek from the Exxon parking lot where they'd left her pickup truck. That, combined with her plans to spend the later part of the evening at Wade's place, had her feeling giddy. She had agreed to drive over after the dance, once she'd dropped Stevie off at the house, and the butterflies had been whirling around in her stomach ever since. She had questioned her decision numerous times, then told herself she would go and see what happened.

"There's Myra," Stevie said, trying to make himself heard over the loud music once they entered the building. He waved at a girl who stood alone on the other side of the gym. He seemed hesitant to leave Lee. "Will you be okay?"

"I should hope so," Lee shouted, noting that most of the men in the room were half her age. "Now, get out of here, you're cramping my style." Stevie grinned and hurried off. Lee immediately made her way to the far end of the gym where the music wasn't as loud. It was obvious the other chaperones and faculty were trying to escape the noise as well, because they had congregated in that area.

Lee waited in a short line at the punch bowl, filled a paper cup, and located an empty chair. She spotted a couple of teachers she knew and waved. They smiled but continued with their conversations without waving her over as she would have expected. She didn't make much of it at first, but as time wore on, she had the feeling they were avoiding her. She knew why.

People were uncomfortable with death, she had discovered in the past couple of weeks. Especially murder. Lee had seen old friends cross the street in order to keep from coming face to face with her. While it hurt, she tried not to blame them. She would not force herself on people and make them feel ill at ease.

After more than an hour of sitting alone and listening to the blaring music, and forcing herself to look as though she were enjoying herself, Lee decided to step outside for air. She grabbed her purse and headed for the exit doors. A slow number was playing, and she caught sight of Stevie and Myra on the dance floor, locked in a tight embrace. She thought of Wade and wished he were there so she didn't have this feeling of being ostracized.

Outside it was cold, but Lee didn't mind. She breathed in the night air and wished she were home, sitting in front of the fire in one of her flannel nightgowns that Stevie had labeled man stoppers. She walked a short distance toward the administration building, where the music faded and she could hear herself think.

A dark-colored Mercedes pulled into the parking lot and a man got out. A pickup truck rattled past, its muffler scraping asphalt, and pulled into the student parking lot on the other side of the building. Lee took some small pleasure in knowing there was a truck in town worse off than hers. She sat on one of the benches and wondered if she would even be missed inside.

The man approached. There was something vaguely familiar about him, but Lee thought nothing of it. She glanced away, even as the sound of his footsteps grew nearer.

"Miss Cates? Lee?"

She snapped her head up. She didn't have to see his face to know who the voice belonged to. Jack McCall stood in front of her, looking dapper in dark slacks and a sport coat. She fought the urge to flee. She would not give in to the fear that'd hit her gut the minute he'd spoken her name.

"What are you doing here?" she demanded.

"It *is* you," he said. "I wasn't sure because of your hair. You look—"

"I asked you a question, Mr. McCall," she interrupted, uncomfortable with his staring.

"I'm a chaperone," he said. "You might say I was bamboozled. I can think of a dozen ways I'd rather spend my Saturday night, but when I heard they might have to cancel the dance, I agreed."

She stifled the urge to laugh. That Herb Henderson would ask a suspected murderer to chaperone a high school dance was more ludicrous than anything she'd ever heard of. But then, Jack had paid a high price to get accepted into the cliquish community.

"I know what you're thinking," he said. "And you're right. Some people can be bought—Henderson is one of them."

"How convenient for you that you have money. Tell me, do you plan to buy every single person in this town, including the people who serve on your jury?"

"I'm innocent of your sister's murder," he said. "Do you blame me for trying to improve my reputation in this town? Besides, my donation was made with all sincerity. The kid has lost both his parents, and I'm sure his mother's estate will be tied up for a while. I didn't want Henderson putting any pressure on you about his tuition."

"And someone from the newspaper just happened to be walking by when you handed Henderson that check, which is why it was plastered all over the front page."

"I'm not the one who decided to turn it into a carnival show, Lee. That was Henderson's idea. He hoped it would spur more donations for the media center. I didn't object because it was in my best interests to go along with it, and I knew it would help the school."

"Why are you suddenly so concerned about my nephew?" she asked. "Last time we spoke, you indicated he might be dangerous."

"I've heard rumors. I think the boy has problems. I worry about you. May I sit down?" he asked, indicating the bench.

"This is school property—of course you may." She stood. "But I don't have to sit here with you. I can't be bought, Mr. McCall. And you can shout your innocence from the rooftops, but until I'm convinced another person killed my sister, I have nothing further to say to you."

Lee picked up her purse and headed back toward the gym. She could hear Jack McCall's footsteps right behind her, and walked faster. She did not wish to be seen entering the gym with him beside her. She jumped when she heard a loud noise coming from the student parking lot. The ratty pickup truck sped away and turned with a squeal of tires onto the road in front of the school. Lee wished they'd change the legal driving limit to age twenty-five. As she neared the entrance to the gym, a young girl seemed to appear out of nowhere, sobbing and yelling for help. Lee's heart took a leap when she recognized Myra.

She hurried over. "Myra, what's wrong?"

"Oh, Miss Cates, it's you. Stevie's hurt."

Jack McCall was suddenly beside them. "What's wrong?"

Myra looked at him. "Stevie and I decided to take a walk. Some boys drove up in a pickup truck and beat him up."

Fear slapped Lee in the face like a gust of cold wind. "Where is he?"

"In the back parking lot. Some kids are trying to help him. He's pretty bad; I think he needs to go to the hospital."

"Myra, go inside and call nine-one-one."

"No, wait," McCall said. "That'll take too long. Let me get my car. I can have him there in five minutes." He looked at Lee. "I'll bring it around back."

Lee didn't have time to argue with him; he was already gone. "Show me where he is," she told the girl.

The two raced to the other side of the building. At the far end of the parking lot, Lee could make out several figures standing or kneeling around someone who was sitting on the pavement. She ran.

"Stevie!" She reached him in a matter of seconds and knelt beside him. There was blood everywhere. It seemed to gush from his nose. He held something white against it, obviously somebody's tee-shirt. "What happened?" she cried.

He tried to talk, but his bottom lip, which had doubled in size, seemed to get in the way. "Kid . . . beat me up," he managed.

"Do you know who it was?"

He hesitated, glanced at those standing around him, and finally shook his head. "It happened . . . so fast. It was dark. Couldn't see his face."

Lee knew he was lying, but there was no time to argue. She heard a car pull up. "Can you stand?"

"I'll put him in the back seat," Jack said, scooping the boy up as though he were no heavier than a sack of flour.

Lee raced ahead and opened the door. She turned to Myra as McCall was putting Stevie in. "Honey, go inside. Those boys might decide to come back. Tell one of the faculty members what happened." She slipped in next to Stevie, trying to stop the flow of blood from his nose. She pressed the overhead light and wished she hadn't when she saw how bad her nephew looked. McCall squealed out of the parking lot.

It seemed to take forever to get to the hospital, although Lee knew McCall was driving as fast as he could. She glanced at her nephew. "You're going to be okay," she said.

"Why is he here?" came his muffled reply, as he spoke from behind the bloody tee-shirt.

Lee knew McCall could hear everything they were saying, but she didn't care. Stevie had every right to ask why the man accused of his mother's murder was driving them to the hospital. "He happened to be standing there when Myra told us how badly you were hurt. He offered to help. I didn't want to have to wait for an ambulance or go for the truck."

Stevie's eyes met hers in the semi-darkness. He lowered the tee-shirt, and when he spoke, his voice was a mere whisper. "I hope he doesn't change his mind and take us somewhere else."

Lee felt a tight, cold fist close around her heart at the thought.

Lee sighed audibly when Jack turned into the hospital parking lot some minutes later and skidded to a halt outside the emergency room entrance. Within seconds he was carrying Stevie inside, with Lee right behind. The boy's wounds looked worse beneath the bright lights; Lee could see there was going to be serious bruising. His hair was matted with blood near the back, where he'd obviously fallen on the pavement. His new outfit was ruined, the knees of his slacks badly torn.

They were led to a cubicle by a tall nurse. Jack lowered the boy onto an examination table, and the nurse took over. "You'll have to wait outside," she said, removing the tee-shirt from Stevie's nose. Lee gasped aloud at the sight of swelling and coagulated blood, and for a moment thought she'd pass out. Jack steadied her by grabbing her elbow.

"Let's go," he said, ushering her out.

They returned to the lobby, where Lee was questioned by an admitting nurse. "I'm certain my nephew is covered by some kind of insurance plan, but I don't know the name of it." She tried to explain the situation.

"If it's a question of money, I'll pay the bill," Jack said.

Lee turned to him. "I thought I'd made it clear that I don't want your money, Mr. McCall," she whispered between gritted teeth. She turned back to the receptionist. "I'm responsible for my nephew. I can write you a check now or you can bill me."

Once they'd worked out payment, Lee asked where she might find a pay phone, and the woman gave her directions. "I have to make a phone call," she told Jack, noticing for the first time there was blood on his sports coat. "Thank you for bringing us here. And send me the cleaning bill for your jacket," she said, indicating the stain. "If there's blood on your back seat, I'll pay to have it cleaned as well."

He opened his mouth to answer but was interrupted by a security officer. "Is that your car out front, buddy?" When Jack nodded, he went on.

"You're going to have to move it immediately."

Jack hurried away without another word, and Lee headed toward the main lobby where she found a pay phone. She dialed Wade's number, and he answered on the second ring.

"I'm at the hospital," she said without preamble. "Some guys beat up Stevie at the dance. I can't make it tonight."

"Is he going to be okay?" Wade asked, sounding genuinely concerned.

"I won't know till I talk to the doctor. We just got here. He looks pretty bad."

"You want me to come?"

"You needn't bother," she said. "They took him right in so I don't suspect we'll be here long. I just wanted to let you know why I can't make it."

"I'm not going anywhere," Wade said. "Call me if you need me."

Lee promised she would, then hung up. She returned to the emergency room lobby and was surprised to find Jack McCall sitting in one of the chairs. He stood the moment he saw her. "Why are you still here?" she asked.

"Your car is at the school. How do you plan to get back?"

She'd forgotten about her car in her panic over Stevie. She'd have to call Wade back and ask him to come after all. "I'll call a friend to come get us," she said.

"Lee, I'm concerned about the boy. At least let me stay until I find out if he's going to be okay."

She glanced around at the other people in the waiting room, but she didn't recognize anyone. No one who could drive her back to get her car. She'd call Wade once they finished with Stevie. "Do as you wish," she told him. She grabbed a magazine and sat. He took the chair across from her.

Lee skimmed an article on good nutrition, read

through a variety of recipes, then put the magazine down. She glanced at the clock. Only fifteen minutes had passed. She yawned.

"Would you like me to get you a cup of coffee?" Jack asked.

A cup of coffee would have been wonderful, even a cup of bad coffee from one of the vending machines, but Lee wasn't about to accept anything else from him. "No thank you," she said, without bothering to look up.

The sliding door whooshed open several times, but Lee gave it no thought. Not until she glanced up and saw Wade come through. He spotted her and hurried over. She knew the moment he saw Jack, because he grimaced and his eyes became as cold as a north wind. He turned around and left.

Lee tossed Jack a dark look as she stood. "You shouldn't have stayed," she said. She hurried out the doors after Wade. She caught up with him as he was unlocking the door to his car. "Wade, wait. I can explain."

He turned. "I don't think so, Lee. That's twice now I've found you with McCall."

"I'm not *with* him."

He ignored her. "I don't know what the hell you're thinking, unless you, too, have been charmed by all his money. But he's still the main suspect in your sister's murder, and I can't stand by and watch you make a complete fool of yourself. You could at least be a little more discreet. Your mother has suffered enough." He climbed into his car and made to close the door, but Lee grabbed it.

"You listen to me, Wade," she said. "Jack McCall just happened to be standing there when I learned Stevie had been beaten up. I didn't know how serious his injuries were; there was blood everywhere.

McCall's car was faster than waiting for an ambulance."

"So McCall saved the day," Wade said, wearing a smirk. "What makes you think the whole thing wasn't planned? If the man has enough money to keep himself out of jail, he can certainly afford to pay someone to beat up a seventeen-year-old kid."

Lee had not thought of that. Even so, it sounded preposterous. "Jack had nothing to do with that," she said. "I'm sure it was the same kid who's been giving Stevie problems all along."

"Jack? You're on a first-name basis with your sister's killer?"

She blushed but ignored the remark. "This is serious, Wade. Stevie could have been killed. I panicked; otherwise I would never have accepted a ride with him. I plan to go to the school Monday and have it out with the headmaster."

"Take *Jack* with you," he said. "I understand he has a lot of pull with Henderson. Excuse me, Lee. I have to go."

She moved her hand from the door so he could close it. As she watched him drive away, she wondered if McCall had indeed planned the whole thing. No, Wade was just being paranoid. When Lee reentered the emergency room, Jack hadn't moved from his chair. He looked up as she approached.

"I'm sorry I caused trouble between you and your boyfriend," he said.

She sat across from him. "No you're not."

"You're right, I'm not. I think he's a jerk." She opened her mouth to protest, but he interrupted. "If the guy really cared, he would've told me to get lost and offered to drive you back to the school himself."

She bristled. "You, of all people, are not in the position to judge anyone, Mr. McCall. Wade just happens to be a very decent man who is concerned for me. He thinks you're using me."

One dark brow lifted. "How so?"

"It would be in your best interest to befriend the sister of the woman you're accused of murdering, would it not? If we're seen together, people will automatically assume I believe you're innocent. They might be swayed."

"I'm not going to lie and say that hasn't crossed my mind, but I don't need your blessing, Lee. I will prove to you and everybody in this town that I'm innocent. I'm not the madman you think I am. The only way I could kill another human being would be in self-defense or if someone I loved was at risk. I wouldn't hesitate to put a bullet through a man's head if that were the case. As for your sister, she was no threat to me. I had no reason in the world to cause her harm."

"But you yourself said that you don't remember what went on that night. How do you know the drugs in the Scotch didn't make you psychotic?"

"I hardly think a tranquilizer could make me psychotic. But I do remember looking at your sister before I left, and she was perfectly fine. The person who killed her was either already in the house or came in as soon as he saw my car leave."

It sounded plausible, but Lee couldn't let herself be swayed. Holden had found enough evidence to charge him with murder, and she had to remember that. She would never forgive herself if she developed a friendship with him, then discovered he was guilty of murdering her sister. It pained her to realize suddenly that she didn't want him to be guilty.

Lee stood and approached the admitting desk. The receptionist looked up expectantly. "I wonder if you could give me my nephew's status," Lee said.

The woman smiled sympathetically. "Sure." She disappeared through a door and Lee waited. When she returned, she looked hopeful. "He's just come back from x-ray. The doctor says there's no concussion, but he's going to be back there a while. Why don't you go get a cup of coffee?''

"I think I will. Thanks for your help." Once more, Lee let herself out of emergency and followed the signs leading to the cafeteria. It was closed, but she found a small room nearby which was lined with vending machines. She put change into one of them and a cup popped out and was filled with coffee. She carried the cup to a table and sat down.

Jack walked in a few minutes later and got coffee for himself. Instead of sitting at the same table, he chose the one next to her. He sipped in silence for a moment. "You should press charges against the Academy."

Lee glanced up. "What?"

"There are very few lights in the student parking lot," he said. "You can barely see your own hand in front of your face. Also, they should have had a security guard on the premises. Henderson is so cheap he squeaks, but he should be forced to spend the money to keep the students and faculty safe."

"I thought you and Henderson were buddies," she said, sarcasm ringing loud in her voice.

He made a sound of disgust. "I was using Henderson, and he knew it. But he's too damn greedy to care."

"Are you using me?" she asked.

He glanced up sharply at the question, and his gaze met hers. "No, I happen to be very attracted to you." A look of vulnerability suddenly replaced his usual guarded expression.

Lee was shocked. She covered it with a sneer. "Because I resemble my sister?"

He shook his head. "You're actually prettier than your sister, but that's not the only reason I'm attracted to you. You're tough. You stand your ground, you say what you believe, and you don't give a damn who likes it." He paused, and when he spoke again, his voice was gentle. "I'd like to see the softer side of you. I know it's there, but I think you've had to be brave for a long time."

Lee couldn't tear her gaze from his face. She cleared her throat, tried to look indifferent, pretending not to be affected by his words. "I don't think we'd be suited for one another, Mr. McCall. I'm not interested in a hard-drinking man who picks up women in bars. And I'm certainly not interested in a man who has a history of spouse abuse."

"Spouse abuse?" He looked perplexed. Then he laughed.

"You think that's funny?"

"Not in the least. I've represented a number of women who were brutalized by men. Not all of them were alive when I took on their cases. But I've never abused a woman, not even my ex-wife."

"So, you're denying the charges?"

"My ex-wife and I were attending a party with a bunch of my colleagues. She got very drunk and began insulting me in front of my friends. It wasn't the first time. I tried to get her to leave, but she refused. Finally, I picked her up and threw her in the swimming pool, and I left the party. My wife was a champion swimmer in high school and college so I knew she wasn't likely to drown. Besides, I threw her in the shallow end."

He paused and took a sip of his coffee. "She pressed charges against me, and her father, the DA who was also my boss, did everything he could to wreck my image. He and I were already at serious odds with the case that caused my disbarment."

"And you did nothing wrong in that instance either, did you?"

"I don't expect you to believe me, under the circumstances. All I can say is that I did what I thought was the right thing. But power and politics sometimes get in the way of what's right."

He glanced down at the floor. "As for my personal life, it's true I've let it go to hell for the past couple of years, but I don't normally participate in one-night stands, and I take every precaution." He wiped a hand across his face. "This business with your sister was a wake-up call for me. I discovered I didn't like myself very much anymore." He paused. "You know, I think you would've liked me had we met before ... before I became what I am."

"And what are you?"

"Bitter. Cynical, I suppose."

"It isn't important what I think, Mr. McCall."

"To me it is."

Lee didn't have a response. She finished her coffee and tossed her cup into a trash can. "Would you mind driving me back to the school so I can get my truck?" she asked.

"What, now?" He stood.

"Yes. That way I can drive Stevie straight home and put him to bed once they release him. I just need to check with the receptionist."

"Sure. Whatever's convenient."

They returned to the waiting area, where Lee was told that Stevie was going to be a while longer and she had time to go for her vehicle. Jack made the trip in record time. If he wondered why Lee's truck was parked by the Exxon station, he didn't ask. She turned to him.

"Thank you for your help this evening, Mr. McCall," she said, "but I want you to stay away from me and my nephew in the future." She opened the door and stepped out.

"What about when I'm cleared?" he asked.

Lee bent down. The light was on in the car; she could see him clearly. His dark face looked hopeful. "I'm not interested in my sister's leftovers," she said, and watched the light go out of his eyes. She slammed the door and walked away.

Jack watched her climb into her old pickup, and waited until she'd started the engine and backed out of her parking space before he did the same. As he watched her drive off, he felt as if she just kneed him in the groin again.

At the hospital, Lee waited another hour before she was called back to talk to the emergency room physician, Dr. Russell. The look on her face when she spotted Stevie must have convinced the doctor he needed to assuage her fears.

"He looks worse than he is, Miss Cates," Russell said. "There's a lot of bruising, but that'll go away. I put a few stitches in his crown, which is why some of his hair has been shaved, but the x-rays showed no concussion. He does have an undisplaced break in his nasal bone, but it should heal just fine on its own."

He patted Stevie on the shoulder lightly. "I'm giving him something for pain. He'll start feeling better in a couple of days." He paused and his look became stern. "I also gave him a lecture on fighting, free of charge."

Lee wanted to tell him Stevie hadn't had a choice in the matter, but she suspected her nephew didn't want to discuss the matter further. He squirmed impatiently; it was obvious he wanted to go home. She thanked the doctor and led the boy out.

"How do you feel?" she asked once she'd helped him into her pickup truck.

"Like I was hit by a train."

She started the engine and pulled from the parking lot. "I hope Myra likes purple," she teased, "because that's what color your face is."

"I doubt she'll have anything to do with me after tonight," he said. "Now that she knows I knifed my mother."

"I'm not listening to this, Stevie," Lee said, knowing it wouldn't take much for him to start feeling sorry for himself. "Besides, you're not giving her enough credit. I mean, it's obvious she's crazy about you. She knows you're not capable of doing something like that."

"Does she? Does anybody?"

"I do," Lee said in a determined voice, "and I'll defend you as long as I have breath in my body."

"What makes you so sure I won't come after you during the night? How do you know you won't end up like my mom?"

Lee shivered. "Stop it!" she snapped. "I don't know what kind of game you're playing, but I don't like it."

"People believe what they want to believe, Aunt Lee. You want to believe I'm innocent because you couldn't handle knowing there was a cold-blooded killer in the family."

She looked at him. "Is that what you think?"

"Think how hard it would be to visit me in prison if I was convicted of killing your sister. And poor Grandma. She'd never be able to face her church friends again. Grandpa would have a major stroke and die." He paused. "Even if all the evidence pointed to me, you wouldn't believe it."

"The evidence doesn't point to you." Lee came to a halt at a red light. She regarded him thoughtfully. "Does it make you feel important to talk like that?" she asked. "Are you so starved for attention that you'll say anything to get it? Even if it means hurting those who love you?" She saw that she'd struck a chord because he looked away.

"I feel like shit," he said after a minute, "and I'm not talking about my face."

"So do I, Stevie," she said matter-of-factly. "I feel worse than shit. I open my eyes in the morning, and my first thoughts are of Lucy. I don't want to get out of the bed, but I make myself because I know if

I don't, I'll curl up and die." She had tears in her eyes. "I'm afraid to cry because I'm afraid I'll never stop." The light changed and she drove on.

"I didn't know you felt that bad," he said, looking at her as if for the first time. "You seem to be handling everything so well."

"I have no choice. I can't fall apart when I know others are depending on me. I keep telling myself that when things settle down I'm going to cry for a month, but face it, Stevie—things are never going to be completely normal again."

"I'll never be able to close my eyes without seeing her as she was that night," he said.

"I suspect the pain will ease off in time," Lee said. "But we're going to have to learn to live with what happened."

"Do you think that McCall fellow did it?"

Lee didn't answer right away. "I don't know. He's very convincing. I think the best thing we can do is stay as far away from him as possible."

"Well, I won't have any trouble doing that," the boy said. "But I'm not so sure about you."

Lee looked at him. For once, she didn't have an answer.

Twenty-two

ON MONDAY Lee drove to the Academy, where she had a four o'clock appointment with the headmaster. She waited close to an hour before he was able to see her, and although he told her how sorry he was to have kept her waiting, his apology rang loud with insincerity.

"I heard about young Steven," he said, as he led her into a paneled office that was so tidy Lee had trouble believing he really did any work there. He motioned her to a chair in front of his desk and she sat. "The boy responsible for brutalizing your nephew will be expelled once we discover his identity."

"I hope you'll keep me apprised of the situation," she said, "because I plan to press charges."

His forehead wrinkled in a frown. "This is a school matter, Miss Cates. A fight between children. I hardly see a need to involve law enforcement. It will only sully the Academy's reputation."

Lee's temper flared. "Mr. Henderson, if you were so determined to preserve the school's good name, you would never have accepted money from an accused killer. That, in itself, was a smear against all the Academy stands for."

The man paled, and his lips thinned in anger. "Miss Cates, you are getting into an area that doesn't concern you. Just because I accepted Mr. McCall's donation for the new media center, that is certainly not an endorsement of his innocence."

"My mistake. Perhaps it just appeared that way because it was plastered all over the front page. I have to hand you credit for that one. Especially since a young black cop was shot the day before in the next county. His story was placed on page two of the newspaper."

He studied her thoughtfully. "You of all people should not condemn me for my dealings with Mr. McCall, Miss Cates. I understand it was he who drove your nephew to the hospital last night, despite the fact there were chaperones and faculty that could have done so just as easily."

Lee felt her cheeks grow warm under his admonition. "It would have been difficult since they all shunned me. Not one of your staff so much as spoke to me—one would have thought I'd done something wrong. But I'm not here to discuss their rude behavior. I'm here on my nephew's behalf.

"I understand he has been tormented by the other students since his mother's death; in fact, there's a certain senior who's made his life intolerable. I believe this same boy is responsible for sending Stevie to the emergency room Saturday night. Unfortunately, no one seems to want to talk. Witnesses claim it was too dark to get a good look at him. I don't believe that for a minute, but that brings me to another area of concern. The school needs to spend money lighting the student parking lot and putting a security guard on campus when you hold dances, sports events, or other social functions."

Henderson leaned forward and clasped his hands together on the desk. "Miss Cates, you obviously have many grievances against the Academy, some of which I agree with. Steven has been with us a long time, but the past couple of years, I've sensed his unhappiness." He paused. "Perhaps he would be happier elsewhere." He smiled. "He could start fresh."

"You're going to kick a child out of school because his mother was brutally murdered and some redneck is making his life miserable?"

"You completely misunderstood me."

"I think I must have. My nephew is not going anywhere, Mr. Henderson. He's going to stay right here in this school, and you're going to see that no one so much as lays a hand on him. You're going to find the boy that beat him up, and you're going to expel him, as well as those others involved."

He looked unmoved. "And I am going to do that because?"

"Because I have a friend on the staff of the *Gazette*, and I won't hesitate to go to them with my story. And I'm going to have one helluva story." She stood and walked to the door, then turned. "Mr. Henderson, how much money did my sister donate to this school?"

"I wouldn't know."

"Like hell you wouldn't. Tell me, did you sleep with her?"

He stood as well, his face red. "Miss Cates, you would be hard-pressed to find a man in this town who hadn't slept with your sister."

Lee laughed out loud. "You came on to her, and she turned you down flat, didn't she?" She could tell by the look on his face she'd struck a nerve. "Good day, Mr. Henderson." She walked out, slamming the door behind her.

Lee had no desire to go back to the studio. Besides, Carol would have already closed the store, and she was skittish about walking in alone after Jack McCall's unexpected visit. Instead, she returned home and found Wade's car in the driveway.

He came out of the front door as she went up the walk. "Well, this is a surprise," she said coolly. "I didn't expect to find you here."

"I'm not going to apologize for my behavior the other night," he said. "I had every right to be angry. It's bad enough that you'd put yourself at risk, but to risk Stevie's welfare as well by getting into the car with an accused murderer is unforgivable and something I can't understand, no matter how hard I try."

"If my behavior is so unforgivable, then why the hell is your car parked in front of my house?"

He looked offended. "I hoped to talk some sense into you. What's gotten into you, Lee?"

"What's gotten into *you*? And what makes you think you can order me around?"

"I was only thinking of your safety. And Stevie's."

"I explained why I was with McCall at the hospital, but you refused to listen. Which meant I had to depend on him again to take me for my truck. So you didn't do me any favors by losing your temper. You've changed, Wade. I liked you better when you were my friend—before you decided friendship wasn't enough and started telling me how to run my life."

"So I'm supposed to overlook the fact that you choose to keep company with an accused murderer—the man who killed your own sister, by the way? And I'm not supposed to care if the people in this town hold you up for ridicule? And you know that's exactly what's going to happen."

"I've already explained my reasons for being with Jack McCall. I'm not going to repeat myself. Now, if you'll excuse me, I want to check on Stevie."

"He's not feeling well."

"He's had his face bashed in, how do you expect him to feel?"

"I'm not talking about his face. He's complaining of headache and nausea. I'm sure it's the flu."

Lee had woken up with a slight headache herself that morning, and feared the same thing. Luckily, it had gone away.

"It's going around at school," Wade continued. "If you need me to pick up something from the drug store, I will."

"Thanks, but I think I have something." She reached for the door knob, then paused when he called her name.

"I don't want this stuff with McCall to come between us."

"Then don't let it." She opened the door and went inside.

Lee found Stevie on the sofa, watching a Claude Van Damme movie. "Wade says you're not feeling well," she said, pausing beside him to feel his head. It was cool.

"Probably just a bug. Wade said it's going around."

She asked him about his symptoms, and it was pretty much as Wade had said. "I've got something I can give you, but I'll have to check with my doctor to see if you can take it on top of pain pills."

He yawned. "Don't bother. Wade gave me another pain pill, and I'm getting sleepy now."

"Okay. Why don't you rest and see how you feel when you wake up."

Lee went about straightening the house and putting in a load of wash. Stevie had followed his part of the bargain about bringing down his dirty laundry, but she was amazed at how much there was of it. Teenagers obviously changed clothes often.

She checked the freezer, found ham slices that her mother had sent home with her, and decided on a simple meal of soup and sandwiches. By the time Lee had finished her chores and had dinner ready, she wasn't feeling so hot herself. Her head had begun to ache, and she had an upset stomach. She took something for both, but although the headache eased off, she had no desire to eat. It would be just her luck to come down with the flu when she had so much to do.

Lee tried to wake Stevie to see if he was hungry, but the pain pill had obviously worked because he was too drowsy to talk. She, too, was feeling sleepy, although she'd taken a nondrowsy flu medicine. She grabbed a blanket and curled into a chair beside the fireplace.

Lee dozed on and off during the night, getting up to check on Stevie. He complained of being thirsty, but she had to lift his head to help him drink the glass of water. "I'll have to take you to the doctor in the morning," she said as he drifted off to sleep.

But when morning came Lee was feeling worse, and it was all she could do to make it to the bathroom. She checked the clock and was surprised to see they'd slept until eleven. Perhaps sleep was what they both needed. Still, she didn't feel any better. In fact, she felt much worse.

She was startled to see the reddish-pink color on Stevie's cheeks. Obviously the boy had a serious fever. But when she touched him he was still cool to the touch. She tried to wake him, but he grumbled. Lee didn't have the strength to fight him. She returned to her chair and tried to ignore her pounding head.

The phone rang, and Lee groaned. Probably Carol wondering why she hadn't come in. With her hands pressed against either side of her head, Lee hurried toward it and answered in a mere whisper.

Jack McCall spoke from the other end. "Lee, is that you? You don't sound like yourself."

"What do you want?" It was a struggle to speak.

"I know you told me not to call, but I was concerned about your nephew. Is he okay?" When Lee didn't answer, he went on. "Are you there?"

"He's not . . . well," Lee managed.

"You don't sound so good yourself," he said in obvious concern. "Have you got someone there to help you?"

"Who is this?" she asked. Silence on the other end. Lee hung up the phone, stumbled to the bathroom, and became sick. She splashed water on her face, made for her bedroom, and fell across the bed.

She didn't know how long she slept, but suddenly she felt as if someone was shaking her teeth out. She forced her eyes open. Jack McCall was there. He was talking to her. His face seemed far away, and she couldn't make sense of what he was saying. Panic struck. Was he there to kill her? Odd that he didn't look crazy or angry; he looked worried. She closed her eyes, unable to keep them open any longer. Living suddenly didn't seem that important.

"Lee, what's wrong with you?" Jack asked, trying to get her to talk to him. "Have you taken some sort of tranquilizer?" She was like a rag doll in his arms. He reached for the telephone on her night table and dialed 9-1-1.

When Lee awoke she was in the emergency room, flanked by a young doctor and a nurse and a third person telling her to lie very still so he could take blood. She winced when the needle went in, then looked the other way.

"Welcome back, Miss Cates," the doctor said.

"Where've I been?" Her voice didn't sound like her own.

"Oz. Next time take your ruby slippers so you can get back easily." He grinned. "Actually, you're suffering from carbon monoxide poisoning."

"My nephew? How is he?"

"He's coming around. We might have to keep him

for a few days. His face looks pretty bad; how'd that happen?''

"A boy attacked him at school," Lee said. "I had him in here a few nights ago."

"I'll look for his chart. He certainly seems to be having his share of bad luck these days. As for you, I'd like to go ahead and admit you so I can watch you for the next twenty-four hours."

Lee's first thought was to protest. She didn't have time to be in the hospital. But at the moment she was too weak to care. "How did I get here?"

The doctor was scribbling something on a clipboard. "By ambulance. You and your nephew were a bright cherry red when you came in. You'd better get your place checked out before you go back in, and I'd invest in a carbon monoxide detector."

"I have one."

He patted her hand. "Might want to test your battery."

Lee just looked at him. She *had* tested it, along with the batteries in her smoke detectors, right when the temperatures had begun to drop and a public service announcement kept warning people to do so. She had gone one step further and replaced the batteries whether they'd needed it or not. But she was too tired to explain it all at the moment.

"We'll have to fill out some forms," the nurse said. "Do you have any idea how this could have happened?"

Lee tried to think. Why did they have to ask her all these questions now? "I recently had a new furnace installed," she said.

The woman nodded. "I'd have the company check it out as soon as possible."

The doctor looked serious. "Had you spent many more hours in your house, you would have arrived in a hearse instead of an ambulance, and that's no joke."

"Will my nephew be all right?"

"Tell you what," the doctor said. "I'm finished up here. I'll drop in and check on him. If I don't come back, I'll send someone."

Lee thanked him and he left. The nurse took down more information. "I need to take this to admissions," she said. "There's a man out there who's been worried out of his mind about you and the boy. Should I send him in?"

"Who is it?" Lee asked.

"I don't know his name, honey, although he claims to be a close family friend. He's the one who found you and called the ambulance."

It had to be Wade. Lee nodded. "Sure, send him in." A moment later, Jack McCall stepped into the room. Lee froze.

"They told me I could come in for a minute," he said.

"You're the one who found me?"

"You don't remember?"

She shook her head. "I remember waking up with a bad headache this morning. After that, everything's a big blank." She regarded him. "How did you know something was wrong?"

"I called to check on Stevie. You were completely out of it. I raced over and found you unconscious."

"All the way from Hilton Head?"

"I have a place in town. When I found you, you were slipping away quickly. Stevie was already unconscious. Scared the hell out of me. I called an ambulance."

The same nurse stuck her head in the door. "Your nephew has regained consciousness, Miss Cates. He's going to be okay, but it'll take a few days."

Lee thanked her, and the woman disappeared. She turned to McCall. "You saved our lives."

He looked sober. "At first I was afraid I'd arrived too late. When I saw that Stevie was in the same condition as you, I suspected there was something wrong inside the house, so I shut off everything and opened the doors and windows.''

"Thank God you came."

"I hope you don't plan to go back into that house until you find out what the problem is. Could it be your furnace?"

"I just had a new one installed."

"Maybe they didn't vent it right. Do you want me to call them for you?"

"I'll see to it."

The nurse returned. "We're going to move you into a room now," she told Lee.

Jack smiled. "Guess that's my cue to leave. Do you mind if I drop by tonight? Just to see how you and Stevie are doing?"

Lee wrestled with the decision as he waited for her answer. "I suppose for a little while."

Wade looked distraught when he entered Lee's hospital room shortly after her dinner tray had been taken away. Without a word, he sat down in the chair beside her. His emotions seemed to be getting the best of him. "You could have died," he said at last.

"How did you know I was here?"

"Holden called me. It would have been nice had you picked up the phone yourself."

Lee realized he was forcing himself not to look at her. "What is it, Wade?"

"Now that I know you're going to be okay, I can't help but wonder what McCall was doing at your house that hour of the morning. Did he spend the night?"

She sighed. "No, he did not. He called out of concern for Stevie. I guess I was disoriented, so he drove over and found both of us unconscious. He saved our lives, Wade," she added softly.

He turned and faced her. "Okay, just hear me out, Lee. That's all I ask. I know you think I'm jealous of McCall, and maybe you're right. But it goes deeper than that. I'm afraid for you and Stevie." When she started to interrupt, he went on. "Don't you think it's a bit strange that McCall just happens to show up at the right moment? Stevie gets beat up, and McCall is there to rush him to the hospital. You almost die from carbon monoxide poisoning, and McCall just happens to be the one who rushes in to save the day."

"What are you saying, Wade?"

"How do you know McCall didn't pay someone to beat up Stevie?" he asked. "How do you know he didn't do something to your furnace to cause the carbon monoxide to escape? All he'd have to do is look under your mat for the key."

"My key is no longer under the mat."

"How hard could it be to break into your house?" He sighed. "I'm not saying that's what happened, Lee; I'm only asking you to consider it." He looked sad as he stood and bent over the bed to kiss her on the forehead. He squeezed her hand. "Take care of yourself, okay?"

Lee watched him go. She didn't blame him for being upset with her, but she hated to lose his friendship. His warning about Jack McCall left a hollow feeling in her stomach.

Holden showed up an hour later, carrying a vase with a single rose and wearing a stern look. "I accompanied the Allen brothers into your house," he said. "They checked out the furnace and found a hole in the exhaust pipe. Evidently it'd been leaking for a couple of days."

"So they repaired it?" Lee asked.

"They were working on it when I left."

"Well, that's a relief. At least it'll be safe to go back."

"I don't like it, Lee." He sat in the chair Wade had occupied earlier. "Unless the pipe was defective when they put it in, there's no reason it should've had a hole in it. The damn thing is brand new. Larry Allen swears he would have noticed a defect, but he also admitted they're as busy as a one-armed paper hanger these days. I guess it could have been overlooked."

"I'm sure that's all it was," Lee said, thinking perhaps Holden was overreacting. As she started to say more, the door was suddenly flung open by Carol, a plant in her hand and a big "Get Well Soon" balloon trailing behind her.

"Holy shit, Lee. Are you trying to scare me to death or what? You're at this hospital so much I figure you're either a hypochondriac or you've met a cute doctor."

Holden stood and saluted them both. "Ladies, I'd love to stay and chat, but I'm sure you'll manage without me."

It was after eight o'clock when Jack McCall walked into Lee's hospital room carrying flowers, a box of chocolates, and several magazines. He'd already dropped a gift off to Stevie and learned the boy was doing better. He found Lee snuggled beneath the covers facing the opposite direction. "Are you awake?" he whispered. There was no movement. He set the items down in the chair and waited a good ten minutes. When she didn't make a move, he decided she probably needed her rest more than visitors. Finally, he left.

Lee continued to lie there very still until she heard the door close behind him. As she lay in lonely silence, her heart was heavy with disappointment.

Twenty-three

HYRAM ATWELL clucked his tongue as he stared at his housekeeper, sitting cross-legged on the floor before the kitchen sink with all the cleaning supplies scattered about. He hadn't even finished his first cup of coffee, and the woman had the whole house torn apart. If he didn't know better, he'd think she'd lost her mind.

"Grace, what in tarnation has gotten into you? I haven't even had my breakfast and here you are pulling everything out of the cabinets. You're in a regular cleaning frenzy. Is the pope planning a visit?"

The black woman didn't so much as look at him. "Mr. Atwell, I ain't in no mood to talk. I've been putting off cleaning out these cabinets for months now, and I aim to see that it's done. Lord knows you ain't about to lift a hand doing anything around here."

He chuckled. "You know danged well that if I got down on that floor I'd never get up."

"I cain't tolerate nastiness," she grumbled. "This whole house needs to be put in order."

"How long do you think this cleaning project will take you? And how much is it going to cost me?" he asked.

She glared at him. "Just you don't worry about it.

I'll be done when I'm done. Besides, you can afford to pay me the extra, so stop acting like you ain't got ten cents to rub together. Now, go on and leave me to my work. I'll bring you a bowl of cereal directly. I got things to do.''

Lee was released that same morning. Although the doctor considered keeping her another day, she finally convinced him she was feeling no ill effects of the carbon monoxide poisoning. She spent an hour with Stevie, trying to draw him into conversation, but the boy was unusually quiet. His bruises had turned a sickly green and lavender, and his bottom lip was still swollen.

She left once he drifted off to sleep. She drove home and found a note on her front door from Larry Allen, stating that the furnace had been repaired and the house was safe to enter. Nevertheless, she stepped inside cautiously, sniffing the air as though she would be able to smell the toxic gas that could have claimed their lives. Nothing. But she already knew carbon monoxide was odorless.

Lee first called her mother, as she had every day since her sister's murder, and pretended everything was normal. She would not burden the woman with more worries. If Shelby Cates suspected anything was amiss, she gave no indication, and Lee could only assume she was getting better at hiding things. Her mother seemed more concerned that her husband wasn't eating as he should.

When Lee hung up, she got the step ladder from the utility room and carried it into the hallway, then set it up beneath the carbon monoxide detector. Flipping on the light switch, she climbed up and reached for the cover, just as she had a few short weeks back when she'd put in a new battery.

And she *had* put in a new battery. She knew it. She'd checked all the detectors for the battery sizes, leaving the covers off until she'd put the new ones in.

She remembered it like it was yesterday.

She popped the cover off and stared for a long moment at the empty slot where the battery had once been.

Grace Jackson found what she was looking for later than morning. She had cleaned all the cabinets and had started on the drawers, tossing old dish towels into the rag box, washing the plastic tray that held the silverware. There were two sets of them, plus a third, less expensive set that looked as though it might have been used on picnics or backyard gatherings.

The late Mrs. Atwell had obviously never thrown away anything, including three drawers worth of cutlery. As Grace pulled the items from the drawers, she was amazed to discover there were eight spatulas, at least as many slotted spoons, a half dozen soup ladles, and four garlic presses.

The knives were in the bottom drawer—at least two dozen of them in different shapes and sizes, some old and so dull as to be worthless. Then Grace saw the butcher knife that had been described to her in detail by Deputy Green—and she wondered why nobody had thought to look there. If you wanted to hide something, you didn't try to think of the last place someone would look, because that always ended up being the first place they looked. You hid it in a place where there were others just like it. Grace realized she had known that all along—that's why she'd avoided the knife drawer to begin with.

As she gazed down at the brown-handled knife, she was thankful Hyram was napping. Already, she could feel the tears sliding down her cheeks.

Twenty-four

L EE FOUND Stevie despondent when she visited him the next morning before work. His doctor, Janet McCarthy, asked Lee to step outside.

"I'm very concerned about your nephew," the woman said. "He won't talk to anyone, and he has no appetite. I know what is going on in his life now; the papers have been full of it—and I'd like to refer Steven to our staff psychiatrist."

Lee couldn't hide her surprise. "You really believe that's necessary?"

"I wouldn't have suggested it otherwise. I think the boy is seriously depressed, and he has every reason to be. But it wouldn't hurt to let someone with more experience have a look at him. Dr. Larson might even want to put him on a light antidepressant."

Lee was thoughtful. "I'm for anything that works, Dr. McCarthy. I just don't want to put him through more pain than he's already been through."

"I'm hoping Dr. Larson can help alleviate some of that pain, Miss Cates. But Steven has to be willing to talk to him. I was hoping you could convince him."

Lee was still pondering it when she arrived at work. The look on Carol's face gave her pause. "What's wrong?"

"I'm worried about you. I mean, how much can one person take?"

"I'm okay," Lee said.

Carol stepped closer. "What if it wasn't an accident?" she said, lowering her voice to a whisper even though there was no one else in the room to hear.

Lee waved it off as though the thought had never entered her mind. "I'm sure it's just one of those freak accidents that happen. Please don't say anything to anybody. I don't want my mother to get wind of it."

"I'd feel better if you stayed with me for a couple of days."

"Believe me, if I think it's necessary, I will."

They argued the point for a few more minutes until Lee finally managed to escape to the back and begin work. When lunchtime rolled around, she left on the pretense of visiting her parents. Instead of heading in that direction, though, she turned onto the highway leading out of town and pulled up in front of a cinderblock building with GUN CITY painted over the door. On the roof, a large gun cut from plywood, its paint long since faded, rested against a metal frame. Inside, Lee found more than she'd counted on: every kind of hunting or sporting equipment she could imagine, and a whole aisle devoted to self-defense products including Mace and hot pepper spray. The handguns and rifles were located in a glass case at the back of the store.

The owner was an overweight man with three chins and a wad of chewing tobacco in one cheek, who selected a small handgun for Lee that would easily fit inside her purse. "Is it powerful?" she asked, thinking it appeared too delicate to be of any use to her.

"Don't let its size fool you, miss," he said. "It packs a wallop."

Lee filled out the necessary paperwork and handed it to him. "I'll have to run a check on you," he said. "You had lunch yet?"

"I beg your pardon?" She glanced up quickly, half afraid he was inviting her. She could imagine sharing a can of cold pork and beans in a grimy kitchen in back.

"If you wanna grab something to eat, I'll go ahead and get on this." He paused and spat, and Lee suppressed a shudder. "Probably have it done by the time you get back."

Lee drove to the nearest fast-food restaurant, where she ordered a burger, took two bites, then pushed it aside. She checked her watch. She'd only been gone ten minutes. She continued to sit there as the place filled up, her thoughts occupied with other matters.

Like the missing battery. And the knowledge that somebody was after her and Stevie. She knew it instinctively. She also knew it was the same person who'd killed her sister. It would have been easier to just tell Holden and ask for protection, but she knew that would keep the killer away. It was up to her to lure him, and she would do that by pretending to be vulnerable. But she didn't have much time. She wanted it done and over with by the time Stevie arrived home from the hospital.

Lee's stomach was tied in knots by the time she arrived back at Gun City. Never in her life would she have believed herself capable of buying a weapon. Perhaps if the threats were aimed at her alone she wouldn't have had the nerve, but since they included her seventeen-year-old nephew, the decision had been made for her. She had no other choice.

The fat man was smiling when she stepped through the door. "It's yours," he said, shoving the pistol across the counter.

Lee stared at the gun for a full minute before reaching for it.

No other choice.

Lee left work an hour early and drove to the public high school. There were only a few cars remaining in the student parking area, but from the looks of the faculty parking, a number of teachers remained. She found Wade's car behind the gym and parked beside it, then grabbed her purse. It was surprisingly light without the gun. She'd locked it in her desk drawer at work. She constantly feared someone would see it or that it would fall out of her purse while she was digging through for something else. She wouldn't rest until it was tucked safely inside the drawer of the night table beside her bed. No, she'd worry even then. She was not accustomed to carrying a firearm and never would be.

Inside, a custodian led her to Wade's office, after checking to make sure there were no male students dressing in the locker area. Wade was clearly surprised to see her. He stood. "Is something wrong?" he asked.

"Does something have to be wrong for me to visit my best pal?" She noted his look of relief as she closed the door and leaned against it. "Actually, I've come to try out for cheerleading."

He chuckled and stepped closer. "You'd have to wear a short skirt."

"Anything for the good of the team," she said, a teasing lilt in her voice.

"And you think my football players will be able to keep their minds on the game once they get a look at those gams? Not a chance."

He smelled of soap. Lee knew he showered before leaving school each day. "I'm tired of fighting with you, Wade," she said softly. "Do you think we can go back to how it was before?"

He met her gaze. "I'd like to think we could do better than that." He took her hand. "I've fallen in love with you, Lee. Which is why I constantly make a fool out of myself by acting so protective. I can't bear the thought of something happening to you—of losing you."

"Who says you're going to lose me?"

"I worry what might happen to you if you're not careful."

She knew he was referring to Jack McCall. "I promise I'll be more cautious in the future," she said. "I won't put myself or Stevie at risk again."

He pulled her into his arms and kissed her, and Lee parted her lips and welcomed his tongue. What would it be like, lying naked in his arms, savoring their lovemaking?

Wade raised his head. The look in his eyes mirrored her own feelings. "You know what your problem is, missy? You're too damn independent for your own good."

"You don't like that trait in a woman?" she asked.

"Maybe I'd like to think you needed me just a little bit."

She reached up and toyed with the button on his shirt. "Of course I need you, Wade. Look how long I've depended on your friendship."

"I'm not talking about friendship."

Lee jumped when she heard a noise in the next room, and realized the janitor was emptying trash cans. "Why don't you take me to dinner tonight, and we can discuss this in a more romantic setting?"

He looked hurt. "You don't think the smell of dirty gym socks is romantic?"

"Frankly, no."

He threw up his hands as though frustrated, but he was smiling. "Okay, I'll take you out for a good steak, how's that?" Lee smiled prettily. "What time should I send the horse-drawn coach?"

"I need to go by the hospital. Stevie's really down in the dumps." She didn't elaborate.

"We can both visit him," Wade said. "We'll try to cheer him up."

They settled on a time, and Wade kissed her again, then walked her out to her truck.

Lee was feeling more optimistic as she drove to her parents' house. She didn't blame Wade for losing his patience with her. She had absolutely no business being in the company of Jack McCall, even if the situation had been an emergency.

Lee was pleased to see her mother looking better, although it was clear she was still grieving. She knew the woman had spent a lot of time with her minister, and her faith had softened the ravaged lines around her eyes and mouth that her daughter's murder had left behind. Lee was not as pleased with her father's appearance. He had the haunted look of a concentration camp survivor. She tried to draw him into conversation, but the dull monosyllabic answers he gave told her he was in no mood for it.

Wade picked her up at seven o'clock, and they drove to the hospital. Stevie was watching TV—a good sign in Lee's opinion—but he said very little to them, and he was almost hostile toward Wade. Finally, Lee kissed him on the forehead and promised to return the next morning.

They drove across town to Jesse's Steak Place, a favorite of theirs. Lee had a glass of wine and Wade ordered a beer while they waited for their dinner. Since the place was packed, Lee knew it would be a while. She was glad their booth afforded them a certain degree of privacy.

"I'm sorry Stevie was rude to you," she said. "He hasn't been himself lately."

"Do you blame the poor kid?" Wade asked. "Look what he's been through."

She told him about her visit with Herb Henderson, and the things he'd said about Lucy.

"And here I thought my opinion of him couldn't get any lower," Wade said. "Way I figure it, he probably came on to your sister, and she told him to go fly a kite. Stevie has every right to stay in that school and be protected against bullies. If Henderson refuses to do it, get the police involved."

Lee sipped her drink and pondered the situation. "Stevie's doctor wants him to see a psychiatrist."

Wade looked thoughtful. "That might not be a bad idea." He took her hand. "Once he gets out of the hospital, I'm going to start spending more time with him. Doing guy things."

Lee chuckled. "Guy things? Does that mean I'm not invited?"

"You'd just get in the way. Besides, you'd never pass the endurance test."

"Endurance test?"

"You know, like going fishing and baiting your own hook. Eating Vienna sausage from a can without a napkin."

"Oh, please, anything but that." She laughed and realized it had been a long time since she'd done so. Just as quickly, her smile faded.

Wade covered her hand. "It's okay to be happy, Lee. Being sad all the time isn't going to bring her back."

She met his gaze. He looked so sincere, and the wine had left her feeling vulnerable. "I sometimes wake up in the night and find myself crying," she confessed.

"Oh, honey." He squeezed her hand.

"That's because I don't allow myself to mourn openly like my mother. I'm afraid once I get started, I won't stop."

"You don't have to be brave and strong every minute, Lee."

He looked so sweet that she was tempted to tell him about the missing battery. But she knew he'd insist on calling Holden or having her stay at his place, and she couldn't risk it. She needed to be in her home, alone.

Their steaks came and Lee was surprised how hungry she was. Wade even offered her part of his, but she assured him she'd had her fill. "I don't always remember to eat these days," she said with a short laugh. "I'm so busy trying to get those panels finished." She had a thought. "Would you like to see them?"

"When, tonight?"

"Sure, we could stop by on the way to my house." It was the only way she knew to get her gun without going back out once he dropped her off.

"That's fine with me," he said, "although I was thinking this would be a good time for us to spend some time alone."

She knew where he was leading. With Stevie in the hospital, they would have her house uninterrupted. "I don't know, Wade. I don't think I could relax with all that's going on."

"We're going to have to put this behind us sooner or later, Lee. And concentrate on us."

"I know. I'm just not ready yet."

Wade paid the check, and they left the restaurant. Her shop was a short ten-minute drive. He parked in back, and Lee unlocked the door, then groped for the light switch.

When the light came on, she gasped and stared in horror at the sight before her. Glass everywhere. Sharp, jagged edges in a rainbow of colors, some still clinging to the solder that had held them in place. Her panels. Weeks of hard work.

Destroyed forever.

* * *

Lee thought she was going to be sick as she surveyed the damage. It was too much to take in at once.

Wade seemed to be having trouble absorbing it as well. "Who would do this?" he asked at last.

Lee shook her head dumbly. When the shock subsided, her eyes filled with tears. She had sunk hundreds of dollars into the materials, knowing she would be reimbursed and paid for her labor once she finished the job. There would be no check now, and it was anybody's guess how she would pay her bills in the future.

"I have to call Holden," Wade said, going straight for the phone. "Sit down, honey, before you fall down."

Lee sat at her desk, staring into space, wondering what she was going to do now. She was vaguely aware of Wade's voice in the background. Suddenly remembering her gun, she reached into her purse for her keys, fingers trembling, and found the one that went to the middle drawer. She unlocked it, then reached for the handle on the bottom drawer.

"Holden's on his way," Wade said, startling her so badly that she jumped.

"Hey, settle down sweetheart," he said soothingly as he patted her shoulder. He knelt beside her. "It's going to be okay, Lee."

She shook her head. "You don't understand."

"I understand more than you think. And together, we'll work through this." He touched her cheek. "Want me to make you a cup of coffee?"

She nodded and he went to the small kitchenette. Lee inched open the drawer. The gun was in a plastic shopping bag in the back. Glancing over her shoulder, she saw Wade rinsing her coffee pot, his back to her. She grabbed the gun and stuffed it in her purse.

Holden soon arrived in civilian clothes with a dep-

uty beside him. "Jesus Christ," he muttered upon
seeing the mess. "Has anyone checked out front?"

Wade shook his head as he handed Lee a cup of
coffee and offered Holden some. "I didn't think to."

"I'll have a look," the deputy said, already headed
in that direction.

Holden sat on the edge of the desk and regarded
Lee. "You got any idea who would've done this?"
he asked.

She shook her head. She had asked herself that
question a dozen times since entering the building.
"What about the boys who beat up Stevie?" She told
him about her visit with Henderson. "If they know
I intend to press charges, they could be doing this
to get even."

"I think it's time I have a little talk with Herb Henderson," Holden said. "He hasn't exactly cooperated
with my deputies, but he's going to find it difficult
to ignore me."

The deputy returned. "There's forced entry," he
said. "Probably somebody pried the door open with
a screwdriver. I'll take a couple of pictures." He
glanced down at the glass. "You want this dusted
for prints?"

"Just get some of the bigger pieces. The rest would
be like looking for a needle in a haystack."

Holden turned back to Lee. "You look like hell,
hon. Why don't you let Wade take you home. I'll
lock up when we're finished here."

Lee agreed, exhausted beyond belief. She thanked
Holden and allowed Wade to lead her to his car.
Although he tried to reassure her along the way, she
said very little.

"Do you want me to come in?" he asked, once he
pulled into the driveway.

She shook her head. "I just want to go to bed."

He helped her out of the car, walked her to the
door, and unlocked it for her. Lee stepped inside and

turned on the light. "Well, goodnight," she said.

"I'll call you tomorrow, honey," he told her. "I'm here for you if you need me. I can take care of you, Lee, if you'll only let me."

Lee thanked him, closed the door, and locked it tight. She started for her bedroom, and noticed the answering machine was blinking on the end table in the living room. She pushed the button. After a succession of beeps, she was surprised to hear Stevie's voice.

"Aunt Lee, it's me," he said, talking slow, as if heavily medicated. "There's a video . . . I was watching it . . . the day I got sick." There was a long pause. "It's still in the VCR. You need to see it."

Lee turned on the TV and rewound the tape, wondering what it could possibly be that Stevie wanted her to see so badly. She was exhausted and wanted nothing more than to go to bed, but something in her nephew's voice told her it couldn't wait. When the tape finished rewinding, Lee hit the play button.

She sat down and waited. When the picture came on it was snowy and distorted. It cleared, and Lee was startled to see her sister standing there, smiling at someone. A man? She made a production of undoing the tiny pearl buttons on her yellow jacket, her movements slow and sensual. Lee's heart leapt to her throat. What was she watching? Did Stevie have footage of Lucy's murder?

Lee noted the date of the video, and her hopes were dashed. It was two years old. This video had been made only days before the house fire that claimed her brother-in-law's life. It was of the old Lucy, before all the plastic surgery.

Suddenly something blocked the camera, and the picture became white. Lee realized someone was standing directly in front of it. Finally, movement, and she was looking at a man's naked back. He approached her sister, who was now down to panties.

The man's head was fuzzy, and Lee strained to get a better look. His hips came into view, he turned slightly, and Lee saw he was erect.

He took Lucy's hand and guided it to the front of himself. With a sinking heart, Lee realized she was about to see a sex act between her sister and another man, who by the looks of his physique was not her sister's husband. She would have turned it off had Stevie not asked her to watch it. Lucy knelt before the man and took him into her mouth.

Lee felt sick to her stomach. Stevie had seen this. Was there no limit to what the poor kid was to be exposed to? Lee reached for the remote and started to turn it off, but something about the man made her pause—something about the way he moved, the set of his shoulders. All at once, he grasped Lucy around the waist and pulled her onto the bed. Lee caught a split-second shot of his face.

It was enough.

Wade Emmett grinned and rammed his sex into Lucy's waiting body. Her sister's lips formed an O of pleasure. Lee hit the off button, ran to the bathroom, and lost her dinner.

Twenty-five

W HAT DID it mean?

Lee was still asking herself that question the next morning as she dressed for work. She had not slept much the night before, and it showed in the dark circles beneath her eyes. Wade and Lucy lovers? For how long? Had they taped their lovemaking session, or had Bill Hodges suspected the affair and managed to tape it secretly? And why was the tape in Stevie's possession? Had Bill simply taped over an old cartoon, then hid it among his son's videos, knowing no one would think to look there? Or had he purposefully put it among Stevie's tapes in hopes the boy would come across it one day?

Lee's mind rebelled against the last possibility. She found it hard to believe that even her brother-in-law would stoop that low.

Perhaps it was a power thing. Bill had always controlled Lucy before. If she had fallen in love with Wade, she might have found the courage to leave her abusive husband. Bill could have threatened to make copies of the tape and mail them to the right people. The school board, for one. If Wade didn't lose his job over it, he would at least suffer public humiliation. And Lucy, who would have done anything to prevent a scandal in those days, would have spent the rest of her life in servitude to her husband.

Lee suddenly remembered the beating Lucy had received only a few days before the fire. When Holden asked her to press charges, she'd refused. Perhaps she'd refused because she and Wade had already figured out a way to make Bill Hodges pay.

No, that was preposterous!

Or was it?

Lee had come to realize that she had never really known her sister.

She had to go to Holden with what she knew. She had to lay her suspicions out before him and depend on his expertise, because she was no longer capable of thinking straight.

An hour later, Holden listened quietly as Lee told him about the tape. Finally, she pulled the video from her purse and put it on his desk. "What do you think?"

He shrugged. "I think you have a video of two adults having consensual sex. I'm sure they're not the first couple to ever tape their lovemaking."

"What if they weren't the ones taping it? What if Bill Hodges had secretly taped it and was blackmailing them?

"Blackmailing them? For what? Wade doesn't have any money."

"He owns some property his folks left him. He's just sitting on it, hoping it'll be worth something one day. And with all the development going on in this town, Bill might have figured that day had come." She pointed to the tape. "That would have destroyed Wade's career."

"Okay, suppose what you're saying is true. Where are you going with this?"

Lee hesitated. She'd barely let herself think it, much less say it out loud. "What if that fire was planned, Holden?"

He looked surprised. Finally, he shook his head. "Lee, I was there the night Wade ran into that house after Lucy's husband. He literally risked his own neck."

"Who investigated the fire?" she asked.

"The fire marshall. There was no evidence of arson."

She leaned close. "Right, Holden. But who is better equipped at hiding the evidence than a trained fireman?"

"And Wade would have done this because?" He waited.

Lee didn't hesitate. "Two point five million dollars."

Holden leaned back in his chair and regarded her. "Sweetheart, I'm going to have to take you off of this case once and for all."

She blinked. "I'm not working this case."

"Precisely. Now, as I see it, you've got a lot of work to do if you hope to get those panels done in time. I'll call you if I need you—how's that?"

She gave a dejected sigh. "Aren't you even going to look at the tape, for Pete's sake?"

"Sure, I'll look at it. I don't expect to find evidence of wrongdoing, but I'll take a gander just in case. Now, scoot on out of here or I'll handcuff you to the flagpole out front."

Lee suddenly felt tired and very sad. "That's the trouble with you, Holden. You never take me seriously." She left his office without another word.

Lee was feeling sorry for herself as she parked outside the Piggly Wiggly supermarket that evening. She and Rob had spent the entire day going through the panels, trying to salvage whatever pieces they could and ordering new glass for those they couldn't. Three panels were completely destroyed, which meant they would have to start from scratch. Lee knew she would have to depend on Rob more than she ever had in the past. She only hoped he was up to the task.

With a heavy sigh, she climbed from her car and went inside the store. Had she not needed coffee so badly, she would have kept on going, but it seemed to be her mainstay these days. She was standing on the aisle trying to find her brand when Jack McCall greeted her. She glanced up to find him close by. She hadn't even heard him come up. She mumbled a response and looked away.

He stepped closer, and when he spoke his voice was concerned. "Lee, you don't look so good. Are you feeling under the weather?"

The gentleness in his voice struck a chord inside of her tired soul, and her eyes stung. She rubbed them. "I'm fine." She reached for a can of coffee, only to upset the one next to it. She reached for the can, but it fell to the floor, loud and metallic. Lee bent to retrieve it just as Jack did the same, and they knocked heads.

"Oh, damn," she said.

"I'm sorry," he told her. "Did I hurt you?"

"No." Tears streamed down her face. She started to turn.

"Lee, wait!" Jack touched her arm. "Hey, I can't let you go like this," he said. He patted his pockets. "Damn, I don't have a tissue either."

"I do." Her voice trembled. Lee fumbled inside her pocketbook and brought one out, tears streaming down both her cheeks.

"Give me your coffee," he said. "I'll pay for it and meet you outside." She started to protest, but he took it from her anyway. "Where are you parked?"

"On the side of the building."

"Okay, go on. I'll be out in a minute."

Lee did as he said, knowing she would only embarrass herself further if she remained in the store. She climbed in her pickup and waited. A couple of minutes later, Jack came out of the store and paused beside her open window.

"Mind if I sit with you for a minute?" he asked.

"I don't need a babysitter."

"I know you don't," he said gently. He rounded the truck and climbed in on the passenger's side. He glanced around the interior of the truck. "I used to have one of these back in high school."

"Now you ride around all day in a limo. You've come up in the world." There was a hint of sarcasm in her voice.

"I got rid of the limo. I'm trying to scale down."

She didn't respond. Her spirits had sunk so low she didn't think she would ever find a reason to smile again.

"What's wrong, Lee?" he asked.

She looked at him as though he'd lost his mind. "What's wrong? You mean, besides the fact my sister was recently murdered, my nephew beaten to a pulp, and someone just tried to kill us with carbon monoxide poisoning? What could possibly be wrong?"

"Okay, stupid question. But something else obviously has you very upset. Will you tell me what it is?"

Fresh tears filled her eyes. She told him about the panels and heard him curse under his breath. "If I work twenty-four hours a day, I might get them finished on time, but it's doubtful. And what do you think my profit margin will be?"

"Zero?"

"Bingo."

"How can I help?"

"Nobody can help. I could hire another stained-glass business to do part of the work to meet the deadline, but it would break me." She glanced at him. "I'm not telling you this for sympathy."

He held his hands up as though surrendering.

"Hey, I wouldn't think of feeling sorry for you."
Then, in a softer tone, "I could help if you'd let me."

"With you it always boils down to money."

"Not always. I know what money can and cannot buy, Lee. But it can make life easier, and I would gladly give you all that I had if it would ease your burden."

Touched, tears welled within her eyes. Under any other circumstances, she might have accepted his help. She had been struggling so long, like swimming against a never-ending strong current. Each time she thought she was getting ahead, she had a numbing setback. But she couldn't allow herself to lean on him when she didn't know what kind of man she was dealing with. "I've already told you I can't be bought," she finally said.

"Honey, I'm not trying to buy you. I just want to help."

The rich timbre of his voice was comforting. Lee was not prepared for the endearment. Her eyes misted. "I don't need your help, Jack. I'll manage. I always do."

He knew he had no choice but to drop it. "Any news on the case?"

"You're the one with the high-priced investigator. Why are you asking me?"

"The sheriff is your cousin. I was hoping he might have told you something."

"If you're trying to pump me for information, forget it."

"You're always jumping to the wrong conclusion, Lee. Do you do it with everybody, or just me?"

"I don't like being used."

"I would never use you. But it's in both our interests to find out who killed your sister." When she didn't respond, he went on. "My investigator has been looking into the fire that claimed your brother-in-law's life."

Lee looked at him. She had put a lot of thought into the fire herself, but she wasn't ready to share it with Jack after Holden had made the whole idea sound ludicrous. "What could the fire possibly have to do with Lucy's murder?"

"Maybe nothing, maybe everything. There were no batteries in the smoke detectors that night."

"There was a perfectly reasonable explanation for that," Lee said, trying to convince herself as much as him. "Lucy had broiled hamburgers in the oven that night, and they'd burned, setting off the smoke detectors. My brother-in-law took the batteries out while they worked to clear the smoke. No one thought to put them back in afterward. The fire marshall found the charred hamburger patties in the trash outside, along with the broiler pan."

"Yes, I know."

"There was no evidence of foul play." Lee waited to see what else he had.

"Right. Just a drunk who happened to pass out with a lit cigarette in his hand on the second floor, and a wife who was sleeping in the spare bedroom on the first floor."

"My sister often slept in the spare bedroom because of my brother-in-law's sleep apnea, which was made worse by his drinking. As for him passing out with a cigarette in his hand, that wasn't the first time. He'd burned holes in just about every piece of furniture they had, not to mention the bed linens and mattress." She paused. "I'm not surprised he burned the house down; I'm surprised he didn't do it sooner."

"I understand the body was burned beyond recognition."

"That's right."

"So there was no way of knowing if he was killed first."

Lee didn't answer right away. "Are you insinuating that my sister conspired to have her husband murdered?"

"I'm just saying some of it looks suspicious. And if she did arrange to have him killed, odds are someone helped her, and that someone was probably a man."

Lee's eyes ached. She couldn't believe these things about her sister. Even if Bill Hodges had deserved to die, Lucy would never have been capable of what Jack was suggesting. Then she wondered if she was being naive. Had years of abuse left Lucy in such a rage that she was able to plan a cold-blooded murder?

"I think the deaths are connected, even if they happened two years apart," Jack said. "I haven't figured out how. Maybe the guy was in love with your sister and expected her to marry him later, when they could do so without looking suspicious. But maybe your sister decided she liked being unattached, and who could blame her after living all those years with abuse? In the meantime, this guy gets tired of waiting. Your sister had a reputation in this town, from what I understand." When Lee shot him a dark look, he said, "I'm just giving you the facts as I know them. Suppose this guy finds out she's sleeping around after he's killed her husband for her and made it possible to collect all that insurance money. He goes into a rage. That would explain the heinous nature of the crime. Destroy her face so that no man ever looked at her again."

"But he killed her. If he'd loved her—"

"He killed her to keep himself from going to prison," Jack interrupted. "Once his rage was spent, he realized he might end up on death row over what he did. And who knows, maybe he was repulsed by what he saw." Jack was thoughtful for a moment. "Did you inherit money from your sister's estate?" he asked.

"Why is that important?"

"Suppose this person decides to try and get his share of the money from you?"

Lee sighed. "This is all very farfetched."

"I know. But I've been looking at it from every angle. I think your sister's murder has something to do with the murder of her husband two years ago. I told you, Lucy was afraid of something—somebody. She didn't die at the hands of a random killer. None of it fits: the fact that she wasn't raped, the nature of the crime. It was personal. He knew her, and he was enraged."

Lee straightened. "I have to go."

"Let me help you, Lee," he said softly.

Once again, fresh tears clouded her vision. She tried to smother a sob, but it escaped, and suddenly there was no stopping it. Jack's arms closed around her. She tried to resist, but he held her firmly against his chest. "Go ahead and cry, Lee," he said. "I've watched you try to be brave for so long. It breaks my heart, what you're going through."

Lee finally gave in to the barrage of tears. She had been holding them back for so long, rationing them in small amounts at night in her bedroom so she wouldn't lose control. But the dam had finally broken, and her control was lost as she cried her heart out in Jack's arms. She was aware of his big hand holding her head against him, of the comforting words he offered.

Jack felt helpless as he held her. It pissed him off that he couldn't help her, that she wouldn't allow it. There'd been a time when he thought there wasn't *anything* he couldn't do. What had happened to that young attorney that had been so full of piss and vinegar the day they swore him in?

Lee pulled away reluctantly. It had been a long time since a man other than Wade had held her in his arms, and the pleasure she had taken in Jack's embrace was disturbing. Her eyes swollen from the tears, she groped for her purse, but knocked it to the floor.

Jack reached for it, and saw the glint of metal. He pulled out the gun. "Jesus," he whispered.

Startled, Lee tried to snatch it from him, but he held it from her. "Give it to me," she snapped.

The muscles in his face hardened. "What the hell are you doing with a goddamn gun?" he demanded.

She bristled with indignation. "You really have to ask that question?"

"Christ, Lee, I've offered to send someone to look after you. I'd do it myself if you'd let me. Is the safety on?" He checked the gun.

"I'm not a complete imbecile." She grabbed it from him.

Jack leaned his head back against the window. "This is bullshit," he muttered. "I'm crazy about you, and you still think I'm a cold-blooded murderer. I fantasize what it would be like spending my life with you, and you're looking forward to watching the state put me to death."

"Jack—"

He looked from her face to the gun and back again. His eyes glittered with hurt and anger. "Or were you planning to kill me yourself?" He didn't wait for her to answer. "Then, go ahead and do it, Lee. Blow my fucking head off and get it over with."

She sagged against the seat, her misery pulling her down like a leaden weight. "I don't think you did it," she said, and choked back a sob. "I think you're innocent."

He gave a snort of a laugh. "No way."

"I wouldn't say it unless it were true. I wouldn't be sitting here, crying in your arms if I believed you killed my sister." She didn't know when she'd stopped believing he was a cold-blooded murderer.

Perhaps at her shop, when he'd walked away without harming her.

It took a moment for her words to sink in, and when they did, Jack reached up and touched her cheek. He half expected her to flinch, but she didn't. His look turned tender, but his eyes were cautious when he raised them to hers. "Are you sure?"

"I have never been more sure of anything in my life."

He pulled her into his arms and kissed her hard on the lips. When he raised up, they were both breathless. "Come back to my place," he said. "You'll be safe there."

She didn't hesitate. "Yes."

Jack's place was an older two-story house located in the business district of Comfrey, where many of the old homes had been turned into commercial property. Lee remembered when the house had belonged to the Jensons, a family of six children who'd played on a tire swing in the backyard and enjoyed popsicles on the front steps because their mama refused to have them in the house dripping all over her rugs. The Jenson kids were grown now, and Martha Jenson, having lost her husband years before, lived in a nursing home.

So many changes, Lee thought, as she stepped inside the house and marveled at the differences. Walls had come down, those that remained were tastefully wallpapered, and the trim was painted. The wood floors looked new, and they were protected by expensive-looking oriental rugs. The furniture was of good quality and blended with everything. An elaborate brass screen stood in front of the fireplace where Lee had roasted marshmallows with the Jenson children when she was a child.

"What do you think?" Jack asked. "I picked out everything myself."

"Very nice."

"I sleep upstairs," he said, following her from room to room. "I plan to use the downstairs for offices."

"What sort of offices?"

"Law offices." At her look of surprise, he went on. "A friend of mine has agreed to assist me in getting reinstated."

"So, you plan to move here permanently?"

"Yeah. Hilton Head is a little rich for my blood." He gave a rueful smile. "I won't actually open my practice until I'm cleared of murder charges, of course. I figure it'll be easier getting clients that way."

She nodded. "You might have a point there, Counselor."

He showed her his office, and a cluttered conference room. He quickly moved to the far end of the table and covered what looked to be a stack of photos.

"Those are pictures of my sister, aren't they?" she asked.

"Yes."

"After the murder?"

"It's necessary to the investigation, Lee. Like I said, we're both interested in finding her killer. Come on, I'll make you a cup of coffee."

The kitchen was cozy but small. Lee sat at a round table and waited as Jack made coffee. Then, he sat beside her and took her hands in his. "Your hands are cold," he said, rubbing them to warm her.

"I get cold easily these days."

"Why don't you stay here tonight? I've got a spare bedroom. It's nice and warm."

It sounded so tempting. Lee knew she had nothing to fear from Jack McCall, and a good night's sleep would go far in restoring her spirits. But she needed to be home just in case.

"I'd better not," she said. "Not because I don't trust you. Stevie might call from the hospital."

He was silent for a moment. "Lee, who do you think murdered Lucy? Do you have any suspicions?"

She thought of Wade but shook her head. Just because she'd found a pornographic video of him and Lucy didn't necessarily mean he was a killer. "I wish I did." She finished her coffee and stood to leave. "I have to go."

"I wish you'd change your mind and stay. I'm really worried about you. Even more so since you have that gun."

"Thanks for listening, Jack." Then, feeling almost shy, she added, "I'm sorry for all the bad things I thought of you."

"I'm just glad you believe in me now."

He walked her to her truck, then kissed her lightly on the lips before helping her in. He watched her pull from the driveway and head down the road, then pause at a stop sign before turning.

As Jack went inside, he couldn't shake the sense of foreboding. He was scared for her.

Twenty-six

THE HOUSE was cold and dark when Lee entered twenty minutes later, and she turned the heat up and prayed it would take the chill from the air quickly. Her eyes burned from crying, and her head ached. Worry and exhaustion had taken its toll. She grabbed her bottle of aspirin from a small shelf over the sink and popped two in her mouth, followed by a glass of water. She changed into her pajamas, brushed her teeth, and climbed into bed, taking a moment to tuck her gun beneath the pillow beside her. She felt groggy, disoriented. As she dozed, her last thoughts were of Jack McCall.

She was jolted awake sometime later by a noise—the old house settling, or a branch scraping her bedroom window, Lee wasn't sure. Maybe it was just another bad dream. The wind had picked up outside, and the broken shutter outside her window creaked and slammed against the house with each gust. She'd meant to repair it over the summer, but had never gotten around to it.

Lee struggled to sit, but it was no easy task. Her limbs felt heavy and clumsy, her brain dulled. She was probably coming down with something. With all the stress in her life lately, her resistance would naturally be low. She groped for the lamp and turned the switch. Nothing. The bulb was obviously burned out.

As she sat there, she sensed a change in the room—as though the air had been disturbed. And she knew she wasn't alone. A cold fist of terror closed around her heart, even as she fought to keep her eyes open. She thought of her sister. Drugged. Mutilated.

She listened, thought she could actually hear someone breathing. A numbing fear hit her. "Is someone there?" she quavered.

Suddenly a light came on, blinding her. Like being on stage. She tried to see past it, but could only make out the silhouette of a man. The goose-necked floor lamp that had belonged to her grandmother was beside him, the bright bulb aimed at her. "Who's there?" she asked, trying to shield her eyes from the glare.

The old Boston rocker near the foot of her bed creaked. "Feeling sleepy, Lee?" a familiar voice asked.

Lee tried to make sense of it, but her brain felt as though it had been stuffed with wood shavings. She was dizzy, sick to her stomach, barely able to hold her head up. "Wade, is that you?" she managed.

"I've noticed you've been having a lot of headaches lately. All that stress is bad for you, Lee. So I put something in your aspirin container to make you relax."

She wasn't surprised. Her own fault for popping pills into her mouth without checking them. "Please move the light from my eyes," she said groggily.

"I don't take orders from you anymore, Lee. You claim to be my friend, but you're no friend of mine. I saw you and McCall necking in the parking lot at Piggly Wiggly, and I followed you to his place. Don't think I don't know what that was all about."

She tried to concentrate on what he was saying,

forced herself to stay awake when all she wanted to do was lie down and close her eyes. If she did, they would be closed forever. "I went to Jack's place for coffee, Wade. That's all. I can't believe you're spying on me." Her mouth was so dry she could barely form the words.

"You expect me to believe that?" His tone was so hateful Lee imagined him wearing a sneer. "You're no different than that whoring sister of yours. Well, she got exactly what she deserved. And she was drugged the night she died, as well. My, my, what a coincidence."

A burst of wild grief exploded in her. He had killed Lucy! He had cut her face to ribbons, then plunged a knife through her heart. She bit her bottom lip to keep from crying out.

He was going to kill her too.

Unless she could think of a way to stop him.

But how the hell could she stop him when her brain wasn't even functioning right, when she couldn't even see him, for God's sake? "Wade, please turn off the light," she said in a pleading voice that gave no indication of the fury building inside of her. "I can't talk to you like this. We've always been able to talk in the past."

The chair creaked, she heard footsteps; the next thing she knew he was on her. "What are you doing?" she cried, trying to push him away with rubbery arms. "Get off of me!"

He slapped her hard enough to bring tears to her eyes. "I'm going to take what the hell I've earned," he said. "Who's had to listen to you whine and carry on every time a man shit on you?" he demanded. "Not once did you ever stop and wonder if it bothered me. You were too caught up in your own feelings. Lucy was the same way. For months, she cried on my shoulder about how bad it was being married to that mean drunk. Then he found out about our affair. Caught us on video. Threatened to send copies to all the staff at school. Do you have any idea how it would have made me look? Well, I helped her get rid of him. I went into his bedroom the night of the fire, and found him crawling like a worm, trying to get to safety. I kicked him in the head till he was unconscious. If it hadn't been for me, the bastard would have made it out.

"Do you think Lucy appreciated what I did for her?" he asked. "Hell no. Once she got her hands on all that insurance money and had cosmetic surgery, she was a different woman."

Lee's head was still reeling from being hit. He had her pinned down so that she could barely breathe. She felt his hand on the waistband of her pajamas. "I thought we were friends," she gasped.

"We're not friends," he snarled as he looked down at her. "I hate whores, Lee. And you're the biggest whore in town now that your sister is gone." He paused. "I tried to end things painlessly when I rigged the furnace. You and Stevie should have drifted off to sleep without a care in the world. But McCall had to rush in here like some hero and screw things up." He paused, and his expression became one of regret. "I even tried to give you another chance. I thought if I destroyed all those panels you'd turn to me for help. I thought you'd finally realize how much you needed me. But you ran to McCall's bed instead. I have no choice now but to hurt you."

The sound of his voice made her wonder if he'd lost his mind. "I'm not a whore."

He grunted. "Sure, you aren't."

He released her for a moment, then ripped her pajama bottoms. Lee cried out and he hit her again, this time bloodying her nose. She struggled, but he managed to pull her underwear free as well. She struggled; he laughed.

"Don't do this, Wade. For God's sake—"

He paused and unfastened his belt. He shoved his pants to his knees. Lee saw that he was already hard. Her temper flared. He tried to part her legs, but she clamped them together tightly. He pried them apart, and she balled her hand into a fist and punched him in the face as hard as she could.

His face turned red with rage. "You bitch. I'll kill you for that."

"You'd *better* kill me you sonofabitch," she spat contemptuously, "because you'll never take me alive."

All at once, his hands were at her throat, squeezing her neck. Lee hadn't seen it coming. Once again, she tried to fight him, but it was useless. He slammed her head several times against the pillow, and she felt something solid beneath it. The gun.

She had forgotten about the gun!

She heard a buzzing sound in her ear, realized she was about to pass out. Fear sent a rush of adrenaline through her body, and she reached beneath the pillow.

The gun felt solid, heavy. It had seemed so light the first time she held it. She brought it up, even as a black curtain began to fall over her, offering relief against the bright light. She pressed it as close to Wade's chest as she could, then fired.

The sound was ear-splitting, followed by the acrid smell of gunpowder. Wade paused, glanced down. Reached for the gun.

Lee fired again. Wade buckled. Collapsed. A lump of human flesh. Lee tried to scream, but couldn't find the air.

Glass shattered from somewhere in the house. Footsteps sounded in the hall. Suddenly, Jack McCall was there, beside the bed. "Holy shit." He grabbed the pistol from her, shoved Wade aside. The injured man fell to the floor with a thump. Lee drank in gulps of air, then screamed for all she was worth.

Jack gathered her in his arms and pulled her close, waiting until her tears and panic subsided. Lee was completely oblivious to the fact that she was naked from the waist down. When she finally calmed down, Jack reached for the phone. "Did he hurt you?" he asked.

Lee shook her head. She didn't trust her voice. She didn't even want to know if Wade was dead.

Jack made the calls, then wrapped her in a blanket and carried her to the living room, where he held her until help arrived.

Holden's face showed the strain when he stepped inside the house ten minutes later, two deputies on his heels. He immediately went to Lee and hugged her. "Are you okay? You think you might need to go to the hospital?"

"I'm fine," she assured him, although in reality she wasn't. "Jack fixed me some cheese and crackers, and I drank a glass of milk so I'm not as groggy." She shivered. Jack had put another blanket around her in the kitchen, but she couldn't seem to get warm. Three paramedics came through the door, two carrying a stretcher.

"He's in the bedroom," Jack said. "I'll show you." They followed him.

"I want one of you to have a look at the lady," Holden said. "She's ingested some kind of sleeping pill." He looked at Lee. "Where's the container they came out of?" he asked.

She pointed to the shelf. Holden put on plastic gloves and picked up the container as one of the paramedics pulled a light from his pocket and checked Lee's eyes and her pulse. He examined the tablet Holden handed him.

"It's Trazedone," he said. "A sleeping pill." He looked at Lee. "How many did you take?"

"Two."

"Do you have any drug allergies?"

"None that I know of."

"Then you shouldn't have any problems other than being sleepy. It'll wear off by morning, then you'll be okay." He started up the stairs.

Lee didn't think she would ever be okay. She had glanced at Wade on the floor, had seen the blood.

Holden said, "If you're up to making coffee, I sure could use a cup." He took the stairs two at a time.

Lee busied herself making coffee and setting out cups for those who might want some. She still felt dazed, and she didn't know if she was in shock or if it was the sleeping pills. Probably both. The coffee hadn't yet dripped through when two of the paramedics came down the stairs carrying Wade on a stretcher. Lee turned away. Holden and Jack joined her in the kitchen a moment later.

"My deputies are taking pictures upstairs," Holden told her. "They'll collect the sheets and everything else." He paused. "Where'd you get the gun?"

"Place called Gun City."

"Jesus, Lee."

She glared at him. "What the hell did you expect me to do, Holden? Just sit here on my ass, waiting for that sack of shit to do the same thing he did to my sister?"

Holden became very still. "Did Wade confess to Lucy's murder?"

"Why do you think I tried to put a bullet in him? Other than the fact he tried to rape me. Thank God I had something to defend myself with, or those guys would have been carrying *me* out in a body bag!"

She didn't realize she was shouting until Jack touched her on the shoulder. "Here, drink this."

Lee gulped the coffee. Her eyes felt gritty, and she desperately needed a shower after having Wade's hands on her. "Is the bastard going to live?"

"Too soon to tell," Holden told her. "He lost a lot of blood." He sipped from his cup in silence for a moment and regarded Lee. "You feel up to answering a few questions?"

"I'm okay now," she said, although she couldn't seem to stop trembling.

"Why don't you just tell me what happened."

Lee told him everything, trying to remember word for word what Wade had said. Holden took notes as they went. "Did Wade claim any responsibility for the fire that caused Bill Hodges's death?"

"He said he went into Bill's bedroom and made sure the man didn't get out alive."

"And Lucy? Did he confess to killing her?"

"He implied it. Said she got exactly what she deserved."

Lee could see the disappointment in Holden's eyes. He and Wade had been friends for years. "I didn't want to believe it either," she said.

"And you took that as a confession of guilt?"

"Yes. I also took it as a threat. I believe he had every intention of doing the same thing to me." She shuddered, and her eyes glistened with tears. "I've never shot anyone before in my life," she said, breathing in shallow, quick breaths. "But I was so scared. He was choking me, and I knew it was a matter of seconds before I'd pass out." She pulled the blanket more tightly around her. "I kept imagining him doing the same thing to me that he'd done to Lucy."

"It's okay, Lee," Jack said, patting her shoulder gently. "Nobody blames you for what you did."

The tears continued to fall. "I don't know where I found the courage or strength to pull the trigger. I just knew I couldn't let my mother bury a second daughter."

"I'm not going to ask you to come to the department tonight, Lee," Holden said, "but I'll need to see you in my office first thing in the morning. In the meantime, I'll leave a deputy with you."

"I'm taking her back to my place." Jack looked at Lee. "You can stay in my spare bedroom till we get this place cleaned up. You'll even have your own bathroom."

Holden looked at the man. "How did you happen to be here when all this came down?" he asked.

Jack explained running into Lee at the grocery store and inviting her to his place for coffee. "I sensed she was afraid," he said. "I was worried something might happen, so I drove over. I hid my car and sat on the front porch, just to make sure Lee didn't have any uninvited guest. I didn't know he was already in the house until I heard the gun shots." He looked at Lee. "He'd obviously been waiting for you to come home. I'm surprised he knew you'd need something for a headache."

"I've been having a lot of headaches lately. Wade knew. It was just a hunch, but it worked."

"Did he have a key to the place?" Holden asked.

"He was responsible for seeing that my new furnace was installed, which he claimed to have tampered with. He would've had a key in his possession for a couple of days. He could have had a copy made."

"And we both know you have a tendency to leave your key under the door mat," Holden muttered.

"Not anymore," Jack said, giving Lee a stern look.

Holden finally seemed convinced with what he had. "Why don't you give me your phone number in case I need to get in touch with Lee," he told Jack. Once he had the information he needed, he gave Lee another hug. "It's going to be okay, honey," he said. "Everything's beginning to make sense now."

Lee struggled with more tears. "He obviously

hated Lucy and me very much to want to kill us both."

"We'll talk more tomorrow," Holden said. "What you need right now is a good night's sleep."

Jack walked him out. As Holden was getting in his patrol car, he paused. "One thing, McCall," he said. "I didn't get a signed confession from Wade Emmett that he killed Lucy Hodges, so you're not off the hook till I find something to link him with the murder."

Jack tensed. It wasn't over. "I didn't kill her, Sheriff."

"I don't think you did either, but you're still a suspect while I'm waiting on more proof. The only reason I'm letting my cousin go with you is because I can tell she likes you and feels secure with you. But don't think for one minute I won't have deputies surrounding your place tonight. You get up to take a piss, I'll know. And if you so much as lay a hand on her, you won't live to see your day in court." He climbed in the car and pulled away.

Lee felt shy as she entered Jack's place for the second time that night, an overnight bag in her hand. She longed to stand under a hot shower until the water ran cold. Jack showed her to her room and left, and she couldn't get out of her clothes fast enough.

In the shower, she scrubbed from head to toe and washed her hair twice. When she was convinced she was as clean as she could get, she dried herself briskly and wrapped her head in a towel. She slipped into a fresh gown and underwear and put socks on her feet.

She noticed the cup of hot cocoa on her dresser when she stepped out of the bathroom, and she smiled and sipped it, wondering how she could ever have thought badly of Jack McCall when he had done nothing but help her. She wondered how long he would've sat on her cold front porch that night just to make sure she was okay.

A tap on the door made her jump, and Lee realized how badly shaken she still was. She felt she could fly into a million pieces with the slightest provocation. Still dazed and shocked with all Wade had told her, she knew she'd never get over having to shoot him. She didn't even want to think about the possibility of his dying.

She pulled the towel from her hair, finger-combed it as best she could, then opened the door to find Jack standing there in sweats and a tee-shirt.

"Are you okay?" he asked.

"Yes. Thanks for the hot chocolate."

He smiled. "Listen, my bedroom is just next door. If you need something during the night, just pound on the wall and I'll be here lickety-split."

She returned his smile. "I'm okay," she assured him, sounding more confident than she felt. Even as she said it, her insides churned with anxiety.

Jack could see the turmoil in her eyes, and he longed to take her in his arms and hold her until . . . until forever. He still shuddered to think what might have happened if she hadn't pulled that trigger. He stepped closer and put a hand on her cheek. "It's over now. You're safe." He kissed her lightly on her forehead. "Goodnight, Lee." He left her then.

Lee was touched by his kindness as she closed her door and prepared for bed. Now that she knew who'd killed her sister, she could fully let down her guard with him. But she had believed Jack was innocent long before Wade confessed to the murder.

Lee pulled the covers down on the bed, but she had serious doubts as to whether she'd be able to sleep. She grabbed a magazine from the night table and thumbed through it but couldn't concentrate. Finally, she switched off the light. But every time she closed her eyes, she saw Wade's face and the crazed look in his eyes as he'd tried to strangle her. She felt hot tears on her cheek and she felt cold, and very much afraid.

Without stopping to think about it, she raised her hand to the wall and knocked gently. Her door was flung open almost immediately. Jack hurried to the bed.

"What is it, honey?"

She sniffed. "I don't want to be alone tonight."

He sat on the edge of the bed and took her hands in his. "Lee, you don't ever have to be alone again."

"Would you just lie here beside me?"

He hesitated. "I'm not dressed. Just my underwear." He chuckled softly. "You scared me so bad I raced out of the bedroom without my bathrobe."

"I'm sorry."

"I'm not complaining." He stretched out on top of the covers.

"Aren't you cold?"

"A little."

Lee gave a jerky laugh. "Then get under the covers, silly."

Jack felt like a clumsy teenager as he joined her between the sheets, where it was warm and smelled soapy and female. Something inside quickened and he pulled her into his arms and held her close. As she fit her head into the crook of his arm, he knew he was lost to her. But then, he'd felt a strong bond with her since the beginning. She was trying so hard to be strong and brave, he couldn't help wanting to be a better man when he was with her.

He felt her tremble. "Are you okay?"

"Yes. It's just, I haven't been held like this in a very long time."

He was perplexed. "I would have thought you and Wade—"

"No." She lay her hand on his bare chest, where

his hair tickled her palm. She longed to explore further, but remained motionless. For the moment she was content just being held by him, inhaling his fresh clean scent. Instinctively, she reached up and touched his jaw.

Jack sighed. He had come in with thoughts of consoling her, but he already had a hard-on that would've won a blue ribbon in any contest. "Lee, what are you doing?" he asked gently.

She snatched her hand away, but he caught it and kissed her palm until it tingled. "I was just—"

"I'm not complaining, babe. But you turn me on, and I don't know what to do about it. I don't know what you want from me . . . what you need from me right now. And I sure as hell don't want to go and do the wrong thing."

Lee liked this vulnerable side of him. She already knew he could be hard and tough as nails, but she wanted to know that he had soft spots as well. She wondered if he had a soft spot for her. "You could kiss me," she said.

He chuckled. "Yes, I suppose I could, couldn't I?" He shifted on the bed, letting her head rest on the pillow beside him. He lowered his face to hers and found her lips. He kissed her gently, tenderly—a kiss to soothe their tired and weary souls. Her lips were softer than anything he could remember.

The kiss quickly took on a life of its own. As he prodded her lips apart and tasted her mouth, he knew he would never be able to get enough of her. He wanted to make love to her, to touch her and taste her and know the pleasure of filling her with himself.

Lee slipped her arms around Jack's neck and held him close, parting her lips to receive his searching tongue. His hand scooted beneath her gown to her breast, and she sighed, feeling as though all was right with the world for the time being. She felt her nipple contract, and he rubbed it between his thumb and forefinger until it was pebbly hard. She explored him, feeling the broad, hair-roughened chest, the hard flat stomach. Hesitating briefly, she lowered her hand, reached inside his briefs, and grasped his erection. She heard him swear softly at her ear.

"You just bought yourself a whole lot of trouble, lady," he said, his fingers already busy unbuttoning her gown. He pulled it free and removed her panties, tossing them to the floor. His briefs joined her clothes a few seconds later.

When his mouth reclaimed hers, Lee returned his kisses eagerly. Any reservations or feelings of shyness disappeared the minute he stroked her legs apart and touched her for the first time. And when he entered her, she moaned in absolute pleasure. He filled her up, and she hadn't realized until now how empty she'd been.

They climaxed together. Afterward, while Jack was still inside of her, he gazed down at her face. "Lee. You humble me."

She slept in his arms. Several times during the night, she awoke to a bad dream, Wade's hands at her throat. Each time she cried out, Jack pulled her tight against him, stroking her, soothing her with his deep voice. Finally at dawn she drifted into a deep sleep, secure for the first time since she'd learned of Lucy's murder.

It was coming up to ten o'clock when Lee awoke to Jack's kisses. They made love, then held each other for a time. Finally, she sat up and reached for her gown. "I have to call my mother," she said, her tone indicating how much she dreaded the task. "I suppose I should call the hospital first and find out if Wade lived through the night."

"I'll do it," Jack said, opening a drawer on the night stand and reaching for the telephone book. He looked up the number and dialed. After being transferred a couple of times, he found someone who could help him. He hung up a moment later.

"Well?" Lee couldn't hide her impatience.

"The nurse wouldn't tell me much. Only that he's in ICU, and that he's stable. He was in surgery all night."

"Do they think he'll live?"

"Honey, she didn't say. But if he survived the surgery and he's stable, I'd think that's a good sign." He took her hand. "Lee, even if he dies, that doesn't mean you didn't have every right to shoot him." He pulled her close. "If you hadn't shot him, you wouldn't be here now. Your mother would be making funeral arrangements this morning."

Lee knew he was right, but it was still going to be hard on her if Wade died by her hand. It amazed her still that they had been friends all those years, and she'd never suspected there was another side to him.

"When this is over and Stevie feels better, I'd like to take the two of you away for a few days," Jack said.

"I have to finish those panels first," she said. "My reputation is at stake."

"Babe, look what you've been through. Don't you think they'd understand if you're a little bit late?"

She looked at him, touched by the concern on his face. "Yes, they probably would. But the church still needs windows."

Lee phoned her mother while Jack made coffee.

Shelby listened quietly. "I never would have suspected Wade," the woman said. "Not in a million years." She sniffled. "I'm afraid this thing is never going to be over."

"It's over now, Mom," Lee said gently. "Stevie and I are safe."

"Did he hurt you, honey?"

"No." Lee decided not to tell her about the bruises on her neck. "Just scared me. I didn't want to have to shoot him, but it couldn't be helped." She could hear her mother crying. "Mom, if we can just get through the next couple of days, everything will be okay. I'll come see you as soon as I can."

When she got off the phone, Lee had tears in her eyes. Jack handed her a cup of coffee and a tissue. "Hang in there, babe. It won't be long now."

Once they'd showered, Jack drove Lee to the sheriff's department to give her formal report. Holden looked tired and Lee suspected he hadn't slept much, either. "Debbie was in labor last night when I got home," he said once they'd reached his office. "She gave birth to a baby boy at seven o'clock this morning."

Lee gave a whoop of delight and threw her arms around him. "Oh, Holden, that's wonderful! You're a daddy."

"That's why I look like I slept in a Dumpster last night," he said, giving a weak smile. "I haven't had a chance to go home and shower."

"Congratulations, Holden," Jack said, reaching out to shake his hand.

Holden hesitated a brief second, but finally clasped his hand. "Thanks."

Lee wasn't sure what to make of the exchange. "I probably won't have time to see Debbie and the baby today," she said, "but I'll drop by tomorrow."

They got down to business. Lee gave her statement. She was trembling by the time it was over; telling it was like reliving the whole event. In her mind, she could see the look on Wade's face as he'd tried to choke the life out of her, and again when he realized he'd been shot.

"Are you okay?" Jack asked, as they waited for her statement to be typed up.

"I will be," she said. Lee mopped her eyes with

the tissue Holden had given her. Then she reached for Holden's phone and dialed the hospital, where she learned Stevie was ready to be released. She chatted with him briefly and told him she'd be there shortly.

"Did you watch that video?" he asked.

"Yes. Wade won't be coming around the house anymore."

"Did you tell him you watched it?"

"We'll talk about it when we get home, okay? I'll be there soon to get you." She said good-bye and hung up, just as Holden came through holding a sheath of papers.

"I need you to read through this, Lee, and sign it."

She took the papers from him, skimmed through the wording, and signed. Finally, she stood and handed them to him. "You need to go home and catch a nap, Holden."

"I plan on it."

She congratulated him again, then left with Jack. They drove straight to the hospital. Lee wondered if Wade was still in ICU, if his condition had worsened. She wished she could stop by and visit Debbie and see the new baby, but there wasn't time.

They found Stevie impatient to leave. He took one look at Jack and turned sullen, and he remained that way until they arrived back at Lee's house. He went upstairs without a word.

"I'm sorry," Lee said, embarrassed by Stevie's behavior but knowing the boy had a right to be angry when he didn't know what was going on.

Jack surprised her by putting a finger to her lips. "Don't worry about it, babe. The kid's been to hell and back. And he saw me in court, accused of his mother's murder. I'll have to win his trust. It'll take time."

"Thanks for being so understanding."

Jack slipped his arms around her. "How about I leave you to get settled and come back this evening with a bucket of chicken? Maybe you'll have time to talk to him by then."

"That would be nice."

He kissed her, then reluctantly pulled away. "I'm going to be thinking of you today," he whispered.

Lee gazed into loving blue eyes. "Me, too."

She watched him drive away a few minutes later. Was she falling in love with the man? It was too hard to tell, with all that was going on around her. She needed time to sift through her feelings.

"Aunt Lee?"

Startled, Lee jumped and swung around to face her nephew. "Oh, Stevie, you scared me."

"Sorry. I just wanted to know if I could fix a sandwich. I didn't eat anything at the hospital."

Lee hadn't thought to eat, either. "Sure, honey. Why don't you have a seat, and I'll make something for both of us."

"And you'll tell me about Wade?"

"It's bad, Stevie. Real bad." She sat down, took his hand, and recounted what had occurred the night before. By the time she was finished, she was crying.

Stevie didn't speak for a moment. Finally, he looked at her. "I knew he and my mom had a thing, and I've secretly wondered if Wade had something to do with the fact my dad never made it out." He paused. "That fire was my fault, you know."

Lee's head snapped up. "What?"

"I had this thing with matches back then. I was always starting fires. I don't know why, I was just fascinated with them. Then I accidentally burned down the tool shed, and my dad hit the ceiling. Told me I was a crazy, fucked-up kid, and he wished he never adopted me."

Lee's heart clenched.

"Anyway, he took me to my bedroom, made me sit on the edge of my bed, and he—" Stevie paused and shuddered.

"What did he do to you, Stevie?" she asked tensely.

"He took out his cigarette lighter and burned blisters on the tips of my fingers."

Lee felt as though all the oxygen had been sucked from her lungs. "Where was Lucy?" she asked, her voice trembling.

His eyes teared. "She was trying to break in the door to stop him." He took a shaky breath. "I was yelling and screaming for him to stop, and my mom was trying to kick the door in. She finally got in and stood in front of me, refusing to let him burn me again. He took the cigarette lighter and burned her face real bad. Everybody thought she got that burn in the fire that night, but that's not how it happened."

"What happened then? Did she tell someone?"

Stevie shook his head. "My dad dared her to do it, but he knew she wouldn't. If the authorities found out how he was abusing me, they would have taken me out of the house. She got on my case later, told me if I didn't stop doing crazy things, then she wouldn't be able to protect me."

"How did you start the fire, Stevie?" Lee asked.

"While I was confined to my room, I got bored, found my matches, and I started lighting them and tossing them into my waste basket. I smoked a couple of cigarettes and tossed them in too, but I put them out first. At least I thought I did." He paused. "I must not've done a good job because when I woke up later that night, my room was full of smoke. The waste basket was on fire, and it had climbed to the curtains. In a few minutes time, the whole room was in flames.

"I ran and woke up my mom, but she told me to

just sit with her downstairs for a while. She said it wouldn't do any good to wake my dad because he'd gotten stoned drunk and would never hear us." He shook his head. "The fire ripped through the house in just a matter of minutes. I can still remember how it roared. I could barely breathe. Finally, we heard the sirens, and my mom said it was time to leave. At first, I was afraid we weren't going to make it out."

Lee could not speak for a moment. Had her sister used the fire as an opportunity to kill her abusive husband? She wasn't ready to answer that question. "Do you still play with matches?" she asked her nephew, thinking it an odd question for a seventeen-year-old.

"No way. Not after that. As much as I hated my dad, I didn't want to see him dead. But I killed him as sure as if I'd taken a gun to him."

"Does anyone else know about this, Stevie?"

"No. My mom told the fire marshall that my dad was a heavy smoker and had a habit of passing out with a cigarette in his hand. She told him about all the furniture he'd burned holes in. He seemed to believe her. There wasn't much of an investigation. Nobody liked my dad anyway."

Shaken, Lee said, "Don't mention this to anybody, Stevie. Besides, you're not the first kid to ever play with matches." She gave him a tremulous smile. "Let's just put all this behind us. You have a new life now, and you don't ever have to worry about being abused. That's a promise."

He looked relieved. "Are you going to start going out with that Jack fellow?" he asked.

Lee hesitated. "Well, now that we know he's innocent, I see no reason not to." She waited for his response. There was none. "As a matter of fact, he offered to bring dinner tonight."

Another shrug. "Could I have that sandwich now?"

"Sure, honey." Lee got up and went to the refrigerator. She had hoped Stevie would warm up to Jack once he knew the real story, but she didn't blame him for being cautious. He'd been deeply hurt by the tragic deaths of his parents, and he was bearing the guilt of one of them. When she felt the time was right, she was going to discuss his going into therapy. The kid was carrying around a lot of baggage for one so young. And she needed to know that he wasn't likely to repeat some of his mistakes.

Once she'd prepared lunch, she set the plates on the table and grabbed a couple of soft drinks from the refrigerator. She tried to drag Stevie into conversation, but he was quiet and withdrawn.

"I'd like to take a nap," he said, once he'd finished eating.

"Sure." She almost offered her room, knowing it would be easier to check on him, then remembered she had to clean it. She dreaded the chore. "I'll check on you in a little while," she said.

"Don't bother," he told her. "I'll probably be asleep."

Lee watched him go, his back bowed, his shoulder blades poking through like tiny pup tents. How would she ever get past the wall he'd erected around himself? How was he ever going to recover from what had happened to him?

Once she'd rinsed the dishes, Lee went into her bedroom and was surprised to find it had already been cleaned and smelled of disinfectant. Even the carpet had been scrubbed, although some stains remained. A fresh mattress pad was in place. Had Holden seen to it? Or perhaps Jack. There was almost nothing to indicate what had taken place only hours before.

Nevertheless, she sat on the edge of the bed and cried.

Jack stepped through the front door of Lee's store and took a moment to study her creations. He was especially impressed by her Tiffany-style lamps. A redheaded woman hurried in from the back room and came to a halt at the sight of him.

"You must be Carol," he said. "I'm Jack McCall."

Carol regarded him as she moved behind the counter. "I know who you are. I've seen your picture in the paper."

"Well, I'm more handsome in person." He smiled, then cleared his throat when she didn't respond. "I've been cleared of all that unfortunate business, Carol. In fact, they know the identity of the real killer."

"I hadn't heard." She glanced around quickly. "Is there something I can help you with?"

"Yes, as a matter of fact, you can. It concerns Lee. I want to help her, but I can't do it without you." Jack saw the guarded look on her face and knew she would take some convincing.

Twenty-seven

B Y THE time Jack arrived with dinner, Lee had straightened the house, taken a hot shower, and carried wood in for a fire. She wore the dress Stevie had given her, hoping it would improve his mood. Her own mood had lightened considerably. Carol had called to tell her Southern Contractors was experiencing problems and couldn't install the panels as quickly as they'd planned. She had an extra month to get them done. Unable to contain the first bit of good news she'd received in days, she hugged Jack the minute he stepped into the kitchen bearing a bucket of chicken and a white sack.

He chuckled. "Let me set this stuff down, and I'll hug you back," he said.

She told him about the extended deadline, and he looked pleased for her. "At least it takes the pressure off," she said.

He slipped his arms around her waist. "Which is exactly what you need at the moment. Where's Stevie?"

"Sleeping. He's not doing so well, Jack. I'm going to have to make an appointment for him to see that psychiatrist from the hospital. I understand she has a private practice in town." Lee didn't even want to think what it would cost.

"Might do him some good, considering what he's

been through," Jack said. "But you might want to see if you can find a doctor at the mental health center. It wouldn't cost you as much." He studied her closely. "How are you doing, Lee?"

"I'm okay."

"Your eyes are swollen."

"I cried a little when I went into the bedroom. Did you have someone clean it, by the way?"

"Guilty as charged," he said. "I grabbed your house key while you were in the shower last night. Hired the woman who cleans my place."

"How did you get it back on my key ring?"

"She dropped it off this morning. Once again, you were in the shower."

"Why all the subterfuge, Jack? Why didn't you just ask me for the key?"

"Because every time I've tried to help you with a problem you get all huffy and bent out of shape and accuse me of trying to buy you. I didn't want you to come back to that mess in the bedroom, and I knew I had to get someone out here fast."

"She came out and cleaned last night? I'll bet that gave her a warm, cozy feeling, cleaning up after a shooting in the middle of the night."

"She brought someone with her. That was part of the deal."

"How much did it cost you?"

"Stop it, Lee."

She regarded him thoughtfully. "Did you have something to do with the contractors giving me an extra month to finish my panels?"

He groaned. "Yes, I did."

"How much did that cost you?"

"Listen to me," he said, pulling her tight against him. "I'm in love with you, and if I want to do something to make your life a little easier, I will."

He loved her? "Without discussing it with me first?" she asked, unable to give in just yet.

He released her and took a step back. "I think, under the circumstances, I acted wisely. If you don't agree, then I apologize for intruding." He shoved his hands in his pockets and stood there, his eyes fixed on a spot just above her head, as though unsure what to say or do next.

Lee saw the vulnerable look on his face and suspected, she too, was falling in love. It was frightening, exhilarating. "Jack?" she said softly.

"What?" He met her gaze.

"Thank you."

He smiled and pulled her into his arms, kissing her deeply. When he raised up, he was smiling. "Would you like to know when I fell in love with you?" She nodded. "When you kneed me in the balls."

"You can't be serious."

"I thought you were the meanest woman I'd ever laid eyes on and how much I'd like to wring your pretty neck, but I couldn't get you off my mind for anything." His smiled faded. "I respected the way you came after me when you thought I killed your sister. Though I was really glad the sheriff was there to pull you off of me," he added with a short laugh.

"Holden called."

"And?"

"He checked on Wade while he was at the hospital. Looks like he'll pull through." She felt her eyes moisten. "I'm trying really hard to deal with all this, Jack, but I can't help crying from time to time."

"I'd like my shoulder to be the one you cry on."

They stood there for a moment, just holding one another. "Are you hungry?" Lee asked.

"Hungry for you. Couldn't you tell this morning?"

Lee shivered at the memory of their lovemaking. "I'm talking about food, silly."

"Yes, I could go for a chicken leg. I haven't had time to eat today."

She pulled away, although she would have enjoyed staying right where she was. "Let me get Stevie." She made for the door. "I might have a couple of beers in the refrigerator if you want one."

"I don't do much drinking these days. You got any soft drinks?"

"Sure. Help yourself." Lee left the room and crossed the living room to the stairs. She hurried up the first flight, then took the short one that led to the attic. Stevie's "Do Not Disturb" sign was firmly in place. She knocked. There was no answer. She tried the knob and found it locked.

"Stevie?" She knocked again. She heard footsteps, and the sound of him unlocking the door. He cracked it an inch and peered out. She could tell he was surprised to see her in his mother's dress because his eyes widened. "Jack's here with dinner, honey. Why don't you come on down and have something to eat?"

"I'm not hungry."

"Stevie, you have to eat something. Would you like me to bring up a tray?"

"I told you I'm not hungry," he said impatiently. "I couldn't get any sleep in that stupid hospital because they kept coming by to check me every ten minutes. I'm tired. I just want to be left alone." He closed the door in her face.

Lee leaned against the wall, waiting, just in case he changed his mind. But he didn't. She had struggled to make him feel welcome in her home, to show him how much she cared about him, but none of it was doing any good. With a sinking heart, she returned downstairs where she found Jack emptying the contents of the bag.

He glanced up. "Where's Stevie?"

"He's not hungry." She was failing with her

nephew, but how could she hope to achieve anything with all that was going on around them?

"Would you rather I leave?" Jack asked. "Maybe it's me."

"No. He wouldn't come down anyway. He stays holed up in that attic, and he refuses to leave except to go to school."

Jack looked thoughtful. "You don't think he's doing drugs or anything, do you?"

Lee went to the cabinet for plates. "I don't know, Jack. I haven't really seen signs of drug use. He's just sullen all the time. I figured it was all part of being a teenager."

"A lot of it probably is." Once Lee had finished setting the table and grabbed something to drink for herself, Jack made a production of pulling her chair out. She chuckled and sat down.

"One night I'd like to take you to dinner," he said, joining her. "I think you could use a little fun in your life. Maybe I could take you to Hilton Head. You could see my place there."

Lee chose a piece of chicken and offered him the plate. "Would I like it?"

He smiled. "No. You'd probably find it ostentatious. At least I do; that's why I put it on the market."

"I should put this place up for sale," she said glumly. "Sell it and get rid of the biggest headache I've ever had." She finished filling her plate and took a bite of her chicken.

Jack looked surprised. "You'd sell this place? I think it's wonderful."

"It needs too much work. My little business can't support it."

"Maybe we could fix it up together," he said.

She looked at him. "I wouldn't touch that with a ten-foot pole."

"Am I moving too fast for you?" He patted her

hand. "I'll back off. For a couple of days," he added with a grin.

"I don't want to rush into anything. Especially now." She gave a weary sigh. "I wonder if I'm going to have nightmares."

"Would you rather I slept here tonight?" Jack asked. "I could sleep on the sofa." When she didn't answer, he went on. "I really don't mind, if it'll put your mind at ease."

She didn't look at him. "I just hate to impose. I know my life is like a horror story right now."

"I've lived through it a little myself, the past few weeks," he said wryly.

"Every time I think it's over, something else happens. I just can't take any more."

He covered her hand with his. "It's over, babe. Now we can begin to pick up the pieces. And I'm going to be with you every step of the way."

They finished their meal, put the food away, and cleaned the kitchen. Jack began to build a fire, and Lee brought in blankets and pillows to make up the couch.

"Don't worry about that right now," Jack told her as he stacked several logs on the grate and wadded up old newspapers. "I'll do it later. I want you to relax."

Once he had a fire going, they sat and talked. Lee told him about growing up in Comfrey, and he told her about his childhood in North Carolina and about his mother. He got up from time to time to put more wood on the fire. Lee was surprised to find it was well after midnight when she looked up at the clock on the mantel. At some point she must've dozed, because the next time she glanced up it was after two, and the fire had burned down. Jack was snoring softly beside her. He mumbled something in his sleep as she pulled free and got up.

The house was dark. Lee went into the kitchen for

a drink of water, then returned to the sofa to cover Jack with one of the blankets. He was sleeping so soundly she hated to wake him. She suspected he was tired after being woken up the previous night with her bad dreams.

Lee started up the steps in the dark, feeling her way from memory. She didn't want to turn on the light and wake Jack, but the old house had an eerie quality to it tonight. She knew it was because she'd almost killed a man in her bedroom the night before.

Lee reached the landing to the second floor and was about to turn toward her bedroom when she thought of Stevie. Perhaps she should check on him once more, just in case he'd awakened hungry in the night. She made her way up the half flight and tapped on the door lightly. No answer. She tried the knob. Much to her surprise, the door opened.

She peeked in. "Stevie?" There was no answer. She hesitated, then stepped inside. The living room and small kitchenette were bathed in a deep burgundy glow from an exposed red light bulb in the overhead socket. Automatically she ducked, as the ceiling came uncomfortably close. She could almost feel it bearing down on her, and she remembered the panic attack she'd suffered last time she was there. She didn't want to go any further and risk going through it again—the choking fear, the impending doom. Just thinking about it sent a wave of apprehension through her.

"Stevie?" she called out softly once more, only to be met with a chill dark silence. A knot formed in her stomach and her facial muscles tensed.

The room was too warm. Her clothes felt hot and burdensome, and they seemed to weigh her down. She moved sluggishly. She sucked in her breath, and as she did, it was as if she'd sucked part of the room inside of her, like something out of a cartoon, distorting the dimensions and periphery. Was she losing her mind or was it panic setting in? Even as she considered it, her ears tried to focus on the peculiar sound in the background, vague but very real; the heavy bass of a song that seemed to be repeating the same chord over and over again. It didn't come from a specific location, but sounded as though it was a part of the room, coming from the very pores in the walls. No, that couldn't be right. Fear had distorted her thinking.

Every instinct told her to run.

"Stevie, are you awake?" she called out. Her breathing was erratic, but the more she tried to control it the worse it got.

The ceiling dropped a notch. She tried to make herself smaller, but she felt squeezed in regardless.

Like being in that trunk, searching for a pocket of air. Wetting herself.

It's all in your mind, Lucy would have said.

Lee closed her eyes and pressed closer to the bedroom door. She imagined the room folding in on her like an accordion, snapping closed like a Venus fly trap. She was inside, suffocating. She could feel sweat beading her upper lip. So warm. How could Stevie take it? She felt the bedroom door in front of her.

She waited, trying to buy more courage. Her heart was beating rapidly, like that of a small animal in the clutches of its prey. The steady rhythm of that bass, over and over and over till she wanted to scream.

One could not scream when there was no oxygen.

She was suffocating. Like being in a jar with the lid screwed tight. Lee gritted her teeth and opened the bedroom door. She was greeted with more red light. "Stevie? Stevie, where are you?" She looked about the room.

And froze at the sight.

The walls were cluttered with photographs. Lee

stepped closer, squinting to get a better look. Pictures of Lucy. Lucy having drinks on her patio with friends, Lucy in her white satin pajamas, Lucy standing beside a Christmas tree, behind a birthday cake. Hundreds of Lucys.

Here a Lucy, there a Lucy, everywhere a Lucy.

Lucy on walls closing in.

Lee turned her head, unable to watch. She grasped the dresser in front of her, disturbing numerous perfume bottles that had been arranged just so. Jewelry on a velvet backdrop. Lucy's jewelry. Lucy in a gilded frame. The scent of gardenias, coming from a small box of potpourri. She had just come upon her sister's shrine. But how had Stevie managed to get his hands on his mother's belongings? She and Holden had been present the whole time. Perhaps he'd taken them earlier and stashed them somewhere so he could get to them easily. Or maybe he'd gone back later.

She picked up the picture frame and gazed at her sister, wearing her hair in the style that Stevie had recently convinced Lee to try. The dress was familiar as well; it was the same dress Lee was wearing now.

In shock, Lee glanced at the mirror, comparing herself to the picture of her sister. The resemblance was startling. Stevie had obviously tried to turn her into a replica of his mother, and from the looks of it, had succeeded very well. At least on the outside.

Still gazing into the mirror, Lee caught movement in the shadows behind her. It struck her as odd that she was not afraid; in fact, her panic had subsided, and she felt numb. Dazed, perhaps. She simply stared as the shadow took on form and materialized into a seventeen-year-old boy with a pitifully thin face and sunken eyes. And a bowed back that showed he'd taken too much on his young shoulders.

She saw the butcher knife in his hand, recognized

it as one of her own. Fear rippled through her stomach. "Hello, Stevie," she said, trying to stay calm.

"I knew you'd come back," he said.

Lee saw the crazed look in his eyes and tried not to show any fear. "I was worried about you, honey. I thought you might like something to eat after all."

He seemed oblivious to what she was saying. "How could you come back? I saw you dead. I saw the hole in your chest! And I put enough pills in your Scotch to kill a fucking horse! How could you survive something like that?"

Lee knew her only chance was to play along. "I came back because I owed you an apology. I—"

"And who the hell fixed your face? I destroyed it. All the muscles and tendons and everything."

Lee gave a startled gasp. Her eyes flitted from the boy's face to the knife and back again. He looked quite mad. In the background the music chanted an ominous song. The room was shrinking. "I was a terrible mother, Stevie. I came back to make peace with you. To ask your forgiveness."

"You're a whore and a liar, that's what you are. I used to feel sorry for you when he hurt you. I used to lie on my bed, my ears covered with a pillow so I wouldn't have to hear you beg him to stop hitting you." He choked back his tears. "I used to try to think of ways to kill him. Finally, I did." He paused. "When I saw my waste basket on fire that night, I carried it straight to his room. He was passed out. I made sure the fire would spread fast and it did."

He was quiet for a moment. "I would never have cut you up had you not changed so much. I got tired of you ignoring me all the time." His voice broke. "I wanted it to be like old times."

"Oh, Stevie, please—" She reached out to him. "I do think of you, and I want to help you."

"Don't come any closer," he said, hissing the words at her. "You don't want to help me. You want to have me locked away like an animal. I begged you to give me another chance, but you wouldn't listen. You just wanted to send me away so I'd be out of your hair. So you could be with all those men. This time I'm going to make sure you never come back."

All at once, he brought the knife up. Lee screamed as it arced high in the air; she only had a split second to move away. He brought it down hard, and it slammed into the dresser, splintering wood. Frozen, Lee watched him try to pry the knife loose, then ran for the living room, pausing when she saw how low the ceiling was.

She would never be able to make it to the door leading out of the apartment. Once again, she tried to make herself small, tried to ignore the ceiling that was pressing down on her, the floor rising up to meet her. Coming together.

Stevie pulled the knife free with a grunt. That was all the impetus she needed. Lee screamed again, ducked, and ran. Through the living room, out the door, to the stairs.

Utter darkness. No time to search for the light. She stumbled down the short flight leading from the attic, found the landing, started down the next. Where was Stevie? She couldn't hear anything except her own heavy breathing and the pounding of her heart. She expected her nephew to bury the knife in her back any moment.

So many steps. No end to them. If she tripped or faltered, she'd be dead.

Suddenly, she heard Jack's voice. "Lee? Is that you? What's wrong, baby?"

Lee almost missed her footing in her hurry to reach him, weeping with relief. She collided into something solid and warm and his arms came around her. "It's Stevie! He's got a knife!"

"Where's the goddamn light?" Jack demanded, feeling for a light switch.

There was a loud thump above. Lee heard her nephew curse. Then, a muffled sound of something falling. A body tumbling. Lasting only a few seconds, lasting forever.

Then, it was quiet.

"Stevie?" Lee called his name softly.

Nothing. Only blackness.

"Where's the damn light switch?" Jack demanded.

Lee's voice trembled. "Stevie, are you there?" She imagined him poised on the steps with the knife as she reached for the light. She flipped it on.

Her nephew lay in a clump at the bottom of the stairs, his neck tilted at an odd angle. She shook him. His head fell back and he stared at her through the eyes of a lifeless doll, his gaze wide open and fixed. Lee cried out her anguish and fell to her knees, burying her face in his soft hair.

"Oh, God, no!" she screamed, feeling as though a giant claw had reached into her chest and ripped her heart out. She pulled him into her arms and rocked him, unable to stop the sobs that racked her body.

"He's gone, Lee," Jack said, trying to pry her arms free.

But she refused to let go. She held the boy and wept.

Twenty-eight

IT WAS 9 a.m. by the time Holden arrived back at his office, having dropped Lee off at her parents'. He was worried about her. Stevie's death had been the final straw. Even Jack couldn't seem to reach her. After questioning her briefly and listening to her wooden responses, he'd decided she was in no condition to give a formal statement.

As Holden sipped yet another cup of black coffee, he wrote out his report, stopping now and then to rub the grit from his eyes. He needed a vacation. As soon as he wrapped up this case, and he promised himself it would be soon, he would go home, lock the doors, take the phone off the hook, and spend time with his family.

He was daydreaming about doing just that when his secretary knocked on the door. He waved her in.

"There's someone here to see you, Sheriff," she said. "Claims it has something to do with the Hodges case."

"That case has been put to bed, Teresa. I have no interest in discussing it with anyone else."

"Whatever you say, Holden, but it might be important."

He leaned back in his chair and frowned. "Who is this person hell-bent on causing me more headaches?"

"An elderly man by the name of Atwell. He's got a black woman with him."

The neighbor and his housekeeper, Holden thought. "Okay, send them in," he said.

A few moments later, Hyram Atwell took a seat in one of the chairs facing Holden's desk. The black woman, who introduced herself as Grace Jackson, sat in the chair next to him.

Hyram didn't speak right away. Finally, he looked at the woman. "Go ahead and give it to him, Grace."

The woman reached into an oversized bag and pulled out something wrapped in a towel. She placed it on Holden's desk. He unwrapped the object and found himself looking at a butcher knife.

"I believe that's what you've been looking for, Sheriff," Hyram said. "The murder weapon. I put it through Mrs. Hodges's heart with every intention of killing her."

Holden was clearly shaken. "Why?"

Hyram looked down at his hands. "I couldn't stand to see her suffering like that. She was near death anyway. All that blood. She wouldn't have lasted long."

"How did you happen to be in Mrs. Hodges's bedroom in the first place?" Holden asked, knowing he should be recording this, but too curious to do anything more than listen. He could always bring out the recorder later and ask Atwell to repeat it.

When Hyram hesitated, Grace prodded him on. "Might as well get it off your chest, Mister Atwell. You know how it's been bothering you."

The old man took a deep, steadying breath. "I'd found a half-dead tomcat on the property the day before, and I put him out of his pain, and wrapped him in a blanket so I could bury him later. I didn't think it was a good idea for my neighbors to see me burying animals so often, so I waited till I was sure everybody would be asleep. I dug a grave at the back of my property in the wee hours that morning, buried the cat, and I was walking up the side of my house when I heard a terrible scream coming from Mrs. Hodges's place." He paused. "I tried to peek in the windows, but I couldn't see. I waited, paced a bit; finally, I went in. The front door was unlocked."

His eyes glistened with tears. He reached into his pocket for a handkerchief. "As long as I live, I'll never forget what I saw. Looked like somebody put her face through one of them shredding machines. Blood everywhere. I leaned over, and I saw the look in her eyes. She was pleading with me to end it. I walked into the kitchen, pulled that knife from a wooden block, went back in the room, and—" He took a shaky breath. "Finished her off." He wiped moisture from his eyes. "Just as I'd done hours earlier for that poor cat."

"What happened to the cat?" Holden asked.

"It had been tortured. Found it lying in the woods, too hurt to even cry out. Wasn't the first time I came upon something like that. I broke its neck. Just as I'd done the others. One quick snap, and they're gone."

"Do you know who was torturing the animals?"

"That boy. Steven Hodges."

Holden regarded him. He looked to be telling the truth. "And you never thought to report him?"

Hyram looked ashamed. "I'd considered it. But I felt sorry for him. Poor kid had no daddy, and his mama—" He paused again and dragged in a long breath. "I knew what kind of woman she was."

"So you're saying it was a mercy killing," Holden said.

"Yes sir. She wasn't long for this world. The person who did it wanted to make sure she died a slow, painful death."

"Did it occur to you at the time that her son did it?"

"I didn't know," Hyram said. "I'd heard a car drive away earlier so I had no way of knowing that maybe it wasn't the person in the car. And since I hadn't seen the make or model, I wouldn't have been much help in that respect. I decided it would be better if I just went back home and pretended that I hadn't seen or heard anything. Then that deputy got to snooping around."

Grace Jackson spoke. "Sheriff, I been working for Mr. Atwell a number of years now, and I have to tell you, he's a good man. He wouldn't hurt a fly. But he wouldn't allow suffering, either. I know what he did was wrong, but he did it out of kindness. I hope you'll take that into account before you throw him in jail."

Holden pondered the whole thing for a moment. Hyram Atwell was frail. He wouldn't last long behind bars; he'd never make it to trial. "Did it ever occur to you to call an ambulance, Mr. Atwell?"

The man straightened in his chair. "Yes sir. I would have done just that if I thought Mrs. Hodges's life could be saved. But you saw her. Looked like all the blood had drained out of her. And even if she could have been saved, she probably would have taken her own life at a later date. Who wants to live when they look like some kind of ghoul? Plastic surgery wouldn't have been able to repair that kind of damage."

Holden sipped his coffee in silence. "Have either of you discussed this with anyone else?" he asked at last. They shook their heads. "Then don't. Go home, and I'll call you if I need anything more."

"Am I going to jail, Sheriff?" Hyram asked, staring at his feet. His liver spots stood out on his bald head.

Holden wasn't about to send the old man to jail.

"I need time to think about it. But if either of you start flapping your jaws, I'm liable to send you both down the river. Just go on home and don't give me no more trouble." He watched them hurry out, confident they would never speak of it again.

Twenty-nine

JACK HAD spent a busy eight weeks trying to get his life in order and settle his father's estate. He purchased a six pack of diet root beer to celebrate the Supreme Court's decision to reinstate him. Now, all he had to do was study for the South Carolina bar.

This was the moment he'd been waiting for.

But it no longer mattered much. He was missing Lee.

And kicking his own ass for agreeing to back off. She'd needed time, she'd said. And he'd understood. But the weeks had turned to months, and now he was afraid he'd lost her for good.

He'd driven by her house a number of times before he realized she wasn't living there. She was staying with her parents. Even though he could understand her need to be with them, he was impatient to find out how she felt about him, if indeed they had a future together. What if she'd merely reached out to him because she couldn't bear what'd been going on in her life at the time? Now that she felt stronger, she might have decided she was better off without him. His name had been cleared, of course, but he was still the man who'd taken her sister home for sex and one of the last to see her alive.

I'm not interested in my sister's leftovers.

That evening, he closed his office and climbed the stairs for bed. He'd have to rent a real house soon—at least before he opened his practice. He couldn't very well live in the rooms over his offices once clients started coming in.

Oh, hell, what did it matter one way or the other?

Outside, Lee sat in her pickup truck and watched Jack cut the downstairs lights. It was after eleven; no doubt he was going to bed. All week, she had sat in this very spot and watched him perform his nightly rituals. The bathroom light came on, and she imagined him showering. She tried not to let her mind conjure up images of a naked Jack McCall with water running down his body, or of the night they'd made love in one of the bedrooms. She felt a tear escape one corner of her eye, and she swiped at it.

Two months. She had been forced to deal with a lot in that time: her sister's grisly murder, shooting Wade, Stevie's death. Burying Stevie in the plot next to his mother. Too much to handle in such a brief time.

Was she really ready for a relationship? She had watched her mother slowly heal while her father continued to deteriorate. Holden seemed to have recovered; he was more concerned with his wife and new son. Lee had worked impossible hours to get her panels done, and she, Rob, and Carol had watched the contractors put them in place. Rob had given her a high five.

The nightmares had stopped. She no longer woke up gasping for air. Perhaps it had something to do with forcing herself to go inside that tiny attic apartment that night, facing her fears.

Lee waited until the bathroom light went off, then climbed from her truck and made her way toward the front door. She was nervous. Jack might think she needed more time. To sort through things.

She had sorted. Boy, had she sorted.

She rang the doorbell. Several times, in fact, before the downstairs light came on, and she saw him moving toward the door in his bathrobe. He looked surprised to see her, but as he opened the door his face broke into a grin, and he gathered her into his arms.

"Oh, sweetheart," he said, anchoring her head between his palms and kissing her until she was weak and breathless. "It's about time."

Lee's heart sang, and she wondered if maybe the bad times in life were really necessary in order to appreciate the good ones. Whatever the reasons, she knew she had never been more ready for love.